ALSO BY KATE GREATHEAD

Laura & Emma

The Book
of George

GEORGE
GEORGE
GEORGE
GEORGE

The Book of George

a novel

Kate Greathead

HENRY HOLT AND COMPANY

NEW YORK

Henry Holt and Company
Publishers since 1866
120 Broadway
New York, New York 10271

Henry Holt® and ⊕® are registered trademarks of
Macmillan Publishing Group, LLC.

Distributed in Canada by Raincoast Book Distribution Limited

ISBN 9781250351029
Designed by Meryl Sussman Levavi

Printed in the United States of America

For Teddy

You are not an evil human; you are not without intellect and education; you have everything that could make you a credit to human society. Moreover, I am acquainted with your heart and know that few are better, but you are nevertheless irritating and unbearable, and I consider it most difficult to live with you.

—Johanna Schopenhauer in a letter to her son,
Arthur Schopenhauer, November 6, 1807

The Book
of George

1. THE SHOPPING PROBLEM

George, 12–18

To George's D.A.R.E. graduation in the Cochran Gym, his father wore a suit. The suit hadn't registered as embarrassing to George, who couldn't even remember what it looked like when he overheard his mother mention it to a friend on the phone later that week, but from her derisive tone in describing it—*custom-made, seersucker, J. Press*—he understood that there was something inherently foolish about it. Or perhaps it was his father's wearing it to such a silly occasion: George and his classmates on the bleachers singing a song about abstaining from drugs and alcohol, the culmination of the substance-abuse unit of their seventh-grade health class.

George struggled to grasp the nuances of his mother's contempt, but it was the beginning of his awareness of a problem in his parents' marriage that had to do with his father's love of expensive clothes.

Ellen didn't discuss it with her kids, but she wasn't exactly sotto voce when venting to her friends on the phone, and there were certain cutting remarks that George wished he hadn't heard. *Not normal. Shopping the way a woman shops—a woman with a shopping problem.*

It was hard for George to imagine his mother having any vices. Ellen, who wore very little makeup and had let her hair go gray, rolled her eyes when people referred to her as beautiful, but she maintained the body of the ballet dancer she'd been in her youth and there was an awareness of her own grace in the way she moved. Her posture could be forbidding. She had a way of silently materializing at the threshold of her children's rooms at incriminating moments, though she rarely intervened beyond expressing her opinion.

"It's just not very attractive," she'd told Cressida the first time she'd caught her smoking.

George recalled, as a young child, a tender, involved mother, but as he got older she withdrew. By the time he and Cressida were teenagers, Ellen seemed to view them as fully formed people who were going to do what they were going to do. She supported their endeavors and applauded their successes, but their accomplishments were not a particular source of pride for her. Nor was she inclined to interpret their struggles as a referendum on her mothering.

Denis had always been the more parental of the two, though between working and commuting, he was not around as much.

* * *

"Do you ever think how random it is, that Mom and Dad are married?" Cressida asked George as they rifled through a gift basket someone had sent their parents, who'd just left for JFK. It was their twentieth wedding anniversary, and they would be spending a week in London. Cressida, who was living with friends in a house upstate after finishing her first year at Bard, had come home so that George, who had just turned fourteen, wouldn't be in the house alone.

George shook his head as he examined a furry brown specimen that turned out to be a dried apricot.

"It's pretty random." Cressida used her teeth to uncork a bottle of champagne.

The sun was setting, and the kitchen was slathered in electric orange. For the third day in a row the temperature had been over ninety, and the house was ripe with the musk of heat-saturated materials, old rugs and cedar closets, Ellen's acrylics. The uphol-stered window seat was still warm, almost hot to the touch.

"We should go swimming in Sugar Pond," George said.

Cressida rejected the proposal with a flared nostril.

"That's disgusting," she said as he dipped a prune into a jar of olive tapenade, mistaking it for chocolate.

"It's good," George claimed, too proud to admit otherwise.

* * *

That evening, Cressida had some college friends over. Like her high school crowd, they were not friendly and dressed in mostly black. They slept over, and the following afternoon more arrived. They kept trickling in, an unsavory cast of characters who regarded George with sardonic amusement—*hey, little brother*—on the rare occasion they acknowledged him at all.

George did his best to avoid them as they colonized various rooms of the house, eating and drinking and smoking.

The second night, as George was reading in bed, his bedroom door creaked open and one of them entered. She was shockingly skinny, with a shaved head and septum ring, but her most arresting feature was her eyes: a metallic gleam in her irises that must have been colored contacts. There was something fantastically sinister about the effect. Demonic. Earlier that day, George had caught himself staring at her as he ate a bowl of cereal at the kitchen counter.

Perhaps she'd taken it the wrong way.

George said nothing as she stripped down to her underpants and climbed into his bed. Her primitively angular breasts and hips that jutted out like spears were the first he'd encountered. They kept their underwear on, but the experience left George unsettled, and even a little depressed.

"How was your night?" Cressida asked with a knowing smile when he came downstairs the next morning.

* * *

George spent the next few nights at his friend Pete's. On Thursday he returned to change his clothes. He was surprised to discover the driveway, which had been jammed with cars belonging to Cressida's friends, was now clear. The house was still a mess, but quiet. His mother's suitcase was at the bottom of the stairs.

Ellen was in the kitchen, leaning over the sink, drinking straight from the faucet.

The countertops were covered with dishes, takeout containers, liquor bottles, things that were not ashtrays but were filled with cigarette butts. Open cabinets revealed bare shelves. The gift basket remained in the center of the kitchen table like a disemboweled carcass, its wicker skeleton surrounded by empty tins, tufts of paper confetti, pistachio shells, and husks of cellophane.

The late afternoon sun embalmed the tableau in a listless copper glaze.

"I thought you weren't getting back till Saturday," George said.

"Five nights was enough," Ellen said, wiping her mouth on the back of her hand as she turned off the water.

"Where's Dad?"

"He's still there."

George was confused. "In London? By himself?"

Ellen nodded. "He's fine. He's having a good time, doing what he likes to do." She smiled wanly. "He *really* likes to shop."

To hear her put it like this, without the snideness she adopted on the phone with her friends, was disconcerting.

"Sounds like a midlife crisis," George said with chipper authority.

He associated the term with *New Yorker* cartoons and sitcoms. He'd hoped the comment would inject the mood with a little levity.

But Ellen seemed to give it earnest consideration.

She started talking about how Denis never made partner at his law firm. He had gone through life feeling in the shadow of taller, more charismatic men. Men who weren't necessarily as smart, hard-working, or loyal as he was, but who had a certain swagger that earned them respect and credibility, resulting in opportunities that Denis felt he'd been denied.

"He doesn't feel very good about himself," she concluded, "and there's no question that the shopping has to do with that."

* * *

Ellen, whose family had money, had a small trust, to which Denis had access. That fall she discovered that he had secretly been dipping into it to pay off credit card debt he had amassed shopping for clothes. George made a point of being out of the house the Sunday his father moved out. When he returned that evening, George was relieved to find that Denis hadn't taken much; the house didn't feel very different.

Ellen set the table for two and defrosted a lasagna for dinner. Just as they sat down to eat, the doorbell rang.

"It's probably just a Seventh-day Adventist," Ellen said as George got up to answer it.

It was Denis.

The two hadn't exchanged a word about his moving out, or any of it. George hoped he wasn't about to initiate some kind of conversation now.

"I forgot to buy silverware, and everything's closed," Denis said.

George had recently surpassed Denis in height, and the difference was exaggerated by his standing in the house, which was higher than the stoop, where it appeared Denis planned to remain.

He waited outside while George went to the kitchen, opened the silverware drawer, and plucked out a fork, a knife, and a spoon.

"You can give him more than *that*," Ellen said. George took out another fork, spoon, knife, and then whatever they had duplicates of: garlic press, carrot peeler, corkscrew.

"What's this?" George held up an instrument.

"Lemon zester," Ellen said. "He can have that."

George put everything in a ziplock bag and returned to the front door.

"This is more than I need," Denis said as George passed him the bounty. "I was thinking just a fork and spoon to hold me over."

"Mom said to give you more," George said.

"Oh. Okay. Well, thank you. I'll bring it back."

"Just keep it," George told him. "We don't need it."

Denis looked as if he were about to protest.

"It's fine," George said. "But I should go back in. We're in the middle of dinner."

George hadn't meant to sound cold.

"Thanks," Denis said, holding up the bag like a prize.

"Enjoy," George responded, and shut the door.

Enjoy.

* * *

When George heard himself say something that was not natural, that sounded like something someone else would say, it troubled him. His goal in life was to be authentic, no matter the consequences. It was the subject of his college essay. After procrastinating, he wrote the whole thing in a single sitting two nights before applications were due to be postmarked.

When he was done, he didn't let anyone read it over, lest he be susceptible to their opinions and suggestions. To alter what he'd written seemed disingenuous, at odds with the spirit of his essay.

George didn't get into either of his top-choice colleges.

"It used to be *any*one could get into Harvard or Yale," Ellen told him. "Things are different now. Much more competitive."

George knew he shouldn't be surprised—in the middle of tenth grade he'd pretty much stopped doing homework—but still, it felt like a slight when he wasn't accepted to a single Ivy.

* * *

Later that month, Ellen took the kids to Bermuda, their first trip without Denis. The weather was terrible, and they spent most of the time inside their cottage. Mostly they read books, but sometimes George and Cressida watched TV in one of their rooms.

One afternoon they watched the show *Jackass*. In one sketch a guy goes to a restaurant and orders a vegetarian platter. After being served he furtively procures a log of human feces he'd brought with him, deposits it on his food, and then summons the waiter to complain that there's something on his plate that looks like a sausage. George noticed Ellen standing in the doorway, looking bewildered.

"What happened to this country?" she asked.

Cressida laughed, but George was embarrassed. He'd always felt implicated in his mother's disgust with lowbrow contemporary culture, as though he were somehow responsible for it by being a member of the generation it was directed toward.

"I'm going for a walk," Ellen told her kids. "In case either of you wants to come . . ."

She lingered.

"Well, okay," she said, and turned to go.

"I'll come," George said, getting up.

The rain had stopped, but the sky remained bleak.

At the bottom of the path that led to the water, Ellen removed her sandals and placed them neatly beside each other. George kept his sneakers on as he followed her down the beach.

A breeze frisked her linen skirt, revealing the contours of her legs.

She took long, purposeful strides, occasionally leaning down to pick up a shell, which she gingerly deposited in the breast pocket of her shirt.

When they reached the end of the cove, George assumed that was it, but Ellen scaled a barrier of large rocks to access the next beach.

"*Mom.*" George pointed to a sign that read THIS BEACH IS FOR THE EXCLUSIVE USE OF GUESTS OF CLOVER COVE BEACH CLUB. PLEASE TURN AROUND.

Ellen shrugged and continued walking. George followed.

Eventually they turned around. When they reached the spot where Ellen had left her sandals, she sat down.

"This is where I learned that Dad was afraid of the ocean," she said, hugging her knees to her chest. George sat down beside her.

"You came here with Dad?"

Ellen nodded. The wind was blowing her hair in her face.

"Right after I discovered I was pregnant with Cress. The weather was perfect. Sunny. Warm. It was the first time I'd been to the beach with Denis, and he never said anything about not liking the ocean, but as the week unfolded, I noticed he never went in deeper than his thighs. 'I'm a pool guy,' he kept saying.

"One afternoon I swam out, and as he stood on the beach watching me, I pretended that I was in trouble. That I needed him to rescue me."

"You pretended that you were drowning?" It was hard to imagine her doing this.

"I pretended that I had a cramp and needed help getting back in. Do you know what he did next?" Ellen looked at George. "He ran to get the lifeguard. Who was about half a mile down the beach.

"I was *pregnant*."

George nodded. She'd included this detail already.

"Afterwards, instead of apologizing, or admitting the shame I'm sure he'd felt, he told me about that dream he had as a kid."

"The ocean dream," George said.

"The reincarnation one," Ellen said dryly.

Growing up, Denis had had a recurring dream that he was on a beach when the tide abruptly receded. Where the ocean had been became a silky carpet of sand strewn with rocks and shells and thatches of seaweed. The beach was full of people, and there was an air of adventure as they all began walking out toward the horizon. When Denis first heard screaming in the distance, he assumed it was from excitement, but then he noticed that the people farthest up ahead had turned around and were running back in the direction they'd come. Behind them, a wall of water was advancing.

Denis, who believed in reincarnation, claimed he'd begun having the dream before he knew what a tsunami was. He speculated that it was a memory from a previous life. This explained his dread of the ocean.

As a child, George had been fascinated by the story. Enchanted. Spooked. He shared his father's interest in things that could not be explained.

But now he understood his mother's contempt. On top of its being ridiculous and self-mythologizing, to think that it justified such cowardly behavior.

* * *

The evening before their flight home, the sky cleared. They got dressed for dinner. As they approached the main house, a chorus of male voices singing "Runaround Sue" carried through the French doors. An a cappella group from Yale was performing in the dining room.

"Are they going to be singing all night?" Cressida asked the maître d' as he showed them to their table.

"They'll take breaks," the man answered.

Ellen asked if they could sit at one of the tables outside.

"We should've always eaten out here," she said as they were led to a flagstone terrace overlooking the water.

"It was raining," Cressida reminded her.

As a waiter filled their water glasses, Ellen asked Cressida if she'd called Denis.

Cressida nodded conspiratorially.

"Was he upset?" Ellen wanted to know.

Cressida shrugged. "He understands," she said quietly.

"What are you talking about?" George asked.

Ellen looked at Cressida, who took a long drink of water.

"That house Denis rented over Memorial Day weekend"—Ellen put on her reading glasses to look at the menu—"it turns out Cressida has a concert that Saturday, so it'll just be you and Dad."

"A concert?" George was incredulous. "You're skipping the trip to go to a *concert*?"

"She's *in* the concert," Ellen explained. "She's performing."

"It's my friends' band," Cressida said. "I'm filling in for the vocalist."

"You're *singing* in a band? Since when do you sing?"

Cressida glowered. "I've always sang."

"You got kicked out of middle school chorus," George reminded her.

"That's because of what happened on the Disney World trip. That had nothing to do with my singing ability."

"That was a fun phone call to get as a parent," Ellen said drolly. "Never thought I'd hear the words *Mickey Mouse* and *indecent exposure* in the same sentence."

"It was a *dare*," Cressida said. "The whole thing was totally overblown. I was fourteen. I barely had tits."

The waiter came to take their orders.

"What happened to the vocalist?" George asked Cressida when he'd left. "The one you're filling in for?"

"She has to go to a wedding," Ellen answered for her.

"Her sister's getting married." Cressida emptied a packet of sugar onto her bread plate and, using the dull end of a butter knife, began pushing it around, divvying it up like lines of cocaine.

"Where's the wedding?" George asked.

"Why do you care?"

"Where is it?"

"You think I'm making this up!" Cressida's jaw dropped in theatrical outrage.

And now George knew for sure she was making it up, because this was her strategy in these situations, to feign outrage at having her credibility questioned. It almost always worked. Flustered, beleaguered, her interrogator backed off.

"What's the band called?" George asked.

"The Angry Pussy," Cressida said.

Ellen looked out at the water. "Well, this is pleasant."

She patted George's wrist. "It'll be nice for you and Dad to spend some alone time together."

The prospect of spending a three-day weekend alone with his father in a stranger's house in a random town in Pennsylvania filled George with dread and anxiety. That Cressida had managed to weasel her way out was infuriating. Typical and infuriating.

Cressida left the table to have a cigarette. She sat on a stone bench at the edge of the lawn. George watched one of the a cappella guys approach her. He could tell from her embarrassed smile that the guy was asking her something. And that she didn't want to hurt his feelings, but the answer was no.

Ellen also noticed.

"He's handsome," she said when Cressida returned to the table.

Cressida rolled her eyes. "He invited me to hang out with them on the beach after."

Ellen smiled. "You should go."

"Are you kidding? You think I want to hang out with those herbs?"

"Herbs?" Ellen said.

"Dorks," George translated.

Their drinks arrived.

"Thanks for paying for all this, Mom," Cressida said, licking the salt off the rim of her mojito. "It's got to be really expensive."

"It's nice to take a vacation together," Ellen said. "Even if the weather was crummy, I'm glad we did it."

"How much did Dad take from that fund?" Cressida asked, as though the question had just occurred to her.

When Ellen had made the discovery three years earlier, she'd refused to disclose the amount, but tonight she said, "You really want to know?"

George did not, so Ellen wrote the figure on a piece of paper, which she passed across the table to Cressida, who looked impressed.

"Man loves his clothes," she said, popping an olive in her mouth.

George pointed to the horizon. "Is that a UFO or an airplane?"

"It's a UFO, George," Cressida said. "You found one. Congratulations." She turned to Ellen. "Mom, would you have been as upset if Dad had spent the money on something other than clothes? Like what if he'd had a thing for boats, or power tools?"

Ellen looked taken aback. "I'm not sure what you're insinuating, but in fact he did spend the money on more than just clothes."

She paused deliberatively.

"He also used the money," she said, "to pay for a hair transplant."

"A *hair* transplant?" Cressida repeated.

Ellen nodded. "He was very concerned about his receding hair-line." The skin above her upper lip crinkled; she was trying to restrain a smile.

"How exactly does a hair transplant work?" Cressida asked. "Like, where does the hair come from, and how do they attach it to the skin?"

"I don't know," said Ellen.

George rotated his chair so that it faced the ocean rather than the table.

"But is it from another part of his body, so his scalp doesn't reject it? Like, is it from his back? He has a lot of hair on his—"

"Let's discuss this later," Ellen said crisply. "It's upsetting George."

She reached over and patted his head. "Don't worry. Balding comes from the maternal grandfather. You won't have that problem."

George wasn't worried about losing his own hair. He had so much of it. Had been born with it. His whole life, people had commented, *Nice hair. So thick. What a waste on a boy!*

George wasn't worried. He was bewildered. He'd never known anyone who'd gotten a hair transplant. It wasn't something people they knew did. It didn't even sound like a real thing. *A hair transplant.* Had it not occurred to his father that getting a hair transplant was infinitely more embarrassing than losing his hair?

Their food arrived. George rotated his chair back to the table, though he wasn't very hungry.

For the past few years, his sadness over his parents' divorce had been complicated by the embarrassment of what had triggered it, a tender little knot of grief and shame—what kind of a father had a shopping problem?—but with this new revelation, his feelings coalesced into something more definitive. Something cold and hard. A stone he could pick up and hurl into the ocean.

"Fuck," George said.

Ellen held a finger over her mouth. A well-dressed elderly couple had just been seated at the next table.

"*Fuck*," George repeated in a whisper. "I just remembered that I signed up to volunteer at Kids' Day."

"What's Kids' Day?" Ellen asked.

"It's like field day for kids with special needs. There are obstacle courses. Team-building exercises. That kind of thing."

Ellen's brow rose. "And what's the problem?"

"It's Memorial Day weekend," George said. "I forgot that it was the weekend Dad was renting the house."

"Is this something that your school does every year?" Ellen asked. "I've never heard about it before."

"It's an annual event." George chewed his lower lip. "I mean, it's been happening since I was a freshman . . ."

Ellen stayed silent.

"Not really sure when it started," he added with a shrug.

"I remember it," Cressida spoke up. "It was around in my time."

"And did you participate?" Ellen asked.

Cressida shook her head. "I wanted to, I was going to, but they made you sign up a few months in advance, and they made this big deal that you had to be one hundred percent sure you could make it, because each student gets paired with one special-needs kid, and there has to be the same number, and so you couldn't back out."

"It was too big of a commitment," Ellen said.

Cressida nodded. "You remember how I was in high school."

George appreciated Cressida's corroboration.

"Well." Ellen sighed. "Poor Denis. I hate to think of him going there all alone."

This was directed at George. She knew he was lying, but, rather than call his bluff, she was trying to manipulate him into feeling sorry for Denis. She was going to let him get away with the lie, but not without making him feel bad about it.

And it worked. George's relief that he wouldn't have to spend the weekend with his father was eclipsed by a terrible sadness imagining

Denis's disappointment. George resented this; how unfair that, on top of everything, he should have to feel sorry for his father.

And then an unforgivable thought: George wished his father were dead. How much easier it would be if he never had to deal with him again.

2. CANADA

George, 18–21

The first night of college, George drank nine beers. The room he
drank most of these beers in was small, and the air was thick
with the odor of the bodies of his classmates who had convened in
this room to get drunk—the smell of fresh sweat and pheromones,
of gin from huge plastic bottles and spearmint gum. George got
pressed into a corner with a guy named Benji, who had no trace of
the jocky aggression that George associated with his Boston accent,
and toward whom he felt an immediate affinity. As he stood there
taking it all in, Benji's expression was equal parts amused, embarrassed, and giddy, which was precisely how George felt. There was
something ridiculous and cliché about the scene, but he was excited
to be a part of it. At one point, George overheard someone nearby
say something to the effect of "And the best part is, no curfew, no
parents," and it was clear from Benji's expression that he had, too.

"No parents," George said.

"No parents," Benji repeated.

Later, Benji would take credit for the chant that quickly took hold
of the room, but it was George who had initiated it—a bold move,
considering how foolish he would've looked had it not caught on.

"No PAR-ents!" the freshmen all yelled for a good five minutes.
"No PAR-ents! No PAR-ents! No PAR-ents!"

George was assigned to a triple in the only dorm on campus
that had two halls segregated by gender. He had not requested this.
When it came to residential preferences he distinctly remembered
circling *single, coed*. Even worse, it had several hockey players who

proudly referred to it as "the Sausage Hall." At least he wouldn't have to endure the awkwardness of sharing a bathroom with girls. His roommate Solomon had cited this as his reason for requesting the all-male hall.

Solly (as he went by) was short and barrel-chested, with an impressively thick beard and a collection of oversize T-shirts featuring the names of concerts and music festivals he'd attended. Among the possessions he'd brought with him to college was a special cereal bowl that had a built-in straw to drink the leftover milk. Solly knew a lot about a lot of things and was an enthusiastic dispenser of obscure facts and trivia—except in the company of girls, when he fell mute. He spoke to his parents every evening, providing them with a detailed account of his day, from impressions of his professors to what he'd eaten for dinner. After getting off the phone with his parents, Solly would share dispatches from their days with whoever was in the room, referring to them by their first names and depicting them with reverent amusement: "And then Miriam tells Ira, 'To think your grandfather spent his days peddling peanuts on a corner of Flatbush so you could sit around in your underwear criticizing society!'"

Solly was very proud of the fact that his father was a newspaper columnist.

George's other roommate, Jeremiah, was not particularly proud of his father, George gleaned from his curt answers to questions about what he did (real estate) and the kind of person he was ("You know, he's of another generation"). He had just turned eighty, and Jeremiah was the youngest of his five offspring, a product of his third marriage, to a former elementary school teacher who was now a member of various boards. George respected Jeremiah's detached critical assessment of his socialite parents and his privileged Manhattan upbringing—which was not something he was eager to brandish as central to his identity, unlike the other city kids in their freshmen class who had self-segregated the very first day, dressing like one another and trafficking in insider references.

The first few days of the semester, Jeremiah was often mistaken for Solly, which George thought was odd, since to him they looked quite different. Jeremiah also had a beard, but it was much more kempt, and he was taller and a preppy dresser. On occasions when the two of them got confused, or were told they could be brothers, Jeremiah did not look pleased. George had observed a tensing of his jaw, a subtle sharpening of his features.

He had come to this school for the film program. "It's one of the top film programs in the country," he told George, who hadn't known this and was a little surprised a university in Connecticut would have this distinction.

Jeremiah had to have things a certain way. He was a meticulous bed-maker and no one was allowed to sit on it. He got mad when someone ate his food, especially if they ripped the packaging "like an animal" or finished off the last of something without disposing of the container. It didn't take long for the roommates' polite accord to dissolve into the playfully contentious rapport of the familiar. Jeremiah was not amused when he returned from taking a shower one morning to discover George in his bed, an assortment of crumpled food wrappers scattered over the blanket (Solly's touch).

As George emerged from his sheets, Jeremiah pointed to his feet. "You know there's something called a nail clipper, and it was invented for a reason."

George found that the type of bond that took months or even years to develop in other contexts happened much faster in college, nurtured by proximity and the inherent lowbrow comedy of campus life: cafeteria dining, the herdlike shuffling from this location to that, the absurd intimacy of dorm living—taking a shit in a stall while a few feet away someone brushed their teeth. There was a collective self-mythologizing that took place in Foss 7 room 114. In the generation of nicknames, the accumulation of private jokes, the ritualistic recapping of the previous night's drunken escapades, there was a sense of laying the groundwork of a communal psychic landscape—through which their future selves would roam, pining, *Oh, to be back in college!*

Jeremiah was a true cinephile. He knew films, he appreciated their technical craft, and it did not feel affected. He didn't dress the part or drop last names of obscure directors or unnecessarily say things like "mise-en-scène," which was the one esoteric movie term George knew. He was shocked to learn that neither Solly nor George had ever seen *The King of Comedy*. He owned the DVD and played it for them on his computer.

In the first twenty minutes of the film he pressed pause several times to relay some piece of trivia. George found this distracting and asked him to stop, but Jeremiah couldn't help himself. Sometimes he'd pause just to repeat his favorite lines.

"'He's touching everything, he's ruining the house!'"

"That was funny," George conceded.

"Yeah, and he improvised that line. Also, the part where he has trouble opening the front door wasn't in the script. He really couldn't open the door, and he just went with it."

At the end, Jeremiah marveled, "Completely anticipates the modern fantasy of mediated fame."

George was envious of his ability to summarize it so pithily.

* * *

The second morning of classes, a plane crashed into a tower of the World Trade Center. And then another plane crashed into the other tower.

There was a room in the campus center with a giant screen featuring live news coverage. George stood in the mass of students watching. The screen was so tall that you had to crane your neck to look up, creating the impression of standing on the street below the burning towers. At one point something fell from above, and at first George thought it was a part of the building, a piece of debris, but it was a person. Everyone saw it. There was a sort of collective groan in the room. A low, guttural sound, like a large animal in the final throes of painful death. More than the image of the first tower collapsing—

which would happen a few minutes later—George would be haunted by the memory of this sound.

When the second tower collapsed, George headed to his dorm to call home, but Jeremiah had beaten him to the phone. "I've got a lot of people to check on," he said, when George asked how long it would be. George returned to the campus center, where there was a line to use the pay phones. Everyone was eager to call their family. The line was long and moving very slowly. A dean approached and asked if anyone in line was from Manhattan. Anyone with relatives in New York City was invited to come with her.

George, whose father worked in the city, though not downtown, followed the dean into the science center, where a bank of phones had been set up in the corner of the lobby. There was no line to use these phones, and George felt a kind of numb panic as he dialed Denis's office number. Since George's departure for college, Denis had left several messages, but George had not called him back. He was a shitty son.

The call did not go through. There wasn't a busy signal, just silence. The dean told George to keep trying. "So many people are calling New York, the system can't keep up," she said.

George kept hanging up and dialing. He thought of a bike accident he'd had when he was five. George had face-planted in the driveway. There was lots of blood. After carrying him inside and cleaning him off, Denis had removed several low-hanging mirrors, concerned that George would be further traumatized by his wounded appearance, a gesture Ellen had found hilarious.

Eventually George got through. Hearing Denis's voice, George worried he might cry.

"Don't worry," Denis said. "The worst is over."

But it wasn't over. When he got off the phone, George learned that another plane had crashed into the Pentagon.

* * *

For a little while things felt grim, uncertain. Planes were grounded. There was talk of war, of being drafted.

"I guess this makes us the new greatest generation," Solly said.

Off campus, American flags proliferated like mushrooms after a rainstorm, and the shop windows of Main Street were plastered with signs featuring the likeness of Osama bin Laden and the words WANTED DEAD OR ALIVE. Solly, mistaken for a Middle Easterner, was refused service at a local barbershop.

It all felt a bit surreal and at odds with the levity of being a freshman in college.

One Friday night, when they were pregaming in the girls' hall, George got bored. He'd drunk three beers and was ready to go out. One of the girls in the room they were in had converted her desk into a vanity table. Amid the clutter of beauty products, George spotted a bottle of talcum powder. When no one was looking, he picked it up, twisted the top open, and gave it a shake. A cloud of white powder descended upon the group. "Anthrax!" he shouted. There was a silence, and then everyone laughed.

An irreverent hilarity persevered. In a way, it felt like a kind of patriotism, to carry on as if nothing had happened, or else, as people were now fond of saying, the terrorists had won.

* * *

Jeremiah was obsessed with the teaching assistant in his Introduction to Film class. If he recognized that it would never happen, that didn't stop him from talking about her and her resemblance to Monica Vitti. Her likeness was so striking that Jeremiah, paranoid that others might overhear them discussing her, insisted they change her nickname from Vitti to Lewinsky.

They had private nicknames for lots of people, some people in their dorm, others they'd never spoken to but who were hard to miss. Queen Frostine, Belligerent Mike, Creepy Mike, Dollface, Russian Spy, Punky Brewster, Hot Mormon, Friendly McGee.

"Odds are we have nicknames, too," Solly mused. "And we'll never know what they are."

Within room 114, George was known as "Half Jew." Both Solly and Jeremiah, who were fully Jewish, had been surprised to learn George was Jewish on his father's side.

"You don't look Jewish at all," Carrie Michaels agreed. "Not even Jewish-ish."

Carrie lived upstairs. She was always forgetting her key and having to climb through their window, which was on the first floor. She had a little dog, Frankie, that she took everywhere she could get away with.

Sometimes she lingered, sitting on Solly's beanbag chair and talking about whatever was on her mind.

"If I'm fat and single at thirty-five, please do me a favor and euthanize me," she said one afternoon.

"*What?*" she asked, looking at George. "Does it make me an *antifeminist* that I have certain biological urges?"

"I didn't say anything," George said.

"Thirty-five isn't even that old," said Solly. "My parents met when they were thirty-eight and forty."

"Well, I plan on having a bunch of kids," Carrie explained, "so I need to start earlier."

"How many kids do you plan on having?" Jeremiah asked.

"Six."

"Six," Jeremiah repeated. "Are you not concerned with overpopulation?"

"We're going to have a low carbon footprint, we're going to live on a farm," she said. "My husband's going to be this hot carpenter, and while he's out chopping wood, I'll be all barefoot and pregnant in the kitchen, baking bread, sewing our own clothes . . ."

"A lot of women have that fantasy," Solly remarked with authority. "Back to the land."

"Are you saying I'm a cliché?" Carrie stood up, clutching Frankie under her arm, to make one of her theatrical exits. There was a tear in the back of her skirt, and she wasn't wearing any underwear, and as she strode across the room you could see a slice of her butt, which was somehow more shocking than if you'd been able to see the whole thing. It wasn't erotic—more embarrassing that she didn't know.

Then again, maybe she did. You never knew with Carrie.

* * *

George did not get confused with his roommates, or anyone else. He was someone people noticed and approached, acknowledged and remembered. He suspected part of the reason for this was a benign eye condition that required him to wear an eye patch for the first several weeks of the semester. He'd been given the choice between a black patch and a flesh-colored sticker, but Cressida had convinced him to go for the less discreet option.

"I feel like a kid dressing up as a pirate," he said.

"Trust me, you look cool," she said. "People will be like, 'Who's *that?*'"

* * *

In October, George was invited to join a secret society. The first meeting took place in an underground tunnel. George and several other recruits were escorted to the location by a guy wearing a fedora and holding a rifle. A BB gun, George assumed. When they arrived at the club's headquarters, a dimly lit graffitied cement dungeon, they were told to sit on the floor. The perimeter of the room was lined with old couches, upon which sat the members of the club. George had assumed these would consist of a motley cross section of campus characters—roller skate girl, tambourine man, the nude saxophonist, those guys who stayed up all night playing poker in the laundry room—but the people on the couches were all run-of-the-mill hipsters. They'd mistaken George for one of their own because of his eye patch.

"Not my thing," George told Jeremiah when he got back.

Jeremiah was irate. "Are you kidding? You don't turn something like this down. Things like this could get you things later in life. Professionally speaking . . ."

Jeremiah's initial bitterness over being snubbed himself had subsided. Now he wanted George to be a member so he could enjoy the benefits by proxy.

"Not doing it," George said.

"You're an idiot," Jeremiah said.

But Carrie nodded approvingly. "That's a punk move," she said. "Not joining society *or* a secret society."

* * *

"The problem with improv is the people who do it aren't funny," Jeremiah remarked on the way back from an improv show.

Solly, who'd made them go to the show, began to protest, but George agreed with this statement. "Look at me, I'm a clinically depressed penis going through airport security . . ."

Without overthinking it, George did an impression of a clinically depressed penis going through airport security, complaining about having to take off its shoes and get searched, and it was very funny—much funnier than anything in the show. It was so funny, George was inspired to try it out on a larger audience at a party later that night. It was a hit, a real crowd-pleaser. People loved it, even those he'd never have expected to be susceptible to such lowbrow humor, such as George's poetry TA, Rose—whom he had a crush on. Everyone had a crush on Rose, whose dimpled, freckled beauty was accentuated by a distracted, sad look in her eyes. But at George's impression of a clinically depressed penis going through airport security, she laughed. And there was a brightening in her eyes as she talked to George afterward. They went outside for a cigarette, and then headed to another party, and when George woke up in her bed the next morning—never had he imagined!—she asked him to do it again.

* * *

George didn't understand why it was a big deal that Jeremiah got an A minus in his Introduction to Film midterm until Solly explained, "In order to major in film, you have to get an A in Introduction to Film, and now that's impossible."

Jeremiah was lying in bed with his shoes on. His eyes were open, and he was staring at the ceiling.

"But it's *one* test," George said. "Can't he talk to the professor?"

"Could you be quiet?" Jeremiah said. "I'm trying to take a nap."

George walked over to Solly's side of the room. "I'm sure they make exceptions," he whispered.

Solly shook his head solemnly. "It's a strict policy. It's to weed out the poseurs."

"But *Jeremiah*'s not a poseur."

Solly nodded, looking remorseful. "Life's a bitch."

Jeremiah slept through dinner and the rest of the night.

The next morning, Solly tried to give him a pep talk. George did his impression of a penis going through airport security. Carrie told him the department was overrated, that it was actually UCLA that had the best film program in the country.

Jeremiah wasn't having any of it. He was angry, distraught, depressed. For a few days he didn't make his bed. He barely got out of it.

On Friday, Solly tried to get him to go to a screening of an alumnus's film in the campus theater. A low-budget indie about an autistic boy who gets lost in the New York subway system. Afterward there'd be a Q and A. Jeremiah said, "I'd rather stick a needle in my eye."

Solly was worried. One night when Jeremiah was in the bathroom, he left a flyer with the number of a suicide hotline on his pillow.

This pissed Jeremiah off. "Fuck you, I'm not planning to kill myself." He crumpled up the paper and tossed it across the room, where it landed in the trash bin.

"Nice shot," George said.

"Maybe I'll join the NBA," he said dryly. "First Jew in the NBA."

A few weeks passed, and slowly Jeremiah began to become his old self again. One day he announced that he would double major in sociology and English.

"You don't have to choose your major for another year," Solly reminded him. "It's not like you have to decide now."

"What's wrong with sociology and English?"

"Nothing," Solly said. "It's a respectable choice."

* * *

As a sophomore, George lived in a condo-style dorm on the edge of campus with Solly, Jeremiah, and Benji, whom they'd befriended during their year on the Sausage Hall. It was an upgrade; they each had their own room, and there was a kitchen and a common room that came with an oversize pleather sofa the previous occupants had left behind.

Carrie Michaels lived across campus but occasionally swung by to ask Benji if he could spare a Ritalin. Once she knocked on George's door to loan him a book of poetry she thought he'd appreciate: *Actual Air* by David Berman.

"I don't know why, but it made me think of you," she said. "Read it and let me know what you think."

George, who'd never discussed poetry with Carrie, was flattered. The poems were very good. Direct, unpretentious, funny. They were the kind of poems that made George think he could write poetry. When he was younger he had.

George tried to write some poems, but they all felt like imitations of David Berman, and he abandoned them. Out of frustration he wrote a poem about trying to write a poem. *Look out the window. / See a leaf falling. / Think an original, profound thought . . .* It went on in this vein for a while. He couldn't decide if it was brilliant or garbage, if he was talented or a hack, but its acceptance by a campus literary magazine made him consider the possibility of the former.

There was a party to celebrate the publication. It was a distinctly literary crowd, and after feeling a little alienated, George had a few drinks and found himself engaged in some interesting intellectual conversations. As the evening progressed he began to wonder if these were his real people and who he'd be had he fallen in with them as a freshman. From afar it was easy to deride the members of this scene as affected, as trying too hard, but how much of that was based on their easily stereotyped hipster aesthetic? His own cohort's lack of a coherent group identity suddenly seemed pathetic. What did George and his friends have in common beyond being lumped together in the same dorm when they were eighteen? What made them special?

When he got back to his apartment, it was empty except for Dominic, a kid who lived down the street whom they'd somehow gotten to know and who came over a few times a week. He was playing Xbox.

"Dominic," George said, taking a seat on the futon next to him. "Of all the apartments in Low Rise, why do you choose to hang out at ours?"

Dominic didn't respond.

"Like Gabe and his buddies across the patio, they're nice guys. Why don't you go to their place? And the girls in C who are always baking vegan desserts . . ."

Dominic ignored him as he continued playing.

"Dominic, you're being rude. I'm asking you a question. Pause the game. Why do you come over here? What do we have on everyone else?"

Dominic paused the game.

"You have an Xbox," he said.

"That's it?" George asked. "Just an Xbox?"

"You always have Double Stuf, too," Dominic said.

"C'mon." George was getting frustrated. "Anything else? Really think about it."

Dominic thought.

"Gatorade sometimes," he said.

"Go home, Dominic," George told him. "It's almost eleven. You should be in bed."

* * *

On the eve of the day he was required to declare a major, George filled his flask and went for a walk. It was hard not to envy those who knew what they wanted to do, who made a plan and stuck to it. Solly, who wanted to work at the UN, was majoring in international studies and economics. Jeremiah, who'd spent the summer as a production assistant on the set of a documentary about rural poverty in America, had decided upon American studies, an interdisciplinary major that incorporated anthropology, English, history, religion, and sociology.

George's indecisiveness when it came to picking a major was rooted in a lifelong conviction—which he was beginning to question—that he was exceptional in most regards. Things came easily to him, always had, so many things, that he'd never felt the need to hone a particular skill set or talent, to tether his identity to a singular subject or activity (often done, George had noticed among his peers, in order to compensate for deficits or mediocrity in other areas). To be expected to narrow his pursuits, to pick a lane at the exclusion of others, felt restrictive and ultimately compromising.

It was a Monday night; the campus was quiet. At the crest of Foss Hill, outside the conservatory, George witnessed something bizarre and beautiful. Someone had poured detergent in a waterfall in a plaza on Main Street, and a hunk of frothy lather the size of a minivan had cleaved and was drifting up the hill. But George didn't know the explanation yet. All he knew was that something celestial was advancing in his direction.

He was listening to Dvořák's seventh *Humoresque* on his headphones. The most beautiful part of the piece coincided with the moment the mysterious mass passed above where he stood. George marveled at his luck to have stepped outside when he did, to have taken this particular route.

And yet it felt like more than luck, more than a coincidence, when upon returning to his dorm, George noticed that someone had written in chalk outside the entrance:

> *What labels me, negates me.*
> *—Kierkegaard*

George's choice of major didn't feel so much like a decision as a revelation—precipitated by that walk—that there was an obvious, all-encompassing alternative to siphoning himself off. George would major in philosophy.

* * *

In May of George's junior year, Denis had a stroke. No one contacted George the evening it happened. He learned about it the next morning when Cressida called from the hospital. She was with Denis, who was recovering in the intensive care unit. When George started to ask questions, she handed the phone to Denis.

George was relieved he was well enough to speak.

"It was very mild," he said. "Should be getting out of here very soon!"

After getting off the phone, George called Ellen, who disputed Denis's claim of an imminent discharge. When she'd spoken to one of the doctors the previous night, she'd been told that Denis would have to stay at least a week for observation.

"It's probably just an insurance liability thing," George said. "Why didn't you call me last night?"

"I figured it would be better to let you get a good night's sleep."

"I'm in college, I never get a good night's sleep. I have three housemates who are constantly getting drunk and blasting music at all hours. Most nights I don't even bother going to bed until three. Last night I had to listen to Benji coming home at four and puking his guts out."

"It would be nice if you visited him," Ellen said.

George sighed. "It's reading week. It's the week before finals . . ."

"I thought you said none of your classes had exams this semester."

"I have term papers."

"Well, as soon as you're done with them, I think you should come down and see him."

"Of course, I will," George said. "You don't have to tell me to do that."

"I'm not. I'm just saying I think that would be a nice thing to do."

George called Cressida back later that afternoon. "So, it sounds like he's fine? Like he'll make a full recovery?"

"His doctor said he probably lost something, but they don't know what it is yet."

"'Lost something'? What does that even mean?"

"Some cognitive function or set of memories. I don't know, George, I'm not a neurologist. I'm just telling you what they said."

"Well, if they don't know what it is, that probably means it's not very serious," George said.

Cressida didn't corroborate this sentiment.

"I'll come visit him as soon as I'm done with reading week," George promised.

* * *

George had only two term papers, and he finished them the second afternoon of reading week. When he returned to his apartment, Solly and Benji were smoking a bong and arguing about how many miles it was possible to drive in a week. They were also done with the semester.

"After five hundred miles in a day, you're statistically as likely to get into an accident as a drunk driver," Solly was saying. "But if you had multiple drivers and could rotate without stopping for the night . . ."

They soon had a plan. They would leave that night! There would be no itinerary and no maps, just a compass. They would take shifts at the wheel so that they could drive continuously. The idea was to drive north, to see how far they could go. When they'd had enough, they'd turn around.

Jeremiah, who derided the plan but was terrified of missing out, requested they delay their departure until he finished his psych paper due in the morning.

George called Denis.

"Should be getting out of here soon," Denis said, sounding chipper. "Possibly tonight or tomorrow morning."

"That's great," George said. "That's very good news. In that case . . . I was going to come straight down and see you, but if you're about to be discharged . . ."

"No rush," Denis said.

"So I'll see you in about a week," said George. "Maybe a week and a half."

* * *

They set out shortly after sunrise the following morning. Benji, who drove the first shift, waited until they'd safely crossed the border to reveal he'd brought a generous stash of weed. Jeremiah was furious. Did Benji realize that, had he been caught, all four of them could have been charged with drug smuggling?

"Apologies for jeopardizing your future senatorial campaign," Benji said.

They pulled over just outside Montreal to piss and rotate seats.

"Are you planning to smoke that in the car?" Jeremiah asked as Benji began packing a bowl.

Following a contentious exchange, Jeremiah requested to be dropped off at the nearest bus depot. Having no map, they didn't know where this was, and so they circled back toward Montreal, where it didn't take long to locate one. George felt a twinge of pity watching Jeremiah wheel his overnight bag into the terminal (unlike the others, he'd packed several changes of clothes). But it was nice to have more room in the back seat.

Onward they proceeded. George, who'd never been to Canada, was awed by the scale of the landscape and of the sky. The geography felt familiar but enhanced, bigger, greener, bluer. That it was an extension of his corner of the world made this feel less like a trip than an exploration, a venturing, a voyage—they were Vikings!

But there were also stretches of restless boredom and irritability. Solly had brought three albums of CDs that were organized alphabetically. On the second evening he requested a Gordon Lightfoot album. Benji objected. "Gordon Lightfoot! Are you kidding? *Gordon Lightfoot.*"

"You don't know Gordon Lightfoot," Solly said. "Name one Gordon Lightfoot song."

They listened to Gordon Lightfoot. Benji, stoned, started crying. "He's so good, man . . . He's so fucking good."

The mood in the car oscillated between these two poles.

"I haven't taken a shit in three days," Benji announced as they got back in the car after a rest stop. None of them had. The car reeked of Doritos and BO, of weed and farts and aerosol Old Spice deodorant—which Solly liberally applied every few hours, much to their objections.

Later that afternoon, the road ended at a body of water. To proceed north they had to take a ferry.

After parking, they worked their way to the upper deck. It was chilly, and most of the other passengers were inside the cabin. It was too windy to work the lighter, but Benji refused to give up, his thumb pink and chapped from trying to produce a flame. Eventually he located a semi-sequestered crevice in the stern where the wind couldn't get. Crouching, they took turns taking hits. Afterward they stumbled up to the front and stood at the bow. The wind was so intense it was difficult to take a full breath. At one point, Benji starting shouting and gesticulating.

"A whale!" he yelled. "*A fucking whale!*"

George stared in stoned astonishment at the majestic gray bulk protruding from the water not a hundred yards from them. He had never thought much about whales, but in this moment the simple fact of their existence seemed like a miracle, a remarkable thing.

They stopped at McDonald's for dinner. There was a kiddie area, and Benji dared Solly to get in the ball pit, which was currently occupied by half a dozen small children.

"Why would I do that?" Solly said.

"Because it's funny."

George agreed: it would be funny if Solly got in the ball pit and sat down so that only his head was visible. He'd look like a child molester.

"I'll do it for two hundred bucks," Solly offered.

They got him down to one hundred. George and Benji would each pay him fifty dollars to get in the ball pit, but only if he stayed there for twenty minutes.

As Solly waded in, the children continued playing, seemingly oblivious, but a parent must have complained, because it wasn't very long before a manager approached and Solly was asked to leave the establishment.

George's second driving shift involved navigating a winding dirt road with a steep drop-off. Benji gave him a hard time about going so slow, but George was scared that if he went any faster he might skid off the cliff. Gradually he became more confident and picked up speed, after which he rounded a curve too fast and lost control of the car. They were drifting, as if on snow or ice, toward the precipice. Nothing like this had ever happened before, and George was struck by how it wasn't just a cliché that time slowed down—it slowed enough for him to have that thought. Despair over his own impending death was mitigated by the guilt of causing two others. "I'm sorry," he said. "I'm so fucking sorry."

With inches to go, the car stopped. After a minute of silence they got out and hugged.

Without the punctuation of stopping for the night, the days blended together. One afternoon they arrived at another ferry. This one was overnight and charged per head rather than per vehicle. George proposed they cut costs by having two of them hide in the trunk as they boarded the ferry. Solly and Benji thought it was a great idea. Benji volunteered to be the cargo, and after some hesitation, Solly said he'd join him.

"So, I guess this means if we get caught, I go to jail for human trafficking," George said. "I guess that's the sacrifice I'm making."

The ferry wasn't leaving for a few hours. They circled back to a gas station to stock up on beer and snacks. As they pulled into the parking lot, Solly said, "Are we sure there's enough air circulation back there?"

They decided to test it out. After emptying the contents of the trunk onto the pavement, Benji and Solly got in. It was hard for them to get comfortable. They attempted fetal positions before realizing it made more sense for them to spoon.

After five minutes George popped the trunk, and Benji and Solly climbed out.

"It's hot in there," Solly said, looking a little pink.

"I'm fine," Benji said. "I could've gone a lot longer."

They arrived at the ferry station five minutes before it was time to board. George had not anticipated a long line of cars waiting to go through the checkpoint to get on.

"You guys okay back there?" George shouted when fifteen minutes had passed and he was still five cars from the ramp leading onto the boat.

There was no reply. It was obvious they couldn't hear him, but still, George was unsettled. They should have tested that out in the parking lot, just so he'd know for sure.

Another ten minutes passed. George cranked the AC in hopes it would cool down the trunk.

After making it onto the boat, George located a parking spot but was reluctant to pop the trunk, as they were surrounded by people getting out of their cars. He waited a few minutes for the other passengers to disperse before pushing the lever to open the trunk.

He did not hear any movement. He got out and walked to the back.

"That's not funny," George said as they played dead.

They were assigned a bunk room with two very narrow beds.

"This is the worst trip I've ever been on," George said when it was agreed he had to sleep on the narrow strip of floor.

It was the best trip he'd ever been on. It was unlike any trip he'd ever taken before, and it was hard to imagine it ever happening again. There would never be another trip like this.

* * *

Four days later, shortly after George had returned to campus, Jeremiah told him he was driving to the city and could give him a ride home.

George was in no rush to get back in a car.

"I'll take the bus in the morning," he said.

"That's silly," Jeremiah said. "I'm driving right by your exit. If you need to shower and get your things together, I'll wait until you're ready."

Jeremiah, who was typically selfish and unaccommodating when it came to offering rides, was adamant that George accept the offer.

As they pulled off campus, Jeremiah said, "Sounds like I missed a pretty epic adventure."

George assumed he was being facetious, as it was Jeremiah's instinct to ridicule things he felt left out of. But then Jeremiah admitted that he regretted bailing so early, that he wished he weren't so uptight and neurotically fixated on achieving his goals. He feared that his avoidance of situations he could not control would mean a more boring life.

George had always begrudgingly admired Jeremiah's discipline and singularly focused ambition—which would no doubt translate to the success he coveted—and so it thrilled him to hear Jeremiah talk like this.

After putting himself down, Jeremiah praised George for being the opposite kind of person: spontaneous, unafraid, destined to have an interesting, unconventional life. And then he went even further, citing George's rejection of the secret society as evidence of his superior character and integrity. George wasn't sure he agreed with Jeremiah's assessment of himself as pure and uncalculating, but he was touched.

He was also unnerved. It was not like Jeremiah to offer such concessions. George wondered what had prompted it.

As they cruised down the Merritt Parkway, he began to get a weird feeling. A terrible feeling. A physical lump in his gut.

They arrived close to eleven, well past Ellen's bedtime, and as they pulled into the driveway, George was disconcerted to discover multiple lights in the house were on.

He glanced at Jeremiah, but Jeremiah would not look back at him.

Cressida was home. She was curled up in the crook of the old green couch, her bony feet resting on Ellen's lap, whose bonier feet were propped on the edge of the card table, which was covered in flowers. White flowers, yellow flowers, lavender, more white—there were so many flowers—and more on the side table—and George, who didn't know much about different kinds of flowers, knew enough to recognize that they hadn't come from Ellen's garden but a store that sold flowers—which he forgot the word for—or maybe they'd come from that commercial from his childhood they used to prank call, 1–800-FLOWERS—but if his mother had gone flower shopping, they were not what she would've chosen, because Ellen liked wild flowers or flowers that looked like the type you'd see in the illustrations of an old-fashioned or whimsical children's book, and these flowers had a cheesy, artificial gleam, and the mingling of their treacly scents masked the familiar smell of the house, which suddenly felt irrevocably altered, stripped of some elemental feature of home there was no word for, because it was something you didn't register until it was gone.

"He died," George said to preempt hearing the words spoken by one of them.

Ellen confirmed the statement with a nod. Cressida hugged a pillow to her chest and closed her eyes.

"Dad," George said.

3. PANIC ATTACK

George, 22–23

George's initial enthusiasm for Kierkegaard and Nietzsche was complicated by their popularity. In fall of his senior year, he switched his honors thesis three times before settling on Arthur Schopenhauer's *On the Basis of Morality*. Schopenhauer, he argued, who was known to be a deeply cynical pessimist, was actually an optimist.

George's advisor took a personal interest in him, inviting him over for dinner, asking him questions about his life. George was flattered. Carl was the head of the philosophy department. He was in his seventies and had written many books. But once the novelty of the friendship wore off, Carl started to get on George's nerves. He was very confident in his opinions and would make ridiculous generalizations about "youth": *The trouble is you take life much too seriously.* He seemed to view everything from a lofty remove.

When George introduced him to his mother at graduation, Carl said, "He's internalized just enough philosophy to make his life more difficult, but not enough to translate into professional credentials."

Ellen laughed in a real way, and Carl looked pleased. George suspected it was not the first time he had delivered this line to a parent.

* * *

After a week of postgraduation parties, George returned to his mother's house in Westchester. Unlike many of his classmates, he didn't have a job or an internship lined up.

He should probably go back to school for another degree, an MFA in film or creative writing.

But he hadn't ruled out pursuing a more civic-minded profession, such as war correspondent or public defender.

He could also be a scholar.

In July, George emailed Carl to ask if they could speak on the phone to discuss PhD programs. He assumed Carl would be excited by this potential development, but Carl, who called him right away, strongly discouraged George from pursuing philosophy further, as there was no guarantee that it would lead to a career. The academic job market was oversaturated.

George was stunned. For Carl to say this implied he didn't think George had a shot.

Perhaps he was thinking of the growing emphasis on diversity in academia.

"Is it the white male thing?" George asked. "Departments don't want to hire another white guy?"

Carl said, "George, do you know what percentage of PhD students drop out?"

George did not.

"Forty to fifty percent," Carl said. "Some with only a year or two left to go."

"I don't think I'd do that."

"You don't *think* you'll do that," Carl repeated.

"No," George said, wounded by Carl's patronizing tone. "Why would I quit after investing all that time?"

"That's the other danger," Carl said. "Some people spend years and years in a program and are unable to finish their dissertation. Not out of laziness or incompetence, but fear. Fear of seeing their project all the way through and allowing it to be judged."

George knew Carl was thinking about his thesis. After having switched his topic three times, with just a few pages left in his first complete draft and a month to go before the deadline, George had had a crisis of confidence about what he had written. He'd wanted to start something new, but Carl had forced him to follow through with his proposal.

* * *

George's grandparents had paid for his college tuition. His mother bought and prepared him food, and he'd inherited his father's Peugeot, which, after its having sat for more than a year in the garage, George was finally able to bring himself to drive.

George's college health insurance would be expiring in September. He did not share his mother's anxiety about this. His primary concern was cash to cover his basic living expenses: alcohol, cigarettes, books, gas.

In August, George interviewed for a job at a restaurant a few towns over. When asked if he'd ever worked at a "fine dining establishment," George confessed to having no experience in the service industry at all.

"We'll start you on the lunch shifts," the manager told him. "You'll be a quick learner."

His name was Rory, and his confidence in George was short-lived.

Being a waiter was more challenging than George imagined. Anything anyone asked for that he didn't immediately write down, he forgot. Carrying a tray of cocktails across the room was a harrowing endeavor that once ended in disaster. The cacophony and cartoonish aftermath of the spill, which would have elicited a hearty round of cheers and applause in the cafeteria, had the opposite effect upon the room, which fell into an embarrassed silence.

There was more to the job than taking orders and relaying them to the kitchen, a certain posture one was supposed to assume when interacting with diners, which also did not come naturally to George. Fortunately, none of the diners was mean to him. If anything, they seemed charmed by his ineptitude, especially older and middle-aged women, the predominant demographic of the lunchtime crowd.

George's coworkers were less forgiving—with the exception of Jenny, the hostess, who often left her post to assist him. At the end of his shifts, George would try to give her a portion of his tips. She always refused, but sometimes she asked him for a cigarette.

One afternoon he pulled out a fresh pack, and as he unwrapped the package, Jenny asked if she could keep the cellophane.

"I make dioramas," she explained. "I want to use it for the windowpanes in a pair of French doors I'm working on."

"That'll be five dollars," George said, offering it to her.

Jenny laughed. Her reaction to his humor was often delayed and outsize, and this made George want to tease her, though he was reluctant to encourage her crush on him because he didn't think he was attracted to her.

She was tall, only two or three inches shorter than George, and he was distracted by a birthmark on her face. The size and color of a kidney bean, it began on the left corner of her lower lip and extended beyond the border. George imagined on more than one occasion that some poor soul had mistaken it for food and had tried to alert her to it by making a wiping gesture.

* * *

"You're a terrible waiter," Rory told George after his second full week on the job. "The worst I've ever had. If you weren't good-looking, I'd have fired you yesterday."

George absorbed the lashing with a stoic reserve, but it was demoralizing to find himself the object of such contempt from a person who was not his older sister.

Jenny followed him out to the parking lot.

"You're not the worst waiter we've ever had," she said. "And you shouldn't take anything he says personally."

She told him that Rory was an angry, bitter person. Racist. Misogynistic. Homophobic.

"You should hear some of the things he says at the end of the dinner shift, after he's been drinking."

George nodded soberly as she repeated some of these things. There was something endearingly juvenile about her earnest outrage, a whiff of the unfettered idealism of early adolescence, although she was actually a year older than he was.

Though Jenny held herself upright, her height felt like an extension of her vulnerability, which George had trouble attributing to anything specific about her beyond her thereness, her eagerness to please. She seemed, at any given moment, wholly present and sincerely invested in the task at hand, as if this were it for her, the summit of her life's ambitions—though it was not. She was planning to go to law school to become a public defender. George found this sweet. He didn't think she would make a good lawyer. She was too guileless, too deferential. She lacked a certain calculating reserve.

"Could I bum a cigarette?" Jenny asked when she was done talking about Rory.

"How did the French doors turn out?" George asked, handing her one.

"Haven't gotten to them yet. They're part of the master bedroom. I just finished the kitchen. Now I'm working on the living room. Couches. Tables. Lamps. Wallpaper. Rug . . ." She paused as George passed her his lighter. "Bookshelves. Fireplace. Mantel. Paintings . . .

"It's a lot of work," she said.

George had trouble gauging if she was trying to be cute or if she had any awareness of how ridiculous she sounded.

"Are you on Friendster or MySpace?" Jenny asked.

George shook his head.

Perhaps he looked a little scornful, because Jenny said, a bit defensively, "It's good for keeping in touch after college."

"I don't need to keep in touch with everyone I ever met," George said. "And as far as my real friends, I don't want our friendships to take place over the computer. That's depressing. Why not just pick up the phone?"

Jenny nodded thoughtfully as George made his argument.

"I respect your boycott," she said.

* * *

"Want to see a photo of the kitchen?" Jenny asked during a smoke break later that week.

Before George could respond, she'd pulled out her phone, forcing him to pretend to be interested.

He was actually a little impressed. "Okay," George said, "I was picturing a shoebox with some Play-Doh sculptures. This is pretty good. If you squint, the stove almost looks real."

Jenny looked pleased. "I've gotten better at appliances."

"You've made a lot of dioramas?" George asked.

She paused to consider the question. "This is only my fifth. But each one has taken me a while."

"How long?" George asked.

"Each one, from start to finish, I dunno . . . a hundred hours? Maybe more?"

George was quiet for a moment. "You're telling me you've spent *hundreds of hours* making tiny things that look like things?"

Jenny acknowledged this with a sheepish smile.

"Why?" George asked.

She looked confused.

"Do you do anything with them after they're done? Is there a national competition, a lucrative market? Are you creating inventory to launch a business?" George exhaled through his nostrils. "Or are you just eccentric? Are you a character in a Wes Anderson movie?"

Jenny's face brightened. "I love Wes Anderson!"

"What I'm asking," George continued, "is have you considered talking to a therapist about this?"

George inwardly cringed at the shitty-sitcom-level banter that came so easily to him, but Jenny laughed. It really was easy to make her laugh. It was obvious that she liked him, and George felt bad that he was always shutting down her attempts to make plans outside of work.

The fall after his dad died, George had briefly joined a bereavement group on his campus. He didn't get much out of the meetings, except for something that someone had said: "It's like your whole life you've been in this one room, and now you're not in that room anymore, and you can never go back."

Jenny was very much in the first room of her life, and George increasingly found such people difficult to relate to, naive, and a bit simple. Rather than being uplifting, their cheery innocence was like an abrasive on a wound.

* * *

Two months into the job, George had a panic attack in the middle of a shift.

It was triggered by the appearance of his high school history teacher, whom he had once lied to about a paper he hadn't written. It wasn't the only time he'd lied about an assignment, but this particular occasion haunted him, because, in convincing Mrs. Tate that he had left a copy on her desk, he inadvertently led her to believe she was at fault for misplacing it. Her apology had alluded to some personal issues—a missing cat, an ill parent—as an explanation for why she'd been so distracted. George had received a conciliatory A.

She was not seated in his section and didn't appear to register his presence, but George was very aware of hers. Here was an opportunity to confess and apologize, and yet he could not bring himself to approach her table. The mere thought of doing it made his mouth go dry.

And then he did it. There was a lull, and he walked over. After George introduced himself and reminded Mrs. Tate who he was, he started to try to explain himself, but he couldn't get any words out.

It was George's first panic attack, and it manifested as a medical episode: vertigo, racing heart, shortness of breath, a sudden weakness. George fainted, and though he came to very quickly and was able to get back on his feet unassisted, everyone was concerned. The paramedics were called, and the next thing George knew, he was being wheeled off the premises on a gurney and loaded into the back of an ambulance.

George was too humiliated to return to work the next day. Or the day after that. He never called Rory to formally quit; he simply stopped showing up.

* * *

A few weeks later, George received a bill from the hospital for $3,859.23. He called the hospital's billing department and was put on hold for nearly an hour. When a person finally confirmed that, for a patient without health insurance, the figure was correct—nearly four thousand dollars, for an ambulance ride, a diagnosis of generalized anxiety disorder, and a prescription for an antidepressant—George said thank you and hung up.

Then he punched the wall above his desk.

He'd never broken a bone before, but he could immediately tell that was what had happened. The pain was unlike anything he'd ever experienced; he thought he might throw up. He definitely couldn't drive. His mother was out. He called Jenny, who was about to get off her lunch shift.

She came straight away and drove him to the hospital.

Just as she pulled into the parking lot, George vomited.

"Don't worry about it," she said in her warm, reassuring way. "I was about to get the car cleaned anyway."

Jenny dropped him off at the entrance and went to park.

The automatic doors swooshed open in a clinical embrace, as if expecting him.

"You're already in the system," the intake nurse told George as he gave her his information.

"Great," he said. "Just put it on my tab."

When asked to rate his pain on a scale of one to ten, George, noticing the nurse was pregnant, said eight, even though it was more like nine and a half.

George kept telling Jenny to go home as he waited for a doctor to see him, but she insisted on staying.

"Is this how you imagined our first date?" he said as a nurse cut his shirt off with a pair of scissors.

Jenny blushed, and George regretted making the joke. First date implied future dates.

The doctor came in, took one look at George's arm, and ordered an X-ray.

As they waited, Jenny begged George to tell her the reason he'd felt so anxious seeing his teacher in the restaurant that he'd had a panic attack (he'd told her this much), and so he told her what he'd done.

Unimpressed by his transgression—"You think you're the first high school student who lied about a paper?"—Jenny told George a story about a trip she'd taken to the city as a kid with her parents.

As they'd walked up Fifth Avenue to Central Park, they passed a bunch of vendors. Six-year-old Jenny wanted an I ♥ NY baseball cap.

"It was completely overpriced. My mom said no, but my dad, who couldn't say no, took out his wallet. 'She'll lose it,' my mom said. 'She loses everything.' At the park they took me to the carousel, the zoo, the castle. We passed by that pond where you can rent a rowboat. Naturally I wanted to do that. As we rowed out, I leaned over the edge of the boat, and my hat fell off into the water. I waited for my mom to yell at me, but she didn't seem to notice. It was floating, and I thought I could reach over and get it without them noticing, but my arm wasn't long enough, and it drifted away. As we were leaving the park my dad asked me where the hat was. I pretended I'd only just realized it was no longer on my head. I don't know why, it's not like I'd done anything wrong, but I was too ashamed to tell him the truth. My mom said, 'See? You never should've gotten her that hat, she's already lost it!' I felt this deep, sickening kid guilt, like I was this careless, spoiled brat. It's completely irrational, but to this day I feel sad when I think about that hat. So, so sad."

Jenny looked like she might cry and, noticing that George saw this, she explained, "My dad died later that year, so it probably has to do with that."

George was surprised by this piece of information. "I didn't know your dad died," he said.

Jenny nodded. "Car accident. I was six."

"My dad died, too," George told her. "Stroke. My junior year of college."

Now Jenny looked surprised. "That's pretty recent."

George shrugged.

A nurse came to take George to his X-ray. He was right; it was a fracture.

Jenny drove George home. There was a charged silence after she pulled into the driveway.

"Do you want to come in?" George asked.

Jenny had to work but volunteered to come over tomorrow, when she had the night off.

George's mother was back. He told her what happened, then passed out on the couch in the TV room. When he woke up, he heard voices in the kitchen. His sister was over. George listened as Ellen told her the story.

"Now he's going to have another medical bill," Cressida pointed out. "I wonder if he'll break his other wrist when that one arrives."

"Hopefully he'll have learned his lesson," Ellen said.

"Are you going to help him pay for it?" Cressida asked.

"I don't think so." There was a silence, and then a more definitive, "No."

She continued. "He already has free housing, a free car. He never grocery shops. Everything he eats, I bought. At a certain point, he needs to learn to take care of himself."

Cressida reminded Ellen that she had paid for her abortion earlier that year.

"That's different," Ellen insisted. "George lost his temper and punched a wall. He did this to *himself*."

"So did I, basically," Cressida said. "I told the guy not to bother with a condom."

"Cressida, *please*," said Ellen.

"You had an abortion?" George asked Cressida as they crossed paths on the stairs later that evening.

She held up two fingers and winked.

* * *

To pay off his medical debt—his subsequent bill was over five thousand dollars—George accepted an internship at a hedge fund, which offered health insurance and a generous weekly stipend on par with the entry-level salaries at many nonprofits.

When George told Jenny this, she said, "If this is about money, and the money is equivalent, then why don't you try to get an entry-level job at a nonprofit?"

"Because then I'd have to sign a contract saying I'll stay there for a year or whatever," he explained. "An internship at a hedge fund I can leave whenever I want. And I wouldn't feel guilty about it."

They were sitting at a table outside a Starbucks. Cars rushed by. At the table next to them, two women commiserated about the going rate of SAT tutors.

George had just had his cast removed and could drive again. Jenny had wanted to meet in a local nature preserve, but George proposed they meet here instead, thinking the less intimate setting would dispel any notions she had of a romantic future.

The last time they had hung out, it had become clear that Jenny expected something to happen, and their parting had been awkward. George still wasn't sure if he was attracted to her, and it seemed too late to find out without hurting her feelings. He really didn't want to hurt her feelings. She had been so kind to him.

George took out his cigarettes.

"Damn," he said, seeing that he had only one left.

Jenny shook her head when he offered her a drag. Then she confessed that she wasn't really a smoker. She'd asked George for cigarettes only as an excuse to talk to him after their shift at the restaurant. This had been obvious to George, but he didn't say so.

Jenny told George about something that had happened the

previous night at the restaurant. A man had gotten down on one knee and proposed to his girlfriend in front of the whole restaurant. Everyone stopped talking as they noticed what was happening. She said yes, and the whole room applauded.

"He seemed like kind of an asshole," Jenny said. "He acted really put out that we were out of one of the specials and then he sent back a perfectly good bottle of wine. Both times she looked really embarrassed and made an effort to smile and thank me, but as far as I could tell she didn't say anything to him. And then, immediately after she'd accepted the proposal, like right after, she got up to use the bathroom. And when she came out I could tell she'd been crying."

The reluctant acceptance made George think of a British girl who'd attended his elementary school just for fifth grade. Helen had made no friends and had kept to herself. He would probably have forgotten her were it not for a poem she'd recited at the culmination of their medieval studies unit. Each student was assigned a role in a fictional feudal village. They had to dress up and compose and give a speech in character. Hers had gone:

Oh no! Oh horrors! Oh, woe is me!
My family has selected a man for me!
He's rich and of great nobility—
And now he wants to marry me!
Guidance and help I surely do need
And your advice I promise to heed.

Jenny was impressed that George had committed the poem to memory after all those years.

"Do you have any idea what it would mean to her?" she asked.

"It was much better than anything else in the class," George said. "I don't even remember mine. I think I was a blacksmith or something."

George wondered where Helen was now. If she'd been aware of her precocious talent, and what she was doing with it.

He flicked the embers out of his cigarette and put what remained of it back in his pack for later.

"Is something wrong?" Jenny asked. "The whole time we've been here, you've had this distracted, depressed look on your face."

"That's just my natural expression," George said. "I'm a distracted and depressed person. A clinically depressed penis."

"What?"

"Dumb joke from college," he said.

"And you keep doing this." Jenny gripped the side of the table and leaned back in her chair so that it was on two legs.

"Old habit," George said. "Don't even know I'm doing it.

"Drives my mom nuts," he added.

"Feels like nervous energy," Jenny said.

"Yup. Definitely got that, too. Distracted, depressed, nervous energy. The complete package."

"What are you nervous about?" Jenny asked.

"Death," George answered.

Jenny smiled.

"And life," he said.

The women at the next table were now discussing a teacher at their kids' school, an excessively harsh grader. It was not fair. Everyone knew! Why did the administration allow it?

"I don't know if this ever happened to you right after graduating . . ." George started doing the chair thing again, and then stopped himself once he realized he was doing it. "But sometimes, for a moment, I forget that I'm not on summer break. I think I'm going back to college. And then I remember it's over. This is it. This is my life."

Jenny left this hanging. She sucked the last sips of her Frappuccino and announced that she had to leave for her shift at the restaurant. George suspected that she just wanted to go. She'd had enough of him and his nervous energy.

As they walked to the parking lot, George knew this would be the last time they saw each other, and even though they hadn't known each other for long, he felt a little sad about this.

"I have something for you," he said.

George reached in his pocket. He had ordered a pizza earlier that week, and it had come with that little plastic table in the middle of the pie that propped up the box. He thought Jenny would like it for her diorama, but, looking at it now, he realized it wasn't her style. The furniture in her dioramas was made out of balsa wood, which she carved using an X-ACTO knife and then applied real wood stain to with a Q-tip. This would look junky in comparison.

But Jenny looked touched as he presented it to her.

"It came in a box of pizza," he explained. "Sorry it's plastic. I thought it looked like a little kitchen table."

"It does. That's exactly what it looks like."

George noticed that one of the table's legs was crooked. When he tried to straighten it, it snapped off.

"Fuck me," he said.

Jenny thought this was funny. "Oh, George," she said with a certain tender familiarity, a fondness that made George feel like she could see all the parts of him. This was something he'd never experienced with a girl.

Jenny opened the door of her car.

"Hey, Jenny," George said, and when she turned her head, he leaned in and kissed her.

4. KARPOS GIVES BACK

George, 23–25

The hedge fund where George was an intern was called Karpos. George's uncle Blake (who was also his godfather) was the CEO. Karpos's headquarters were located in midtown Manhattan, but to ease the commutes of its suburban employees, Blake had opened an outpost on the third floor of a commercial building in Greenwich, Connecticut.

Blake had his own private office; the rest of the traders worked in cubicles on an open floor.

At the desk adjacent to George's sat a man who had just gotten divorced. Clark was funny in the way people can be when their lives are abruptly upended. To entertain himself he would carry on imaginary conversations with celebrities, which often took the form of pep talks about how Clark needed to get his life together. Sometimes he just did impressions from movies.

"Come on, Chief!" he'd say to himself as Jack Nicholson from *One Flew Over the Cuckoo's Nest*. "Get your hands up!"

Clark was a talented impersonator. On George's mother's birthday, he asked Clark to wish her a happy birthday on her answering machine in the voice of Woody Allen. Clark got really into it. "I'm normally into younga women, but I'll make an exception for a shiksa like you . . ."

Ellen loved it. "Your friend should be on *Saturday Night Live!*"

George liked Clark but thought the rest of the traders were simple, one-dimensional men who subscribed to mottos like "work hard, play hard." That was the extent of their soul-searching. "He's a good guy," they'd say of anyone they had a favorable business interaction with. Happiness, or at least their version of it, came easily to these men for whom life was a game. Money was the prize, and they were the winners.

On casual Fridays, the traders swapped their suits for colorful polo shirts, khakis, and Vineyard Vines belts embroidered with golf clubs or sailboats or some other emblem that screamed "I'm rich!" As the hour crept toward five, someone would turn on a playlist. They liked hip-hop. One of their favorite songs contained the line, "It's the freakin' weekend, baby, I'm about to have me some fun." They had no idea how they looked, the traders at Karpos, singing and nodding along at their desks like a row of bobbleheads.

It was an embarrassing sight to behold. These were not George's people. He did not belong there.

So that George would be able to put some money away in addition to paying off his hospital bill, Blake had offered to let him live for free in a converted carriage house in their backyard, which was a fifteen-minute drive from the office.

When George first moved into "the cottage"—as they called it— it was hotel-clean and stocked with essentials. It was an open space with a little kitchenette and steps leading up to a sleeping loft. A soaring vaulted ceiling made it feel much bigger than it was. Across from the fireplace, a bank of casement windows looked out over a field and then woods. ("It's like one of my dioramas come to life!" Jenny gushed, coming to see it for the first time.)

George's aunt—his mother's younger sister—took pride in showing him where everything was kept: toilet paper, light bulbs, cleaning supplies, fan, mousetraps, flashlights in case of a power outage. There was even a drawer full of takeout menus, arranged alphabetically. That it was obvious Addie had gotten great pleasure, even joy, out of doing all this made George feel sorry for her.

But mostly he felt sorry for himself. Because these things did nothing for him. And recognizing this made him feel spoiled and ungrateful.

* * *

One of George's responsibilities at Karpos was to take everyone's lunch orders. Sandwiches were popular. Big sandwiches, with lots of things in them, which the men would bark out in distracted voices as they stared at their computers: roast beef, turkey, ham, salami, prosciutto, Swiss, American, cheddar, Muenster, bacon, pickles, onions, peppers, tomato, mustard, lettuce, mayo, *make that extra mayo* . . .

George would circulate the room writing it all down. Some days it seemed like each order was longer than the last, and that the length of each order was a challenge to the next one. Almost like a contest. A macho thing.

"Would you like a baby with that?" George once asked in response to an order that included three different kinds of meat. "For extra protein, I could ask them to toss in a fresh newborn baby."

No one laughed. Everyone was looking at him.

"His wife just had a miscarriage," Clark whispered when George returned to his desk.

George hadn't known this. He felt terrible. He should say something. Or would that make it worse? Preoccupied, he forgot to call in the order, and though no one was going to yell at the boss's nephew, he could tell everyone was angry at him.

"Let's get a drink," Clark said to him before they left that day. To avoid their colleagues, they went to a working-class bar. A crew of Department of Public Works employees walked in right after them, and the bartender—who knew them all by name—served them first. George didn't mind, but Clark looked visibly annoyed, which made George self-conscious. He didn't want to play into any stereotypes.

When it was finally their turn, Clark asked for a Budweiser and a shot of Jameson.

"We'll have two of those," he said when George couldn't decide what he wanted.

They took their drinks to a booth in the back. After a second round, George began to confide in Clark about how depressed he was. About how much he hated being an intern at Karpos, the loneliness of going home at night to the froufrou cottage, his sense of dread upon waking in the morning.

George stared sadly into his drink. "This is not how I imagined my life."

Clark was a laugher, but George had never heard him laugh this hard.

When he finally stopped laughing, there was a residual smile on his face, and it was a little mean.

"You're, *what*, twenty-fucking-five years old?"

"Twenty-three," George corrected him.

"Twenty-three!" Clark resumed laughing; then he stopped and his face turned dark.

"When I was your age, I was an NBC page," he said. "If you grow up watching *Saturday Night Live* and you think, I could write that shit, I could do that, you apply to be a fucking NBC page. You work lots of hours, and then on the weekends, you do stand-up at little hole-in-the-wall joints, practicing your material. You date. You sleep around. Life is good. Then you meet a chick who's out of your league, but she thinks you're very funny and gives you a shot. Everyone thinks you're very funny, and you *are* very funny—for a regular person. The problem is, you're not *quite* funny enough for a stand-up or comedy writer. You're like a single-A minor league baseball player at best—better than nearly everyone except the pros. Eventually, you realize not everybody can be Will Ferrell. You let the comedy thing go. You switch to finance, because the girl has certain expectations for her life, and you do it because she's still out of your league and you want to make her happy. It's as boring and soul-crushing as you expected, but you got the girl, so it's worth it. You're in love. You get married. You buy a house. Have two kids. You're doing the thing, you're a fucking adult. And then, *boom!*" Clark slapped the table with such force, George had to steady his beer. "One day she decides she don't love you no mo' . . ."

Clark started to explain how divorce and alimony worked. How what you earned the year of your divorce dictated what you owed your spouse for years to come. His wife had filed for a divorce the year Clark had earned his biggest bonus ever, which meant Clark was expected to make that kind of money every year, which left him no options but to spend the rest of his life in finance, which he hated.

"You could've had one life, but because of her, you chose another, and now the whole thing's ruined." Clark pressed his lips together and shrugged.

George didn't know what to say. Clark's life really did seem ruined. But it sounded like he hadn't been talented enough to make it as a comedy writer, either.

This was the first time they'd socialized outside of work, and George regretted it. It would be hard to go back to seeing him as the comically disgruntled guy at the next desk.

"Moral of the story"—Clark adopted his Louis Armstrong voice, his best impression—"never get married. Just don't do it. Just not worth it."

George expected Clark to follow up with an acknowledgment of his kids, to say that it actually had been worth it, if just for them, but instead he kept going with his impression.

"Oh, *yeaaaah*," he sang, like Armstrong at the end of "What a Wonderful World."

* * *

The office was often over-air-conditioned, but today it was ridiculous.

"Is it just me, or is it freezing in here?" George kept asking the room.

No one else was cold. George wondered if he was sick.

His teeth started to chatter. He could have controlled the sound by tensing his jaw but chose not to.

The traders noticed.

"Dude, you don't look so good."

"Bro, you should go home."

"Only you would get the flu in June," Clark said as George packed up his things.

George drove back to the cottage. He felt shivery and weak. With what little energy he had, he lit a fire.

On his way up to the sleeping loft, a step dislodged from its base and clattered on the floor. George stumbled backward and landed on his tailbone. Shrill tendrils of pain fanned into a dull ache.

When he managed to get to his feet, George picked up the step and chucked it into the fireplace, where the wood, being dense and not very flammable, had a smothering effect. As the flames withered, smoke feathered into the room.

The smoke detector went off.

It was too high to reach.

George located a broom and began prodding the contraption until it fell on the floor, where it cracked like an eggshell under the force of his stomps.

George had a temper, and sometimes it got out of control.

When he calmed down, George collapsed on the love seat and fell into a deep, dreamless sleep.

When he woke up, it was the next morning. George felt a little better, but that didn't really mean anything, as it was often the case when you were sick that you woke up feeling better and then deteriorated as the day went on.

George called his mom. When he told her that he was sick, she said, "Well, I'm sure it's just a little virus." And then she told him about a neighbor who had just been diagnosed with lung cancer. "Never even picked up a cigarette."

George thought of calling Jenny. They had been seeing each other on a sporadic basis until one night, several weeks earlier, Jenny had said, "I can't do this anymore. This casual sex thing. Do me a favor, and don't invite me over again unless you're interested in a relationship."

George called Jenny.

She arrived later that afternoon with a bag of groceries. "I was passing by Food Emporium and thought I'd pick you up a few things . . ."

"Thank you," George said. He shuffled over to the kitchenette to help her unload the bag. Over yesterday's clothes, he wore a blanket like a cape. He was definitely feeling better but felt the need to keep up appearances, lest she see him as a hypochondriac.

"You just sit," Jenny said. "I'll make you some tea."

"Okay," George said, returning to the love seat.

Jenny joined him on the love seat. They sat in silence sipping Earl Grey. Normally when Jenny came over, it was late and they drank their way through any initial discomfort. But it was too early for alcohol.

Jenny noticed the missing step. "What happened?"

"It broke," George told her. "Like everything I touch."

Jenny laughed.

"It's true," George said. "Don't say I didn't warn you."

She laughed again.

"It's in there." George pointed to the hearth.

"You tried to *burn* it?"

"I was in a mood." George got up and pulled the step out of the ashes so that he could put it back on its base. It was only a little charred.

"Oh, George," Jenny said, in the manner of someone who'd known him for much longer.

She seemed to relish saying that. *Oh, George.*

Jenny spent the night. In the morning George felt almost completely better, but he called in sick anyway.

As they drank coffee on the love seat, Jenny gasped and ran to the window. There was a flock of wild turkeys in the field. George, who'd seen them many times before, pretended to share her awe.

It started raining. George proposed they watch a movie on his computer. He apologized for the dearth of options in his DVD collection: some David Lynch films, *Harold and Maude*, and the first and third seasons of *The Larry Sanders Show*.

"Let's watch *Harold and Maude*," George said.

Jenny looked hesitant.

"You've never seen *Harold and Maude?*"

George started to summarize it, but Jenny interrupted. "I know what it's about, I know how it ends, and I don't want to see it." There was an uncharacteristic edge to her voice.

"My dad killed himself," she said. "I don't like movies that end with suicide."

"I thought your dad died in a car wreck."

"Sometimes that's what I tell people when I don't feel like getting into it." Jenny spoke crisply, without looking at George. "When you grow up in a small town, and it's the first thing people know about you . . ."

"I understand," George told her. "That makes sense."

"I'll tell you about it sometime," she said, continuing to avoid his gaze. "But not right now."

George took her hand. Pressed her limp fingers in his. When she remained unresponsive, he leaned forward and kissed her birthmark. As he pulled back, she looked at him, but her big brown eyes gave nothing away. George was aroused by her sudden remote demeanor. That there was more to Jenny, that she was capable of withholding a part of herself, made her more interesting.

They spent the afternoon watching *The Larry Sanders Show*. Even if George appreciated the show's acerbic humor more than Jenny seemed to, he could tell it made her happy, to be spending the day together like this. George felt happy, too.

* * *

Jenny started coming over more often, occasionally showing up unannounced.

One evening George was taking a shower when the shower rod fell. It was a tension rod, and it wasn't difficult to reinstall, but moments after George had done this, it fell again. George turned off the water, picked up the rod, and put it back. It fell.

As the process repeated itself, George lost his temper. After it clunked him on the head, he picked up the rod and brought it down over his knee. He'd imagined its snapping in two, but instead he hurt himself, which made him even angrier. George picked up the rod again, and this time he tried to break it by thrashing it against the pipe beneath the sink. As he stood there, naked, wet, and red with rage, banging metal against metal, he noticed Jenny in the doorway.

That she appeared to find it funny was surprising to George. He couldn't tell if it was a genuine reaction or a choice.

* * *

George was ashamed when Jenny witnessed his temper, which was inevitable given how often she was around.

Understandably, with each successive episode, her reaction was less amused.

"I don't know what a person like you is doing with a piece of shit like me," George told her one night.

Jenny looked sad that he would say this. "You're not a piece of shit, George. You've got a temper, you've got some things to work through, but you're a wonderful person."

George marveled at her compassion for him. That she was so quickly able to shift from her own feelings to his.

He sometimes wondered how much of his appeal to her was his ability to make her laugh. Saying lewd things in a Kermit the Frog voice, doing his Fred Astaire dance routine wearing only a button-down shirt and business socks, whistling "Mary Had a Little Lamb" with a deranged look in his eyes—it didn't take much to get her going. Some acts went over so well they became recurring bits. Like the first time George had walked in on Jenny changing and pretended to have a spontaneous orgasm.

"Is it fun to be able to make someone laugh so hard?" Jenny once asked him.

George nodded. "But what's best is to make a whole group of girls laugh."

Jenny laughed, and George felt like a jerk because he had not been kidding.

"I like making you laugh," he said. "It's a good feeling."

"Does it make you feel like a man?" Jenny asked. "Like you're dominating me?"

George considered this. "There's definitely a feeling of power. Especially when I get you to a place where you kind of lose control, and then it gets even easier. Like the wheels are greased, and we're coasting downhill. Like waves that will never end."

Jenny took this in, blinking, silent. She wasn't exactly an intellectual, but she had a certain curiosity, and George admired this about her.

"Is it fun to be with someone who can make you laugh so hard?" he asked.

Jenny nodded earnestly, almost shyly. "It's the best."

The energy she'd channeled into her dioramas Jenny now put toward the cottage. She was always baking and cleaning and rearranging things to make them nicer. She'd take long walks alone in the woods and come back with a fistful of wild flowers. In October she bought pumpkins for the front stoop and draped the mantel with vines of bittersweet she'd snipped off a tree on the side of the road.

In December she hung a Christmas wreath on the door. George's aunt noticed and told Ellen, who said, "I hear you have a girlfriend and she's decorating your cottage for Christmas."

There was a teasing quality in Ellen's tone, as though she were aware of George's insecurity about their relationship, which was that it was prematurely domestic and they didn't have enough sex— through no fault of Jenny's, she was always up for it. It was George's issue, and he attributed it to Lexapro.

It was a snowy winter. Jenny slept over most evenings, and they almost always lit a fire. One night they turned off all the lights and sat on the love seat drinking whiskey as George read passages of *Finnegans Wake* in an Irish accent.

"Do you understand any of this?" George paused to ask.

After some hesitation, Jenny admitted she did not.

George smiled. "You don't have to be embarrassed about that. No one does."

"I like this, though," she said, resting her freshly shampooed head against his shoulder. "Keep going."

They did. And with each passing month George's affection for Jenny deepened, sometimes manifesting as a physical pang, or even a pain, similar, he suspected, to what a parent felt for a child. His awareness of how happy he could make her, of how large he loomed in her mind, came with a burden.

One night Jenny rolled over, hugged George from behind, and whispered, "I'm in love with you."

George said nothing. Felt nothing. Anything he might have felt was subverted by an awareness of what he was supposed to say, which he couldn't bring himself to utter, not for the sake of it. It would mean nothing if he did. He remained on his side, facing away from her, and pretended to be asleep.

The next night, Jenny said it again. "I'm in love with you, George."

This time they were lying in bed facing each other.

"Do you feel that way about me?"

George told her the truth. "I don't really know what that means. To be in love. I know that I love you."

"Then you're not in it."

Jenny spoke these words very matter-of-factly. She did not roll over.

George felt bad. "I never had a role model for that at home," he said. "That could be part of it."

* * *

Jenny's cousin needed someone to cat-sit for the first week of May. She lived on the Lower East Side of Manhattan, and Jenny suggested they make a little vacation out of it. George, who'd barely taken any time off since starting his internship, consented.

It was a mistake. The lovely spring weather, knowing this was his only pocket of free time for God knew how long, had a paralyzing effect on George. Jenny had made all these plans of things they were going to do, but after summiting the four flights of stairs to the apartment they were staying in, George couldn't bring himself to do anything. He wanted to sleep, to be left alone. He encouraged Jenny to go out on her own, and after some resistance she did. She visited the Tenement Museum, the Met, MoMA; walked the High Line; went to a Moth show. She did all these things by herself, returning with amusing anecdotes, which George, touched by her plucky nature, made an effort to appear entertained by.

It was an effort to pretend to be a normal human. It did not help that the apartment was a cramped studio cluttered with plants, and the walls were painted dark blue. The cat was nowhere to be seen, but made its existence known with its outrageously pungent deposits in the kitty litter box. The plants were everywhere. There was something sinister about the glossy sheen of their thick rubbery leaves, the tendrils spilling out from hanging pots. One afternoon George had a semi-lucid dream in which he woke up—in the dream—to discover that the plants had overtaken the apartment and he was pinned to the bed.

It wasn't the week Jenny had been looking forward to, but apart from a fight about making George go down and up the four flights to buy her a lemon, she didn't try to force him to do anything or make him feel guilty. On the penultimate morning, after she'd left the apartment, George had an idea of something he could do to make it up to her. An inspired gesture. It would take a lot of steps, but imagining how happy it would make her motivated him to take the first one and get out of bed. A few steps later, George's energy started to flag. To commit to following through with his plan, he texted Jenny to meet him at the Central Park boat pond at two o'clock.

It worked. A few hours later, George and Jenny were in a boat in the middle of the pond. George was the rower. They sat facing each other, but Jenny kept craning her head to follow the progress of a mallard and her trio of ducklings. While Jenny was watching the ducks, George rested the oars and discreetly unzipped his backpack.

"For fuck's sake," he said, summoning Jenny's attention. "I hate when people litter." He pretended to retrieve an object from the water. "Wait . . . Is this . . . ? Oh my God . . . What are the odds?"

George handed it to Jenny, who burst into tears upon seeing the I LOVE NY logo on the baseball cap.

"Congratulations!" someone in another boat called out, mistaking her reaction for a proposal.

* * *

In their absence, a bird built a nest in the Christmas wreath on the front door of the cottage. "I was just thinking I should take that down," Jenny said. "I'm glad I didn't!"

Concerned the opening and closing of the door would be disruptive to the nesting process, Jenny insisted they remove the screen from a window and use that instead of the door.

Eggs were laid. They were taking a long time to hatch, George thought, when a week had passed. He was eager to get his door back. Even Jenny got tired of climbing through the window. It was she who suggested it would be okay if they resumed using the door, as long as they were very careful about it. She made a sign and taped it to the door: EGGS!!! CAREFUL!!!!

One morning Jenny woke up with a cold sore. "Goddamn herpes," she said, looking in the mirror. It wasn't too noticeable, George said, trying to comfort her. But over the next twenty-four hours it got bigger, redder, crustier. George requested that she be very careful about not sharing cups and using her own towel until it healed. Jenny, sounding a little defensive, insisted she was being careful, but also claimed that George, who'd never had a cold sore, had definitely been exposed to the virus by this point in his life and could thus assume he was part of the fourteen percent of the population who was not susceptible. George was reassured by that notion, but still, he didn't want to take any chances. "I just wouldn't like to have to show up at work with something like that on my face," he explained.

Jenny looked stunned, and George realized what a stupid, insensitive remark this was. Not only because Jenny was about to report to her shift at the restaurant, with *something like that on her face*, but also because of the birthmark on her lip, which she rarely spoke about, but he knew made her self-conscious.

As he struggled to come up with the right apology, Jenny left. She left in a huff, and in doing so, did not open and close the door with the usual caution.

She didn't realize what she'd done. George discovered the terrible sight an hour later upon stepping outside for a cigarette. He went back in and poured himself a scotch before dealing with the mess. After removing all the solid matter and depositing it in the woods, he unraveled the garden hose and sprayed the concrete until there was no more evidence of the tragedy.

The nest itself had remained intact, on the wreath. The mother was gone.

"The nest is empty," Jenny told George the next morning.

"They must have hatched and flown away," George said.

"Birds don't fly away the day they're born."

"Maybe it was a raccoon," George said.

Jenny's stricken expression turned suspicious.

That night he looked up from his book to find her gaze fixed on him, chilly, interrogating.

"Do you want to tell me what really happened, George?"

George placed his book facedown on the table beside him. He picked up his drink, took a sip, and sighed.

"There was an accident," he said.

"Of course it was an *accident*," she snapped. "I'm not accusing you of intentionally murdering them, you're not a psychopath, but goddamn it, George, could you not have been a little more careful? It's just so typical of you. You're so wrapped up in yourself, it's kind of astounding."

George's clumsiness was indicative of a greater character flaw, Jenny argued: his absentminded disregard for others, his resistance to doing anything that posed the slightest inconvenience to him. It was immature, it was selfish. It was not a good way to be!

As Jenny went on, George felt a kind of relief. The relief of resignation. The shame and self-recrimination he'd felt after the comment he'd made to Jenny were subverted by a searing humility; he had been exposed for who he was, and would suffer for it. There was a dignity in passively enduring such a brutal character assassination—in recognizing that it was deserved—at least he had this.

"Are you going to say anything?" Jenny asked. "You can defend yourself."

George spoke after a silence. "You make a lot of valid points."

"Is that all?"

"I'm sorry," he said. "You deserve better."

* * *

Jenny had never officially moved in, but over the past eleven months she'd brought enough of her things over that it took her the better part of a Saturday morning to clear out.

When she was done, George followed her out to the driveway.

"So, this is it?" he said. "Goodbye, see you never?"

"Take care of yourself, George," Jenny said. "Stop smoking. Look for a job you actually like. Or go back to school. See a therapist . . ."

"Therapists are expensive," George said.

A leaf blower droned in the distance.

"There are clinics," Jenny said. "Find someone who charges on a sliding scale."

George huffed. "I'm sure those people want to give a discount to someone who works at a hedge fund."

Jenny chewed her bottom lip and stared at him. Her face was

still marbled from earlier tears, but she was fully composed. Her eyes seemed to sparkle with a placid resolve.

"Well," she said, "if that's your attitude."

* * *

Once a year, the employees of Karpos took a day off from work to volunteer. Last year, the traders spent the day in a soup kitchen in Harlem. This year they would be visiting an elementary school in the Bronx.

The day had a name: Karpos Gives Back. George was in charge of ordering the T-shirts, booking a photographer, and chartering a van.

When the van arrived, there wasn't enough room for everyone plus the photographer and all of his equipment.

Blake asked George to drive the photographer in.

As he backed out of the parking spot, George asked, "Do you shoot a lot of corporate publicity stunts?"

The photographer looked uncomfortable. "I do a bit of every-thing," he responded. They drove the rest of the way in silence. George had trouble parking and they arrived at the school a few minutes after everyone else.

A security guard spoke into a walkie-talkie as they entered the building. "We got more yellow T-shirts."

After going through a metal detector, they were escorted to a class-room, where George was paired with a second-grader named Iris.

Iris was shy, and that made George feel shy. Their mutual reserve was more pronounced in the midst of the animated banter that sur-rounded them.

"Do you like math?" George asked Iris, who shook her head.

"I never liked it, either," George told her. "I liked reading and social studies much better. What's your favorite subject?"

Iris shrugged and shoved her fists deeper into the pockets of her hooded sweatshirt.

"Do you have a favorite animal?" George asked.

Iris muttered something.

"What's that?" George said.

"Horses," Iris said.

George immediately regretted asking Iris if she had ever ridden a horse—what a thoughtless question to ask a child growing up in the Bronx—but Iris nodded. She had ridden a horse named Applesauce.

He was brown.

He loved apples.

He lived in Van Cortlandt Park.

When George had run out of questions to ask Iris about Applesauce, he volunteered his own riding history.

"I don't like riding horses," he told Iris. "You know why?"

She shook her head.

"Because I always get the bad horse. The difficult horse. There's always one horse in the stable that's trouble, and that's the one they put me on. And some guy who works there is always like, 'Oh, you got *Aspen*? Watch out!'"

Iris had been avoiding eye contact, but now she looked at George in a curious, scrutinizing way.

"You just have to keep trying," she said.

"It's not me," George clarified. "It's not about trying. It's the *horse*."

Iris looked uncomfortable. George didn't blame her.

At the desk next to them, one of the Karpos employees made a farting sound with his clasped hands to the delight of his student.

"It's the horse," George repeated. "I always get the difficult one."

George was usually popular with kids. He felt like Iris had gotten a dud.

"Have you ever touched the ceiling?" George asked.

Iris shook her head.

"Do you want to?"

"What?"

"Do you want me to lift you up so that you can touch the ceiling?"

Iris looked confused. A little nervous. "I don't think my teacher would like that."

George nodded. "Yeah, probably a bad idea."

Iris returned her focus to the math problems. She worked in silence.

A few minutes later, she said, "Mister?"

"You can call me George," George told her.

"I would like to touch the ceiling."

George looked over his shoulder. The teacher was circulating around the room. "What about your teacher?"

Iris shrugged. "Maybe she won't see?"

"Okay," George said. "I'm going to kneel down, and you're going to climb on my shoulders.

"Sort of like I'm a horse," he added. "Do you think you can do that?"

Iris nodded.

George got down. Iris sat on his shoulders. It took a little effort for George to stand up. Iris was heavier than he'd anticipated.

"Are you touching the ceiling?" he asked.

"It's too high."

"Are you sure?"

"It's too *high*."

George knelt back down. Iris dismounted.

"It's not *that* high." George frowned, looking up at the ceiling. "Were you sticking your arm up straight?"

Iris nodded.

"How close were your fingers to touching?"

Iris held her hands several inches apart.

"So, you were pretty close . . ."

George noted the teacher's location in the back of the room. "How about we try again, but this time I'll lift you up by the knees? That should give you a few extra inches."

Iris stood on her chair, and George lifted her up by her knees.

"It's too high," she said.

Now that she wasn't on his shoulders, George could crane his head up and see what was going on. She was very close.

"You can do this, Iris." As he attempted to hold her up higher, George's arms began to tremble from exertion. He felt a dull ache in the wrist he'd broken. Iris listed slightly.

"Straighten your back," George instructed. "Stretch your fingers out more. Come on, Iris, you can do this. You're so close."

"Iris!"

George put Iris down. The teacher looked at both of them, mostly at Iris.

"It was my idea," George confessed.

The teacher said nothing. She didn't need to; her expression said it all.

When she eventually moved on, George looked at Iris.

"I'm sorry," he said. "That was a stupid idea."

Iris said nothing. George felt like an idiot. But then he saw that she was biting back a smile. A triumphant little grin.

"I did it," she whispered. "I touched the ceiling."

5. POWER BROKER

George, 26

In January of 2009, George developed a pain in his penis. Herpes. In the year and a half since he'd been single, he'd slept with a few girls, but he'd always used a condom, and there had been no blow jobs. According to the internet, it was possible to have an outbreak months or even years after having been exposed to the virus.

It was Jenny; there was no other explanation.

George emailed Jenny to let her know, and she'd written back right away. *I don't remember giving you a blow job before an outbreak, but I guess it's possible. I'm sorry, George.*

George had trouble gauging if she was genuinely remorseful. Did she realize what this meant for him? Then a visit to the doctor revealed the cause of the pain in George's penis was not herpes but a hair that had gotten caught in his urethra. George emailed Jenny again, and this time she called him back. She was irritated that he had prematurely accused her of giving him herpes after a self-diagnosis—she'd spent the whole week racked with shame and guilt for nothing.

"Do you have anything to say to me?" she asked.

"I miss you," George said.

Jenny missed him, too.

Now they were a couple again.

The first week of March, Jenny was accepted to Fordham law school in New York. She would be starting in the fall. George, a week away from concluding his three-year stint at Karpos, had decided to put his job search on hold until the job market improved. They decided to have an adventure: to drive out West.

They were brainstorming people they knew in various states along I-80 that they might visit along the way. George wondered if Dizart still lived in Wyoming.

"Who's Dizart?" Jenny asked.

"A family friend who came to live with us when I was a kid."

"Lived with you?"

He'd spent the past several years traveling through Asia, George explained, and needed a place to stay when he got back. Ellen had cleared out the study, which had its own private bathroom and a couch that folded out into a bed. But Dizart didn't use that. He just slept on a mat on the floor.

George was maybe seven or eight. He was impressed that his parents had a friend like Dizart, who knew everything there was to know about nature and animals and didn't believe in buying new clothes, or buying things in general, especially if it was something you could grow or make yourself.

Dizart was very good at making things.

He made a swing for George. Then he built a fence around Ellen's vegetable garden to protect it from the deer. When he was done with that, he got to work repairing a part of the porch that was rotting.

George soon grew bored of the swing. He wanted a tree house.

"Can you make a tree house?" he asked Dizart one night at dinner.

His parents looked embarrassed, but Dizart said, "I know the perfect tree."

Dizart acquired some lumber and got to work. George looked forward to coming home from school so that he could help him.

One afternoon they were out back working when Freckles, their dog, came running out of the woods, a lifeless sack of fur swinging from her jowls. After a few triumphant laps around the lawn, she deposited the specimen—a rabbit—on the flagstone terrace, at the foot of the chaise where Ellen was sitting.

Ellen screamed, "It's still alive!"

"We can't let it suffer," said Dizart, who calmly walked over and finished the job with his own two hands.

Afterward, he skinned and cooked the rabbit for dinner. George refused to try it, but everyone else said it was delicious.

If his parents had explained Dizart's abrupt departure, George had no memory of it. Only of returning from school one afternoon and noticing that his car wasn't in the driveway. And then discovering the study restored to its normal order, freshly vacuumed and smelling of Pledge.

George was bewildered. Dizart hadn't said goodbye or told him he was leaving.

Dizart did not come back after that. His name was rarely, if ever, spoken. If it weren't for the partially assembled platform of what was supposed to have been the tree house, George might have thought he'd dreamt Dizart up.

But when he was in seventh grade, George received a letter from Dizart, who was living in the mountains of Wyoming in a cabin he'd built himself. He had some goats. The rest of the letter was questions about George. Did he like school? Had he read any good books recently? Was he still planning to invent a special kind of underwear that transformed the odor of a fart into a good smell?

Ellen had left the letter on George's pillow. She didn't say anything about it at dinner, but later that evening she came into his room to ask if he'd opened it.

George nodded.

"Where is it?"

"In the box where I keep my personal letters," George told her.

He rarely received mail and resented the assumption that she could read it.

"What did he say?" Ellen asked, when it was obvious he wasn't going to show it to her.

George shrugged. "Just how was I doing and stuff."

Ellen looked unsatisfied.

"He lives in Wyoming," George revealed.

"I saw that on the envelope." Ellen uncrossed and refolded her arms. "Did he mention any details about his life?"

George shook his head.

"Well. That was nice of him to reach out to you after all these years."

Ellen lingered.

"I wonder 'if he feels guilty about recusing himself from being your godfather . . ."

Ellen told George that when he was a baby they had asked Dizart to be his godfather, and that Dizart had agreed, but then he objected to something the minister had instructed him to say during the baptism. Ellen couldn't recall exactly what it was—some kind of vow that implied a belief in Christ—and Dizart, taking the whole thing much too seriously, had said that he didn't believe in Christ, and therefore wouldn't say it, and the minister, being equally obstinate, had paused the ceremony to ask if any of the congregants would assume the role. That's why Blake was George's godfather—he was a last-minute fill-in.

George had never heard any of this before.

"It was classic Dizart," Ellen said. "Pretty immature."

Ellen had more to say on the subject of Dizart's immaturity. He'd never had a job, she told George, not a real one.

George was surprised by his mother's tone of contempt. After all, Ellen—who'd taught a few art classes before getting married and none since—wasn't exactly a thriving member of the workforce.

* * *

If Dizart still lived in Wyoming, George no longer had his address or any contact information. He did remember that Dizart wasn't his real name, just his middle name. His real name was Robert. *Robert Dizart Lowe.*

"He's not on Facebook," Jenny confirmed, looking up from her laptop. "Should I try LinkedIn?"

George shook his head. "That's the last place he'd be."

He had no hope of tracking down Dizart, but Jenny wouldn't give up. An extensive Google search revealed a phone listing with a Vermont area code.

"No answer," George said, after calling the number.

Unbeknownst to George, Jenny kept trying.

"You're never going to believe this," she said, when he returned from his last day of work.

Jenny had spoken to Dizart that morning. When she explained who she was, and why she was calling, he was very excited. He'd inherited some land in Vermont. A farm. He hoped George and Jenny would visit. The house had plenty of bedrooms; they could stay as long as they wanted.

They decided to make it the first stop of their road trip.

Jenny helped George pack, bring what he didn't need to his mother's house, and then clean up the cottage. It took four days.

The morning of their departure, Addie and Blake came outside to see them off. As George pulled out, they stood in the driveway waving goodbye. George had never seen them so happy. "Yup, you're finally getting rid of me!" he whispered, waving back.

It was the first calendar day of spring, but driving north on the Taconic felt like returning to winter. Pockets of snow lined the meridian. Rocky embankments gleamed with ice.

After getting off the highway, they drove an hour on backcountry roads. They arrived just after four. The driveway was long and unpaved. George had pictured a classic New England farm with a hulking red barn and an old clapboard farmhouse, but the property looked more like a British estate. The house was a three-story brick Tudor with multiple chimneys, limestone molding, and a certain grandeur that was incongruous with the motley collection of farm animals—sheep, chickens, a pair of llamas—that populated a fenced-in patch of earth out front.

"That's him," George said. "That's Dizart."

George felt unexpectedly bashful watching his childhood hero trot down the steps of the pillared entrance, his red hair now salmon-gray. Otherwise he seemed quite youthful: trim, freckled, bright-eyed.

He initiated a hug as George stepped out of the car. "Old Gray," Dizart said, the name he'd called him as a child.

The house had been built by Dizart's great-grandfather in 1902. Dizart didn't seem eager to reveal this fact; it had come up only when Jenny asked as he gave them a tour.

It could've been a hotel. There were lots of bedrooms to choose from, and though it seemed Dizart steered them toward it, George was a little embarrassed when Jenny selected the grandest, which had a marble fireplace and French doors that opened onto a balcony overlooking the wooded hills of Vermont.

Jenny tried to get George to go for a walk, but he was too tired, and so she went on her own.

George collapsed on the bed.

For the past few days he'd been running on the excitement of being about to embark on the unknown. Even the drive up, in spite of some tedious stretches, had a momentum-generating thrill. There was something jarring about their arrival: the abrupt cessation of movement, the sudden quiet and still of the country.

George regretted leaving the timeline of their visit open-ended. He wished he had some excuse to leave after a night or two. He wanted to keep going. More than just exhausted, he felt low. A drink would help revive him. George was relieved when Dizart knocked on their door to let him know it was time for dinner.

The dining room, like the rest of the house, felt oversize and excessively formal. Floor-length drapes, English oak furniture, bronze sconces. The faded pineapple wallpaper was punctuated by less faded squares where paintings had been removed.

There were three other people sitting at the table: a man and two women, who appeared to be in their midtwenties. Dizart hadn't referred to them as roommates, but as Jenny peppered them with questions, it came out that they were living in the house with Dizart, and had been for some time.

They weren't particularly friendly. Undeterred, Jenny tried to draw them out.

The women, whose resemblance to each other was not helped by their names—Jaqueline and Janelle—maintained a surly front, but she had more luck with the guy, Adam.

When she asked what had brought him to "the farm"—as they referred to it—Adam's response was a bizarre and rambling story about Dizart rescuing him from the side of the highway after his car broke down on his way back to Harvard Law School, which he ended up dropping out of, a decision his parents did not support, and for which he credited Dizart, who'd invited him to move in.

George had trouble following, as Adam spoke so quietly you literally had to stop chewing to hear him—and George was hungry—but it did not escape his attention that the whole time Adam spoke, his gaze was directed at Dizart, for whom this was presumably not new information.

George wondered when someone would offer him something to drink besides water.

Now that Adam was warmed up, he had more to say about law school, lawyers, and the broken legal system. Jenny took advantage of a pause to disclose that she was starting law school in the fall—but that she was planning to go into public interest, to work for nonprofits dedicated to fixing the problems Adam was talking about.

At this point Dizart took over. "My father was a lawyer," he began. "He was also a liar, a cheat, and a bigot."

Dizart's scorn for his father was matched by his own deep mistrust of the legal system, and government in general, as it was run by men who were all after the same thing.

"Obama is no different than the rest of them," he proclaimed. "No different from the rest."

Dizart proceeded to school the table on why President Obama was just as corrupt as every other politician—with the exception of Vermont senator Bernie Sanders, whose marginalized status was further proof of his colleagues' sinister agendas—especially the ones who ran on platforms that were more or less ideologically aligned with those across the aisle. These people, the neoliberals, were the real blight on the system.

George was impressed by Dizart's familiarity with various representatives' voting records. He recognized an opportunity to hone his own more abstract critique of the government's dysfunction, but remained distracted by the absence of an alcoholic beverage within arm's reach. He should have thought to bring a bottle of something. He'd assumed Dizart was a drinker.

"George is the only other person I know who can wiggle his ears," Dizart announced when he was done talking about politics. "Can you still do it?"

Everyone watched as George wiggled his ears.

"I didn't know you could do that," Jenny said.

"I taught him," Dizart said, demonstrating his own prowess.

"This is delicious," Jenny gushed about the vegetable soup, which Jaqueline and Janelle had made. George's concern that he'd have trouble telling them apart seemed somewhat forgivable upon learning they were not merely sisters, but identical twins. They had a striking look. George wouldn't necessarily call it beautiful. They barely spoke, but several times George caught them exchanging furtive glances.

As they stood up to clear the table, one of them whispered something to Dizart, who looked at George and Jenny and said, "I forgot to ask if you would keep your cell phones in your car.

"Radiation," he explained as they got up to do this.

* * *

Jenny was good at playing the part of gracious guest, but over the course of dinner she had formed some critical opinions that she shared with George when they were alone in their room:

There was something disconcerting about the dynamic between Dizart and his roommates. Dizart was a force, and they were all so passive. The two women barely spoke once the entire meal. And

Adam—did George think it was a good thing that Adam dropped out of law school?

George shrugged.

"He seems a little lost," Jenny said. "A little too susceptible to the opinions of Dizart.

"I don't know if it was such a good thing," she said, unhooking the sash of the curtain and pulling the fabric across the window.

George had no opinion on Adam's decision to drop out of law school, but he agreed there was something strange about the atmosphere.

"We don't have to stay here," he said. "We could leave tomorrow."

Jenny looked relieved. "If that's okay. I think maybe one night is enough."

"How do we explain that we're leaving so soon?" George whispered after they'd turned out the light. "Dizart knows we don't have anywhere to be. I don't want to offend him."

"I don't know," Jenny said. "We'll figure something out tomorrow."

* * *

Jenny woke George up the next morning. It was eleven. George, unable to sleep, had taken Benadryl in the middle of the night. He was groggy and wanted to sleep more, but Jenny looked agitated.

There was blood on her jeans.

"An orphaned lamb imprinted upon me," she told him.

While George had slept in, Jenny had gotten up and gone outside, where she'd come across Dizart assisting a sheep in labor. It was a difficult birth, and the mother died. Jenny had cradled the orphan in her arms while Dizart defrosted some colostrum he kept in case of such events.

When he returned, Jenny stood by as Dizart attempted to feed the bottle of colostrum to the newborn lamb, but it didn't work. He'd thought it was a problem with the lamb's sucking reflex, but then Jenny tried feeding the lamb and it worked. The lamb latched onto the nipple and drank the whole bottle.

George yawned. "Did you figure out how to tell Dizart we're leaving today?"

"*George.*" Jenny sat on the bed. "An orphaned lamb has *imprinted* upon me. Do you realize what that means?"

George suspected Jenny overestimated her importance to the survival of this animal, but he agreed to stay a bit longer.

On the second morning, George asked Dizart if he could do anything, and Dizart put him to work removing stones from a field he was cultivating in back of the house. The next day George planted garlic. After that he turned compost. Over the weekend he helped Dizart install a mesh fence around the chicken coop.

George did not lose himself in any of these tasks. Most of the time, whatever he was doing, he was bored and couldn't wait to be done with it. He was disappointed in himself for feeling this way. On the drive up, he'd had an agrarian image of himself, gleefully tossing bales of hay out of a loft. He felt embarrassed and ridiculous thinking about it now.

One afternoon Dizart needed George's help picking up some fertilizer from another farm a few towns over. On the ride over, Dizart opined on the failures of the Obama administration.

"He campaigned as the antiwar candidate, but he's not reversing any of Bush's policies. Illegal wiretaps, torture, detention, that's all fine with him."

"He hasn't been in office very long," George pointed out.

Dizart glanced at George with avuncular affection, as though he were still the naive child he'd once been, and said no more.

Sometimes George found himself comparing himself to President Obama, an exercise in self-loathing, because it was hard to imagine a person superior to the forty-fourth president. George had nothing on Obama: intellect, integrity, courage—Obama had it all, including humor and humility. And there was no begrudging him, because everything Obama had, he had earned.

On the return trip they drove in silence, except for the end, when Dizart said, "When you were a child, you wanted to write books when you grew up."

George nodded ruefully. "I wanted to do a lot of things."

* * *

Caring for an orphaned newborn lamb was a lot of work. It needed to be fed every six hours.

The mortality rate for orphaned lambs was very high, Jenny reminded George whenever he questioned whether it was really necessary to set her alarm for five a.m.

At George's recommendation, Jenny was reading Robert Caro's biography of Robert Moses, *The Power Broker: Robert Moses and the Fall of New York*, which she'd ordered from the nearest nonchain bookstore.

"I didn't know it was over a thousand pages," she said after driving two hours round trip to pick it up.

Jenny sat down with her book every morning after breakfast, and then again after dinner. She was a slow reader, but George was surprised when, after two weeks, she mentioned that Robert Moses still hadn't graduated from college.

"You can skim parts of it," George told her. "It'll be good practice for law school. To learn how to skim parts of your reading load. Otherwise you'll never get through."

"No," Jenny said. "When I read a book, I read the whole thing."

When she wasn't reading about Robert Moses or tending to her lamb, Jenny helped the twins with meal prep. In bits and pieces, she extracted their backstory.

They'd grown up in rural Utah, two of seven children. Their family was Mormon. As seniors in high school, their parents had taken the family on a trip to New York City to celebrate the girls' acceptances to Brigham Young University. They were waiting on a subway platform when they caught the attention of a modeling scout. Instead of going to college, they became models.

There was a market for identical twins, and they did quite well.

Two years ago, they'd been hired to do a photo shoot on a farm in the area, Jenny told George. Something involving sheep and mist at dawn. The director of the shoot was a creep. In the middle of the night he'd come into their tent and tried to rape them. After fighting him off, they'd run away and gotten lost in the woods. Eventually they'd stumbled onto the property, where they'd met Dizart, who'd just moved in and started the farm.

He seemed lonely, they told Jenny, who relayed all this to George, who thought it was a completely bizarre and possibly fabricated story.

"And so they decided to move in and become his indentured servants?" George asked.

"They'd grown up on a farm," she said. "They hated being models, they weren't cut out for New York City. This is the life they know. They like it here."

"I just don't understand the arrangement," George said. "Do they pay rent? Or do they earn their keep by doing all the cooking and housework?"

Jenny couldn't answer this.

"I just think it's interesting," George continued, "that for Adam, as well as Jaqueline and Janelle, a chance encounter with Dizart led to them giving up their lives and partaking in this . . . whatever you want to call this little thing he's got going here."

"Why do you have to be so cynical?" Jenny responded. "You spoke so fondly of him, then ever since we got here, you act like he's got some kind of sinister agenda."

"You were the one who thought this was a cult and wanted to leave the first night we got here," George reminded her.

"Oh, come on, I never said that word."

Dizart was growing on Jenny, and George knew anything he said she'd interpret as further evidence of his hostility toward him, and so he didn't say anything.

But it was definitely a weird situation—Dizart, the farm, Adam, the Mormon twins—and George was eager for the lamb to turn five weeks, at which point its mortality rate supposedly significantly decreased and Jenny promised they could leave.

* * *

George was helping Dizart install a fence in a newly partitioned section of the barnyard that would soon be home to a pair of baby emus—their grotesquely enormous eggs were currently incubating beneath a hot lamp in the kitchen.

Jenny came out for the lamb's midday feeding. Passing by George and Dizart, she paused. "Wow, you're making a lot of progress." Then she pointed to the section George had been working on. "That might be a little loose."

"I know," George said. "I'm going to redo that part." It was a simple task, securing chicken mesh by hammering metal staples to wood posts, but George kept messing up. His staples were unevenly spaced and the mesh looked crooked.

Jenny smiled encouragingly and strolled off.

George hooked the hammer in his belt loop and removed the staples from the post Jenny had noticed. "Fuck me," he muttered when the hammer slipped out of the belt loop and landed on his toe.

Dizart looked up at George and grinned, which George thought was strange and a little rude. Then he said, in his magisterial way, "We all have something in which we become the thing we are doing."

Squinting, he gestured toward Jenny, who was feeding her lamb in the enclosure on the other side of the field. Dizart was impressed with the way she cared for the animal, he often told George.

The temperature was only in the sixties, but it felt much warmer doing the kind of work they were doing, in the height of the day. After taking a long drink from his metal thermos, Dizart removed his T-shirt, revealing a rather impressive six-pack. His flimsy, precariously knotted drawstring pants *left little to the imagination*, as Ellen used to say of certain outfits Cressida wore in high school. George wondered if Dizart's boycott of underwear was purely a matter of comfort, or a political thing—part of his rejection of all things conventional, restrictive. George hated himself for thinking these thoughts; they made him feel old, cranky, conservative.

"For men, it's more difficult to find that thing," Dizart continued. "From a young age we're given this idea that it's all about money. You've got to *earn* your living. Prove your *worth*."

Dizart was strong and lean, but the visual effect of his muscle definition was enhanced by a slackening of his skin, George realized, noting the folds at the base of his neck. His body hair was patchy and gray. He must have been approaching sixty, if not that already, and yet evidence of this only seemed to underscore his vitality. He was an attractive guy. George, who wasn't in the habit of noticing these things, was aware of this fact, and he suspected Dizart was, too.

Finished with her feeding, Jenny exited the enclosure and started walking in the direction of the house. Dizart beckoned her over.

"I was just telling George what we spoke about earlier," he said as she approached.

Jenny's lips parted in an O. Her eyes darted between the two of them before settling on Dizart, who looked at George.

"I appreciate your help," Dizart said, "but I want you to make better use of your time up here. I want you to think of this time as an opportunity to do the thing you were meant to do, and not worry about anything else."

"We think you should be writing," Jenny said.

* * *

Over the years, George had wondered, were it not required, would he get out of bed in the morning? If he weren't expected to wake up at a certain time and report to a certain place—what would become of him?

A few weeks into life on the farm, George got an answer, and it surprised him. Given the opportunity to sleep as late as he wanted, he woke up naturally around nine. After getting dressed, he would go out to his car and check his phone. As it rumbled to life with new texts, there was a feeling of excitement, but the messages were almost always from his mom:

Just checking in.

Everything okay?

When are you coming back?

Her questions felt intrusive, but George made a point of responding, or else she would call.

After shutting down his phone and returning it to the glove compartment, George went inside and ate breakfast, which Janelle and Jaqueline left on the stove for people to serve themselves. Historically, George had never had much of an appetite in the morning, but that was no longer the case. Eggs, oatmeal, pancakes, French toast made from bread baked the previous night—George liked it all.

After eating, George took his coffee up to their bedroom, where he sat at a desk by the window, overlooking the property. He was not alone; Jenny did her reading on the chaise next to the fireplace. Sometimes she would break the silence with an expressive sigh.

"I don't think I'll ever look at the height of a bridge over a parkway the same way," she muttered one morning.

"The racism behind it," she added.

"What?" George said.

"The *racism* of low bridges."

"I don't know what you're talking about," George said.

"Low bridges make it impossible for buses to use a parkway. Making the area inaccessible to people who don't own cars."

"Oh," George said. "Interesting. I actually never thought of that."

Jenny looked confused. "But didn't you read the book?"

She held up her copy of *The Power Broker*.

"I read sections," George said.

Jenny got a funny look on her face. Her cheeks flushed in smug amusement.

"I never said I read it," he said.

"Yeah, well, it's kind of assumed when someone recommends a book to you."

George disagreed but didn't want to get derailed by an argument, so he let it go.

He was writing a novel about the life of a man named Jasper Barrows. He was born in 1948. When he was six years old, Jasper contracted polio and almost died. Jasper's hypermasculine steel-worker father was ashamed of his invalid son, who spent a good portion of what remained of his childhood in bed reading books. Jasper became the first person in his family to go to college, then went on to pursue a PhD in English literature. While the rest of his generation was getting high and having sex with strangers, Jasper Barrows was reading. To pay for his tuition, he worked part-time in a shoe store. The goal had been to become a writer, but a failed marriage and the subsequent legal repercussions demanded a more reliable income.

And so Jasper Barrows spent the better part of his adult life teaching English at a suburban New Jersey high school, where his soft-spoken timidity and the singular intensity of his passion for literature rendered him a pariah among his colleagues and an object of ridicule to his students, who were much more interested in the mystery of his legs—two different lengths, a result of the polio—than anything he had to teach them.

The book was partly inspired by the novel *Stoner* and partly by George's high school English teacher, Mr. Cummings, who had made a deep impression upon George as a man of superior intellect and character, as well as humility. A man who hadn't gotten his due. Mr. Cummings suffered from a limp, for reasons that were unknown by students. On more than one occasion, George had stood by and watched as a classmate trailed Mr. Cummings as he walked down the hall, mocking his gait. If Mr. Cummings was aware of what was happening, he pretended otherwise.

George couldn't recall the last time he'd been so focused.

Sometimes he would become aware of having to pee, and it would feel very urgent, but he would want to finish his thought. And then an hour would pass, and George would discover he still hadn't gone.

* * *

George's depression typically got worse in the spring, and Jenny thought that this was because it was the anniversary of Denis's death, but George disagreed. He had always struggled with the sudden eruption of green, the fleeting euphoria of a lilac-infused breeze, the unrelenting trill of morning songbirds. It had always been too much.

But this year was different. Spring arrived later and unfolded more gradually up north. The absence of lots of people parading about, hollering about how beautiful it was, made it possible for George to enjoy the season on his own terms. As the days got longer, he began going for walks before dinner. There was a trail that cut through the woods, at the top of which he could see for miles. Even when George was feeling lazy and hadn't wanted to go, he never regretted it.

Once there was a bear. The bear didn't see George, but George saw the bear, just off the path, about three car lengths from where he stood. A bear!

George tried to stay alert to his surroundings on his evening walks, especially after the bear sighting, but he was often preoccupied by his writing. When he wasn't thinking about the story itself, he was thinking about the book as an event in his life.

When it came to this book, and his future as a writer, George was either manically confident or utterly not—never anything in between.

Each night before bed George showed Jenny what he'd written that day, and she was invariably impressed. *It's brilliant, George. You're a beautiful writer. Compelling, relatable, moving, funny*—Jenny was full of praise, and George was touched by her encouragement, but some nights it wasn't enough.

Jenny was just one reader, and not a very discerning one. She'd once given him a copy of *Tuesdays with Morrie*. What if nothing became of this book? What if it wasn't a book, but just hours of his life lost, the sad adult version of a child playing make-believe?

* * *

One afternoon, George looked up from his laptop and saw Jenny and Dizart on the grass beneath his window. She was speaking in her excitable way, gesticulating, making faces, her animated self-possession occasionally undermined by an assurance-seeking glance at Dizart, whose lanky figure seemed to list ever so slightly as he stood there listening.

George felt irritated at both of them, for no rational reason. When had he become such an angry, misanthropic person? It had been a stupid, unproductive day, full of self-doubt and loathing. There was a sentence he had written countless times that still wasn't right.

George returned to his work, but the sentence only got worse. He glanced out the window again. Several minutes had passed, and they were still standing there in the dappled afternoon light. Now it was Dizart who was doing the talking as Jenny nodded along, agog.

George felt something wild in his veins as he saw Dizart reach out and touch her forehead. He watched in disbelief as his fingers lingered against her skin. And then Dizart withdrew his hand and wiped his fingers on his pants, and George realized it must've been a mosquito.

He was just killing a mosquito.

They parted ways. Minutes later the bedroom door opened, and Jenny entered, her cheeks flushed from the exertion of walking upstairs. "Hi," she said. "How was your day?"

"Terrible," George said.

Jenny summoned a look of sympathy, then stepped into the bathroom and started running a bath.

George got up and stood in the entrance to the bathroom. "It just feels like, *what's the point?*"

"Of life, or your book?" Jenny knelt by the tub, holding her fingers under the faucet. The plumbing was very old. It took a while for the water to get hot.

"I was talking about my book." George crossed his arms and leaned against the doorframe. "To be honest, I couldn't even tell you what it's about . . ."

Jenny began to summarize what she'd read of the plot so far.

George interrupted: "*A boy grows up to be a man who is disappointed by life*—boo-hoo. What's the bigger story I'm trying to tell?"

Jenny shook her head. "Are writers expected to know that? Isn't that open for interpretation, for readers and critics to figure out?"

Satisfied with the water temperature, she inserted the rubber stopper in the drain. As she waited for the tub to fill, she stripped down to her underwear, propped her foot on the edge of the toilet, and began applying a goo-like substance to one of her legs using what looked like a Popsicle stick.

She looked a little annoyed, registering George's perplexed stare. "It's a hair-removal product."

George picked up the container and read the label. "Why is it called Nad's? Is it short for gonads?"

"No," Jenny said. "I don't know why it's called that. I think it's Australian."

"Does this mean I'm going to get to go to the land down under?"

Jenny rolled her eyes.

"Aren't you glad I'm not the kind of guy who actually makes jokes like that?" George said.

"You just did."

"But I said it in a voice that indicated I was being ironic."

Jenny nodded wearily.

George wondered if she was thinking about how little sex they had. They rarely spoke about it, but he knew it bothered her. It bothered George when he thought about it. Weren't young unmarried couples supposed to be having sex all the time?

George glanced at his reflection in the mirror. It had been a while since he'd washed his hair. When he ran his hand through it, it left a mold of his fingers—that's how greasy it was. It wasn't a bad look. Feral, slightly unhinged, but in a fun, intelligent way. It could be a compelling author photo.

"George," Jenny pleaded, as he tried out different author photo expressions, "could I have some privacy?"

George closed the bathroom door behind him and returned to his laptop.

He had trouble getting back into his work.

"What were you talking about?" he asked when Jenny emerged from her bath, wrapped in one of the house's ancient towels. A fraying, monogrammed, mold-speckled artifact of a towel.

Jenny looked confused.

"Outside with Dizart. I saw you out the window. It looked like you were having a deep conversation . . ."

"You, actually. Dizart was telling me about what you were like as a kid."

Jenny stood over a decorative chamber pot and wrung out the excess water from her hair by twisting it into a rope and squeezing. Drops of water sounded like pebbles as they smacked the porcelain.

"What was I like?" George asked.

"Sensitive. Curious. Kind. A passionate advocate of the underdog . . ." She smiled tenderly. "You never told me you were a vegetarian."

"That didn't last very long." George wanted more. "What else did he tell you?"

Jenny sat on the chaise and began applying lotion to her legs, which looked painfully pink and raw. "He said that you were always trying to impress Cressida, and that she could be pretty cruel to you."

* * *

George was surprised, and a little alarmed, one morning to discover a text from his sister.

Call me, it said.

George called her immediately, but she didn't answer.

An hour later, he tried again. This time the call went straight to voicemail.

George had trouble writing. It was not like Cressida to reach out unprompted.

Throughout the day he returned to his car to try Cressida. Around three o'clock, he finally reached her.

She laughed when George's first words were to ask if something bad had happened.

"Ever the catastrophist," she said. "Just calling to say hi."

"Oh," George said. "Hi."

"Mom said you're living with Dizart?"

"Yeah. We've been staying at his place in Vermont."

"But I thought you were going on a cross-country road trip?"

"We were—we are. This is just a stop. It's been very productive, actually . . .

"I'm writing a book."

George felt a little foolish speaking this sentence aloud.

"Good for you, George," Cressida said. "How much longer are you going to be there?"

"Hard to predict," George said. "I'd like to finish a full draft. I'm averaging about a thousand words a day, so at this rate, not more than a few months . . .

"How are you?" he asked. "What's going on with you?"

"I'm grand," Cressida said, "but I'm actually calling because Mom is worried. She said you've been really evasive about your plans, and she wants to know how much longer you'll be there."

"But I told her exactly what I told you. What's she worried about? This is literally the most productive I've been since college. And healthy, too. I finally quit smoking, and I haven't had a drink in seven weeks. Every day after working, I go for these long walks—"

"I guess it's just weird for her," Cressida interrupted. "Her son living with her ex-lover."

* * *

Within minutes of getting off the phone, George made a decision: they would pack their bags and leave first thing tomorrow. Maybe even tonight.

He found Jenny reading her book beneath a tree.

"I just got off the phone with Cressida," he told her. "He had an affair with my mom."

Jenny's eyes popped. "Dizart?"

"While he was living with us. Cressida walked in on them. In bed. She was twelve years old."

Jenny held her hand over her mouth.

"He tried to convince my mom to run away with him. Not just to leave my dad, but leave us. Her kids."

"What?"

George nodded. "Cress only found that part out later from reading my mom's journal. Apparently, her main reservation was his unconventional lifestyle. His refusal to have a career, or a bank account, or buy a house. She didn't want to live in a tent somewhere."

"Why would your mom put any of this in a journal? Wasn't she worried one of you guys would read it?"

George shrugged. "Apparently not."

Jenny looked expectantly at George. She wanted all the details, to know everything.

"We're going to get out of here," he said. "We're going to pack up and leave tomorrow morning."

"Where will we go?"

"Out West," George said. "As was our plan all along."

* * *

As Jenny packed up their things, George went for a final walk in the woods. It did not do what other walks had done for him. He did not see a bear or anything magical. As he walked, he tried to think of his final words to Dizart.

He came up with some damning material.

George reached the end of the trail. He stood on top of the hill that overlooked the farm, which was really a mansion that had been built by an oil magnate who'd had dozens of servants. That's why there were so many bedrooms. Really, it was hilarious when you considered it, the absurdity of Dizart, having gotten by his whole life without ever having a real job, living this back-to-the-land fantasy courtesy of his inheritance, thinking it was some kind of protest against capitalism.

George yelled, "*Ha!*" And the *Ha!* ricocheted down the ravine and then echoed across the valley. There was a thrill in projecting so powerfully, in summoning the full force of his disdain for Dizart and expelling it across such a vast distance. George did it again, and again, until his throat burned and his voice started to fray.

On the way back down, George was consumed by thoughts of twelve-year-old Cressida walking in on their mother and Dizart. *Mom and Dizart in bed*, was how she'd put it, her language uncharacteristically delicate in its euphemistic vagueness. How generous of her to spare him the details.

But it was almost worse, as it made him wonder about those details. George found himself entertaining different scenarios—bed, position, acoustics—as if trying to solve a riddle. Intrusive images (in some of which Ellen morphed into Jenny) were interspersed with thoughts of his father.

George wondered if Denis had confronted Dizart after being informed of the situation. It was hard to imagine. His father had never been good at that sort of thing. George recalled his pathetic attempt to reprimand a group of neighborhood teenagers on Halloween as they lobbed eggs at their front porch: *That's not very nice, boys. Cut it out. I mean it. Time to go home now!*

George remembered feeling angry at the teenagers, and indignant on his father's behalf, though he suspected his true reaction was more complicated. There was something deeply embarrassing, disgraceful even, about a man who was so afraid of confrontation. A man who was incapable of taking real action.

When George returned to their room, Jenny had finished packing.

"Let's get out of here," he rasped.

Jenny couldn't understand him. "What happened to your voice?"

George stepped into the bathroom and drank some water from the faucet. "Let's get out of here."

"You want to leave *now*?" Jenny asked. "Don't you want to say goodbye to anyone?"

George thought about it.

"Let's just leave now," he said.

6. ROTTEN RALPH'S ROTTEN FAMILY

George, 27

Cressida invited George to stay in her apartment in Williamsburg while she took a trip to Berlin. Having not seen the apartment beforehand, it sounded like an appealing offer.

"I think you'll like it here," she said, letting him in.

Cressida's skinny limbs and severely blunt bangs made her look like a cartoon character. She folded her arms in a proprietary manner as George surveyed the premises.

The apartment was street level. The front door opened to an L-shaped room, which might have felt spacious were it not cluttered with bookshelves and lamps and furniture that looked like it had been lifted from the curb. In one corner, planks of wood rested haphazardly against the wall, an IKEA project someone had given up on. The shorter arm of the L featured a collection of mini-fridges—George counted three—and a round table littered with plastic utensils and little packets of ketchup and soy sauce.

A single barred window overlooked a recessed alley teeming with trash receptacles.

A garden apartment, Cressida had described it.

"Where's the oven?" George asked.

Cressida pointed toward a plug-in stovetop on a slab of butcher block.

"But is there an *oven*?"

Cressida looked irritated by the question. "Since when do you bake?"

"Just curious."

"There's no oven," she said. "But there's a patio."

A door in the back of the kitchen opened to a small asphalt lot.

"It's really nice in the summer," Cressida said. "We have parties."

"How'd you find this place?" George asked.

"Friend of a friend." Cressida opened the door to her room. It was just big enough to fit a queen-size bed. Underneath, she kept her clothes in giant Tupperware bins, one of which she'd emptied for George to use.

"How many roommates do you have?"

"Just Otto. He's really busy and he keeps odd hours. You'll barely see him." Cressida's tongue probed the corner of a cheek. "Sometimes we do the Airbnb thing.

"Well," she said, uprighting her suitcase, "my car's about to get here."

George walked with her outside.

"It's a really fun neighborhood," she said as she handed him the keys. "There's always something going on at night. Music. Sketch comedy. There's a bar a few blocks down that shows movies from our childhood. *Ghostbusters, Goonies, The Princess Bride.* The apartment's usually empty during the day, so you should be able to get some work done. Mom said you're trying to get a job at a newspaper?"

George scratched the back of his neck and nodded.

"Cool, cool," Cressida said with polite enthusiasm. "But you haven't given up on the book, right?"

"Eh. Putting it on pause for a bit while I look for an actual job that will translate into some kind of career. To be honest, I'm not sure about the whole journalism thing. But I don't know, with the whole market crash, it's hard to get any kind of job . . ."

Cressida nodded rapidly, encouraging George to wrap it up.

"I dunno, at a certain point I guess you just have to choose something," he said, feeling a little fragile.

Last night he'd received a group email from Benji, who'd surprised everyone by joining the Peace Corps and was so popular in the small Ugandan village he'd been placed in that he was getting asked to officiate funerals and marriage ceremonies. The image of blond, blue-eyed Benji, with his shit-eating stoner's grin, literally holding court among a group of African tribesmen—no doubt reveling in his newfound status as a spiritual authority, oblivious to the colonialist undertones of assuming such a role—made George cringe. But that didn't curtail his jealousy.

Minutes later, Solly had responded with his own update: he'd just been hired at a think tank in San Francisco and couldn't have been more pleased with himself. "Yup, getting paid to think!"

Jeremiah, who'd graduated from intern to paid staff member of a documentary production company, was excited to announce that he was halfway to meeting his goal of raising the funds to make his own film—a project he described in vague, elevator-pitch terms as "depicting the victims of America's broken health care system."

George had responded to the thread, "Maybe you can use the profits to buy me some health insurance?"

After pressing send, he immediately felt bad. George had always felt self-conscious deploying reflexive niceties, but he wished he'd responded in a more adult way. He started to write Jeremiah another email saying it sounded like an interesting project, an important topic, but then worried this would come across as compensatory and insincere, and so he saved it to his drafts.

"I should get going." Cressida gestured to a car by the curb. George hadn't seen it pull up.

As he helped her load her suitcase into the trunk, Cressida said, "Otto takes care of cleaning the room in between guests, but, like I said, he keeps odd hours and isn't always around during the day. So I told him you'd be around during the day, in case something comes up with the Airbnb people. You know"—Cressida climbed into the back seat—"sometimes these people arrive and they're like, *oh, where's the this, how do I turn on that.*"

"I see," George said. "So that's why you're so eager for me to stay here. You needed a concierge."

Cressida affected a look of outrage. "You're getting to stay in one of the most popular tourist destinations in the world! For *free.*" She closed the door harder than necessary.

George went for a walk. It was October, but you'd never guess it from the afternoon heat.

The block was dominated by recently erected co-ops, whose sleek, soulless exteriors seemed born out of cold indifference to the buildings they were gradually replacing, tenements like Cressida's. A bodega on the corner appeared to be a hangout spot for what remained of the neighborhood's Puerto Rican population. George felt like an intruder and left without buying anything.

As he headed down Bedford Avenue, he felt light, unencumbered. The people who gravitated to Williamsburg didn't seem like real people but extras in a movie. The onus was on the aesthetic. Whatever look they were going for, whether it involved tattoos and trucker hats, or bow ties and handlebar mustaches, they were all in. To be surrounded by such people, en masse, made life seem like a joke, an ongoing theme party.

George walked into a juice bar and ordered the first item on the menu, which cost eleven dollars and contained bee pollen and honeysuckle extract.

When the clerk rang him up, George couldn't find his wallet.

"I'm sorry," he told the clerk, explaining that his wallet must have fallen out of his pocket. "I'll come right back as soon as I find it."

George retraced his steps back down Bedford, past record stores and vintage clothing boutiques, taco trucks, and destination food shops: HOME OF THE FAMOUS "RAINBOW BAGEL" AS SEEN ON NY1 NEWS.

As he combed the sidewalk outside Cressida's apartment, he caught the attention of some men smoking cigarettes outside the bodega.

"Looking for something?"

"Wallet," George explained. "Lost my wallet."

"You should buy a chain," one of them said, gesturing to his own.

Another chimed in: "No one takes your wallet when it's on a chain."

One of them had taken George's wallet, and this was their way of letting him know. They knew he wasn't the type to do anything about it; he radiated meekness.

"Fucking assholes," George muttered to himself as he let himself back into Cressida's.

Upon returning to his room, George discovered the wallet was on his bed.

* * *

A pair of sisters from Copenhagen was staying in the apartment. Their cousin was marrying an American woman, and they were in town for her bachelorette party. A limo was picking them up in one hour. In the meantime, they were sitting at the kitchen table sharing a bottle of wine. George accepted their invitation to join them.

One was a classic Nordic blonde, and the other had darker hair, a deviation that reinforced the beauty of their otherwise similar features: wide-set brown eyes; dimples; broad, luminescent foreheads.

George sensed his initial attempts at small talk were just as painful for them, but after half a glass of wine, he found his footing. Impressed by his familiarity with Danish cinema, one of the sisters asked if he'd studied film in college. When George said he'd been a philosophy major, they exchanged glances.

"Her ex-boyfriend studied philosophy," the darker one explained.

"What is love?" the blonde said. "Is love real? Am I real?"

Her Scandinavian manner of speaking was very literal and coarse, but George surmised that this was supposed to be a humorous impression of her ex, the philosopher scholar, and pretended to look amused.

"Do you have a girlfriend?" asked her sister.

George shrugged and finished what remained in his glass. "I'm not sure what to call her at the moment."

The girls looked interested.

"We just got back from this road trip," he began. "I'd always wanted to see the rest of the country. It's weird being an American, growing up in the Northeast. There's this whole other part of the country that you feel very disconnected from. As a child, I was fascinated by the idea of 'out West' and 'the South.' I had this romantic notion of these places, this vision of small towns with mom-and-pop shops. But instead, everywhere we went, Walmart."

George helped himself to more wine. "You probably don't even know what Walmart is. It's this huge store that sells everything. Food, guns, clothes, plastic crap Americans buy that ends up in the Great Pacific Garbage Patch."

George shook his head to convey his disgust.

"As we were driving back East, Jenny—my girlfriend—started talking fondly about all the places we'd been and everything we'd seen. It was as if we'd taken two different trips, visited two different countries.

"She's a very enthusiastic person," George explained.

"That's very American," the dark one said. "Excited about everything."

"Yeah, well, I'm not like that," George said. "Which Jenny's known from day one, but continually acts hurt and surprised by. When I told her the truth, that it depressed the hell out of me, that I wished we'd never taken the trip, so that the America I'd imagined could continue to exist that way in my mind, instead of being replaced by visions of Walmart, she got very upset.

"The problem is," George concluded, "she interprets everything as a referendum on her. She takes my depression personally."

The sisters nodded solemnly.

"You are done?" the blonde inquired.

"We're calling it a break." George sighed and drummed his fingers on the table. "I dunno, maybe this is it, though."

After they'd left, it occurred to George that when one of the sisters had said, "You are done?" she might not have been referring to the relationship but his commentary about it.

He'd talked too much. His description of the rest of the country as a bunch of Walmarts could be interpreted as elitist.

He was trying to impress them, and they'd seen through it. A privileged American trying to impress the citizens of a culturally and politically superior nation by pledging his contempt for the less educated swaths of his own.

Recalling his statement about Danish films as "cutting to the bone of the human psyche," George cringed. How *incisive*, to base one's impression of an entire nation's cinematic output on fewer than a dozen films, several of which, now that he thought of it, were actually Swedish.

George wished he'd said:

"The reason Danish cinema—all of Scandinavian cinema, really, and I imagine your novels, too—is so much better than American, besides not being commercial Hollywood trash, is because your societies aren't obviously unjust. Your filmmakers don't feel the burden of being socially responsible to justify their art. They're free to focus on more abstract or niche subjects. And they're not operating out of what Nietzsche called slave morality. Their work can afford to be subtle."

That was smart, George thought. He was impressed with this insight and frustrated that he hadn't gotten to use it. He typed it out for use in some future piece of writing. He was about to go to bed when he heard voices through his door.

"Now we are drinking water," announced the dark one as George poked his head out to find them back at the kitchen table.

"Because we are drunk," explained the blonde.

This was obvious from their rosy cheeks and dilated pupils. There was a slackening of their Scandinavian edges, and it put George at ease.

He poured himself a nightcap and took a seat at the table.

"How was it?" he asked.

The sisters took turns impersonating the bride-to-be: "Woo-hoo! I'm getting married! I'm getting MAAAAARRIED!" At the end of the night, she'd stuck her head out the limo's sunroof to let all of Manhattan know.

The sisters laughed as George shook his head in embarrassed recognition of this idiotic aspect of American culture: the aggressively self-celebratory nature of marking ordinary milestones as if they were some kind of hard-won victory or unique life accomplishment.

As they sat around the kitchen table for another hour, George imagined himself through their eyes, a charming combination of familiar and foreign, someone they related to on an interpersonal and intellectual level, but who also possessed that ineffable quality of being from America—a country for whom their disdain was surely complicated by respect for aspects of the culture that were cool: Bob Dylan, Miles Davis, Brooklyn?—and he was no longer worried.

They were beautiful, the sisters from Copenhagen.

George was sad when he woke up the next morning and they were gone.

It was nearly eleven. A tall, shirtless man George assumed was Otto was vacuuming. They exchanged perfunctory nods. George brushed his teeth, got dressed, and returned to the juice store. A different person was working there. As George explained that he owed them eleven dollars, he felt self-conscious, a little lame. It was the sort of thing he'd relished doing as a child—the opportunity to demonstrate his integrity. "Honest Abe," Cressida had mockingly called him.

On his way back, George stopped in a dumpling shop and ordered eight pork dumplings, which he ate sitting on a stool at a bar overlooking the street. He had a sad, Sunday feeling, though it was still Saturday. The apartment was empty when he returned. He lay down in bed and, without meaning to, fell back asleep. At one point he was aware of someone opening the door to his bedroom and briskly closing it.

When George woke up it was nearly five. The couch in the common room was occupied by two kids. A girl, who looked to be six or seven, and a toddler, who was very fat.

They were watching a show on an iPad. Registering George's presence, the girl looked up from the screen and said, "*Mom.*"

A woman sat at the kitchen table.

"Do you know which is our room?" she asked, barely looking up from her phone.

"I believe it's that door." George pointed.

"Doesn't work," the woman said, holding up a key.

"Hmmm," George said. "Let me try."

The key slid right in, but the doorknob wouldn't budge.

"Yeah, there's something wrong," George said as he tried again.

"Not sure why they lock the door before people come," he muttered, pushing his weight against the door. "Doesn't really make sense, when you think about it.

"I don't live here," he explained. "I'm just staying here while my sister's out of town."

The woman said nothing.

"Here on vacation?" he asked.

She nodded.

"Where're you from?"

"Pennsylvania."

"Where in Pennsylvania?" George jiggled the knob.

"Lewisburg."

"Bucknell," George said. "Isn't that where Bucknell is?"

The woman nodded.

"I have a friend who went there."

The woman looked uninterested. And then she said, "I work there.

"Food services," she volunteered before George could ask.

The girl got up from the couch to watch as George continued to try different things. She had her mother's tightly coiled brown hair and dark, brooding eyes.

"What happens if he can't open it?" she asked, in the petulant voice of a child who knows the answer. "Can we go to a hotel?"

"No, Brianna, we're not going to a hotel."

Eventually George figured it out. "The trick is to pull the door towards you as you turn the key," he said as he demonstrated.

It was similar to the room he was staying in, but without any personal objects. Just bare cinder-block walls, vinyl flooring, fluorescent strip lighting. George wondered if they knew they'd be sharing a full-size bed.

"Not exactly the Four Seasons," he apologized.

* * *

Eager to get out of the apartment, George went to a bar that gave you a free mini pizza with every beer you ordered. He'd brought his copy of *Gravity's Rainbow* but had trouble focusing. The interaction with the woman in the apartment—Robyn, her name was—had left him unsettled. Her curt responses to his attempts at friendly conversation had left him feeling hostile, but that hostility was complicated by her job.

George recalled the cafeteria workers at his college. There were students who worked to develop a rapport with the people on the other side of the Plexiglas, but George was not one of them. Their friendly overtures struck George as reinforcing the power dynamic as they pressured the workers to reciprocate, to pretend they were happy to be there and were charmed by their condescending small talk. But maybe George adopted that view to mitigate his guilt for making no such effort. And maybe the reason he hadn't made an effort wasn't so much "social indolence" (as his college self would have called it) but fear of rejection.

George wondered how much Cressida and her roommate charged people to spend the night in their dump of an apartment, and if they advertised the patio as an amenity. He resented being the face of the transaction.

George stayed out late. Walking home, he passed by a crate of children's books on the curb. In what felt like a grand gesture, he brought it home.

When he woke up the next morning, his door was open. Brianna stood in the doorway, looking coy.

"He opened it." She pointed to her brother, who was crouched in the corner wearing only a diaper. His face was red, and he seemed to be having trouble breathing. He was really fat. He looked like the stock image attached to an article about America's obesity problem.

"Is he okay?" George asked as the boy grunted.

Brianna nodded. "He's pooping."

"I'll give you a little privacy," George said, getting out of bed.

The common room floor was scattered with children's books.

George had to pee but Robyn was taking a shower. He was starting to get desperate when she finally emerged, the rubber soles of her shower shoes squawking as she padded across the linoleum floor.

The apartment was poorly ventilated. George's room reeked after what had transpired in the corner, and the air in the common room, steamy from Robyn's shower, was now infused with a noxious odor—an aerosol product Robyn had sprayed on the children's hair as they sat at the table eating Pop-Tarts off Styrofoam plates.

"What's that?" Brianna asked as George poured an envelope of instant oatmeal into a mug.

"My breakfast," George answered.

He felt like a jerk, hearing himself speak so tersely to a child. His sensitivity to the smells, his resentment at having to interact with strangers so early in the morning, was compounded by his hangover.

"Oatmeal," George spoke a moment later. "I'm making instant oatmeal in the microwave."

Now the child looked at him as though he were speaking to himself.

"What are you going to see today?" George asked Robyn.

"Times Square," Robyn said.

"Is he coming?" Brianna asked.

"Are you coming?" she asked George herself when her mother ignored the question.

"Not really a Times Square guy," George said, and retreated to his room, where he remained until they left.

George spent the morning reading various articles about public schools in preparation for speaking with the woman who had written them, a journalist at the *New York Times* who was married to the son of a family friend.

"George, this is how the world works," Ellen would say of the milking of vague social connections under the pretense of seeking professional advice.

George agreed but wanted no part of it, which was why he'd declined to reach out to the journalist, whose contact information had been forwarded to him for such purposes. It was only when Nicole—clearly at the behest of her mother-in-law—had emailed George, offering to "chat," that the call had been scheduled for four o'clock that afternoon.

At 3:56, Robyn and the kids returned. George retreated to his room and locked the door.

George planned to begin the conversation by complimenting her work, but at the last minute he feared it would come across as brownnosing. Instead he said something about the scarcity of entry-level journalism jobs, which he immediately regretted, as she misinterpreted this as his asking her for one.

"I'm afraid I can't help you with that," she said, and began talking about internships.

George interjected to say that he'd spent three years in an internship and was reluctant to pursue another "at this phase in my life," adding that he also had moral qualms with the whole "internship system," which perpetuated a cycle of inequality—a point she'd raised in one of her articles about the opportunity gap between those who graduated with student debt and those who did not. George cited the article as an example of something he'd read of hers and found "very compelling." With a brisk "thank you," Nicole pivoted the conversation back to George, asking where he'd interned.

George, pacing the few feet of floor space next his bed as he spoke, told her that it had been with a hedge fund, explaining that he had no interest in the financial industry and had only taken the position to help pay off a medical bill. Realizing this was potentially confusing, he clarified that it was a paid internship, though he wouldn't have been able to save a dime had he not lived for free in a cottage on the property of the CEO, who was also his uncle—it all sounded very wrong to George, but there was no way around it, these were the facts, this was his life.

Nicole started talking about Columbia's one-year journalism program, but George was distracted by knocking on his door. When the knocking became pounding, George opened the door, and Brianna spilled in, whining about her brother.

"Excuse me," George said to Nicole, and told Brianna to ask her mom for help.

"She's gone," Brianna said.

"What do you mean she's gone?"

"She went out."

"She left you alone here?"

Brianna nodded.

"Did she say where she was going or when she's coming back?"

Brianna looked flustered. "I'm in charge," she informed George, and flew out of the room.

"Sounds like you have to go," Nicole said. "Which is fine, as I think that about covers everything, as far as any advice I have. Best of luck."

"Thank you," George said. "You, too."

Hanging up, George cringed. "You, too"? What a dipshit.

Whatever the conflict was, when George came out of his room, it appeared to have been resolved. The kids sat peacefully on the couch, hunkered over the iPad, which was playing a terrible kids' song.

Mommy-finger . . . Mommy-finger . . . where ARE you . . .
HERE I am, HERE I am,
how do you do . . .

"Off," George said. "Turn that thing off."

Looking amused by George's imperious tone, Brianna playfully tossed the device aside, as if to say, Now what?

"We're going to read a *book*," George told them, scanning his options on the floor.

Rotten Ralph's Rotten Family was about a cat whose selfish, egomaniacal, and destructive behavior occasionally tests the patience of his doting owner, a sweet girl named Sarah. One night, Sarah gets mad, and Ralph decides to run away. He returns to his highly dysfunctional biological family—the title did not disappoint—whose cruel and belittling treatment of Ralph explains why he is the way he is. Eventually, Ralph has enough. After tearfully bidding his cat mother goodbye—she was the only kind one—Ralph returns to Sarah, cleaning the house and cooking her a grand breakfast in gratitude for the love she shows him.

George had been disappointed by the formulaically sappy end to what had otherwise struck him as a subversively dark children's tale until, on the final page, after Sarah says how nice it is to have Ralph at home, the cat thinks, *Where I can do anything I want.*

"*That Ralph*," George said, closing the book. "He's incorrigible. It's nice that Sarah takes him back anyway."

Brianna shrugged in moody indifference.

"Maybe that's the takeaway," George mused. "Maybe it's not just a cynical depiction of how deeply wounded people, or *cats*, are beyond reform, but a testament to the power of love."

"What do you think?" George asked the boy, who stared solemnly back.

It was hard to look at him without imagining his future: diabetes, social isolation, unemployment. George wondered, if he were to adopt the child, how things might turn out differently.

"He doesn't talk," Brianna said. "He's two and he can only say five words and two of them don't count because they're names."

"Late talking can be a sign of intelligence," George said.

Brianna raised her eyebrows in skepticism.

Robyn returned with a pizza and a liter of orange soda. Seeing George on the couch, sandwiched between her kids, she looked pissed.

"I told you not to bother him," she scolded Brianna, whose eyes popped in righteous indignation.

"But, Mom, *he* started it! He took away our iPad! He said we had to read a *book*!"

"Sorry," George said instinctively.

* * *

They'd already left the apartment when George got up the next morning. Not knowing how long he had the place to himself made him skittish. He kept imagining he heard a key in the door. And then he did. He went into his room and shut the door but it didn't work. Within minutes, *knock-knock-knock. Pound-thump!*

"Some bad guys flew an airplane into a building," Brianna informed George, stepping into his room. "The people in the building were scared of getting burned in the fire so they jumped out the window."

"I remember when it happened," George told her. "It was my first week of college. I was on my way to class and—"

"This is a piece of the building," Brianna interrupted, holding up a nub of cement.

"Where did you get that?" George asked.

"We went to the place where it happened," she answered in a husky whisper.

"Did you find it on the ground, or was someone selling it?"

"Someone was selling it."

"Also got this." Briana reached into her pocket and pulled out a refrigerator magnet featuring a ghostly image of the towers set against the Manhattan skyline, above the words NEVER FORGET.

Brianna spent the evening drawing pictures inspired by what she'd learned from their visit to the 9/11 Memorial. Rendered in the plucky scrawl of a child's hand, the images looked sort of folksy. She was not a bad drawer.

The next morning, Robyn had planned to take the kids to the Empire State Building, but Brianna was refusing to go.

"She's scared a plane will crash into it," Robyn explained in exasperation.

"I can guarantee you that won't happen," George said. "But I can't guarantee that you won't find it really boring. It's a long elevator ride, you get to the top, walk around on this deck, and that's it."

George proposed that Robyn instead take the kids to the Metropolitan Museum of Art.

"Kids like the Met," he said. "Brianna could bring her sketchbook and pencils and sketch some of the paintings. My mom used to be an art teacher, and when we were little she used to take us there to do that. She said it's the best way to learn. Copy the pros."

Robyn didn't look particularly enthusiastic, but Brianna was eager to go.

Two hours after they set out, George heard the key in the front door.

Brianna shot him a dark look as they came in. "Why did you tell us to go there when it was closed!"

"It was closed?" George said.

"Closed on Mondays," Robyn said.

"I'm sorry," George said. In case it wasn't obvious, he added, "I didn't know that."

"She really wanted to draw pictures of the paintings," Robyn said. "You got her all excited."

"You could go to an art gallery," he suggested.

Robyn shook her head. "Not getting back on the subway."

"You don't need to go to Manhattan for that. There's got to be some within walking distance."

Robyn wasn't looking for solutions. Her anger needed an outlet, and it was George. George, who had been nothing but accommodating to this woman.

He volunteered to take Brianna to an art gallery himself.

Brianna begrudgingly accepted the offer.

George took her to a gallery on Wythe where they saw sculptures made out of trash. A photo exhibit of urinals. Bananas duct-taped to blank canvases. A giant cube. Brianna was not inspired to sketch any of these things in her notebook.

"It's conceptual art," George explained. "It's supposed to make you think something. Does it make you think something?"

Brianna's eyes percolated with disappointment and anger. "Can we go back?" she asked.

George didn't look forward to having children. Was it not enough that the world made a mockery of your own expectations?

Brianna's mood picked up when they returned to the apartment and Robyn revealed that tomorrow—their final day of the trip—they would be going to see Elmo at Madison Square Garden.

George was surprised by her excitement. He would've thought she was too old for Elmo.

* * *

George woke up the next morning to a rambling voicemail, recorded shortly after midnight.

Hello, George, this is George. I'm calling because your mother tells me you want to be a writer and I thought I'd save us both some time and give you the CliffsNotes version of the advice I give my students who want to be writers. Do not get an MFA. Did Shakespeare get an MFA? Dickens? Salinger? Roth? The last thing the world needs is another novel harvested in a workshop of navel-gazing twentysomethings who've never left the classroom. Go out and see the world! Have you left the Northeast? Leave the Northeast! Spend a few years in London, San Francisco, Paris, even a small town in Arkansas—you'll come back with a completely different perspective.

The speaker went on to inveigh against the entitlement of George's generation, from their whiny grade-grubbing to their desire for professional advancement without paying dues.

I'm not sure what your book is about, the man concluded, *but I'm confident it'll be a better one if you shelve it for now and get a few years of life under your belt. Work, love, suffer, endure, observe, learn, unlearn, be humbled . . .*

George was confused; he did not recognize the voice. He wondered if it could be his dad's cousin, who was an English professor at NYU. That they had the same name was a coincidence—he and his dad hadn't been close. He must have attended Denis's memorial, but George remembered meeting him only once, as a child at some kind of family function, and the adults chortling as he had teased George, "There's only room for one of us!"

George called his mom, who confirmed it was indeed Denis's cousin. She'd given George his number and asked him to reach out.

"I thought he'd be a good person for you to talk to. That he might have some ideas or advice."

"Well, thank you for that," George said. "It was a great way to start the day. A drunk voicemail telling me I suck."

"Oh, *George*," Ellen said. "He doesn't even *know* you. You can't take it personally."

When George came out of his room, Brianna was sitting at the kitchen table, her face illuminated with tears. They would not be going to see Elmo at Madison Square Garden, after all, because the boy had woken up with a fever.

Robyn was on the phone with Ticketmaster trying to get a refund.

"There goes a week's salary," she said, getting off.

"It's not *fair*," Brianna whined. "Why does it matter if he's sick? Why can't we go anyway? He can just sit there."

"That wouldn't be nice to him," Robyn told Brianna. "He needs to rest, be comfortable."

Brianna's disappointment simmered to a rage. She began to wail.

"Enough of the screaming, Brianna," Robyn said. "I never said life was fair, quit acting like a baby."

This further inflamed things.

George was relieved when Brianna went into their room and shut the door.

The boy fell asleep sitting up on the couch, head slumped over. He wore only a diaper. With each inhalation his belly cleaved into four distinct quadrants of fat, then puffed back up with the silken jiggle of undercooked soufflé.

As George adjusted him into a reclining position, he was struck by how smooth his skin felt. Smooth and firm, the plump gathering in seemingly arbitrary folds, like the contours of an heirloom tomato.

"You have younger siblings growing up?" Robyn asked.

George was self-conscious, realizing she'd been watching him from across the room. "Just an older sister."

"You're good with kids," she said.

No one had ever told George this before. He must have looked surprised, because Robyn nodded thoughtfully. "You have a natural way."

George had an idea: "Why don't you and Brianna go to the show, and he can stay here with me?"

"He'll probably sleep the whole time," Robyn told George. "You won't even know he's here."

The show was at eleven; they would have to leave immediately.

Robyn went to go tell Brianna, who emerged a few minutes later, swollen-cheeked and glassy-eyed, in a purple sequined dress and leopard-print tights.

She looked up at George, and said—with an affected nonchalance that betrayed her pride—"We're taking a *taxi*."

Robyn thanked George on her way out the door. And then she said: "I wouldn't leave my kids with just anyone."

George wasn't sure if this was intended as a compliment or a threat.

"I'll take good care of him," he responded awkwardly.

When they were gone, George opened up his laptop and began working on a cover letter. He left the door to his room open so that he could hear if the boy started crying.

After an hour of silence, George went out to check on the boy.

His eyes were open. He lay there looking miserable.

"I'm going to give you some medicine," George told him. "It'll make you feel better."

Robyn had left a bottle of Infants' Tylenol out on the kitchen table and told George he was due for a second dose at noon. It was eleven-forty, but George figured that was close enough. After carefully extracting the correct amount of liquid into the syringe, George squirted it into the boy's mouth. He immediately spat it back out. It got everywhere—the boy, the couch, George. It was the consistency of semen and smelled like air freshener.

The boy felt very warm.

George called his mother: "What are you supposed to do if a baby has a high fever and refuses to take medicine?"

Ellen said, "I don't know. Give him some juice? Whose kid is this?"

George googled the question and the internet suggested a bath. A lukewarm bath.

George went into the bathroom to start the water. As he waited for the tub to fill, he went back out to check on the boy, who lay staring intently at something in the distance. George started talking to him, but the boy's gaze remained fixed. On what, exactly, it was not clear.

As George picked him up, his body felt stiff, as though he were arching his back.

Something was wrong.

In his panic, George couldn't find his phone, and rather than waste time looking for it, he carried the child out the front door, onto the street, and into the corner bodega.

It was as if they were expecting him, as though they had drills for this sort of thing.

"Lay him on his side," someone instructed. "That way if he vomits, he don't choke."

George gently laid the boy down, one cheek on the cold linoleum floor. People circled around. A pair of hands pressed a carton of ice cream to the child's bare feet, which did not seem to register the cold.

Someone was on speakerphone with 9–1–1. The dispassionate drone of the dispatcher's questions—how old is the baby, does he have any medical conditions, when did the episode begin—seemed pointless to George.

"Just tell them to fucking send someone," he pleaded. "We need them to get here *now*."

A chorus of voices assured George help was on the way.

The boy's eyes remained disconcertingly open. His complexion wasn't right.

George leaned over and pressed his face to the baby's exposed cheek, so that he felt the presence of another human, if not one who mattered to him.

"Here they are!" someone announced.

Police. EMTs. As they thundered into the store, the child stirred. A meek whimper escalated to a wail.

George felt a hand on his back. "Crying is good," a man's voice told him.

"Febrile seizure," an EMT announced after taking the baby's temperature, which was 104.8.

They wanted to take him to the hospital for observation, but febrile seizures were extremely common and they were not worried, the EMT assured George.

Someone handed George a Cherry Coke.

They had to attach a child's seat to the stretcher, which was taking some time. George was reassured by their casual annoyance at figuring out the buckles. If the situation were dire, surely they would just go.

The boy was going to be just fine, they kept telling George, and he started to believe it.

For a moment, his relief was elevated by hope. A sudden conviction that the boy's future wasn't all grim, that along with the inevitable disappointments and hardships, there were bound to be some happy times, some unanticipated victories.

"He's going to be okay?" George asked, one more time, as they boarded the ambulance.

"He's going to be just fine, Dad," said the EMT.

7. CHICKENS

George, 27 ½

The dogs George walked lived in Manhattan, and the room he was subletting was in Sunset Park, and so he spent his mornings commuting to the city, then the better part of his day traveling between the dogs' apartments. His meals came from food trucks and bodegas and were consumed on the go. Once, George was unknowingly photographed for a *New York Post* story about people who ate on the subway. The headline: "New Yorkers Eat like Slobs on Subway." George forwarded the link to people he knew would find it funny. *Oh, George*, Cressida responded. *Have some self-respect.*

At least he was saving money. Through various connections he'd gotten plugged in to a network of rich dog owners and made two hundred, sometimes three hundred, dollars a day, all off the books. He couldn't complain about that. But it was far from the existence he'd envisioned for himself. He felt lonely and adrift, while also stuck and claustrophobic.

One evening George was riding the subway home—back to the shithole apartment he shared with three strangers—when his thoughts were interrupted by the sound of change falling. A homeless man in a wheelchair examined his empty cup as coins skittered across the floor.

George instinctively rose to his feet and began picking them up. As his fingers grazed the filthy, sticky F train floor, he felt a kind of penance. "God bless," the homeless man said as George deposited the coins back in his cup. George returned to his seat, sobered, humbled, in awe of this person's will to keep living. Who was George to feel sorry for himself?

But he couldn't help it.

Later that week he realized it was his half birthday. "It's my half birthday," George told Rocco the Labradoodle as they waited for the elevator. "I'm twenty-seven and a half, which means I'm seventy-five percent between twenty and thirty."

"Happy seventy-five percent to thirty to me," George said each time he picked up a poop that day.

That night he called Jenny, who was in her second semester at Fordham Law. They hadn't spoken in many months. Jenny had requested a "clean break," a total cessation of communication, but he wondered if she'd make an exception on his half birthday.

"It's my half birthday," George said when she picked up. "I'm three quarters of the way to thirty."

"Happy half birthday, George," Jenny said. "Welcome to the final quarter." There was a playful edge, a fruity withholding in her tone.

After a little resistance on Jenny's end, they began seeing each other again. Jenny was busy, and their time together was limited to the weekends. They would meet up at some party or bar, get drunk, and go back to one or the other's apartment, usually Jenny's student housing. It felt like a new and exciting thing but with the comfort of familiarity.

As the conclusion of George's sublet approached, he asked Jenny if it would be okay if he crashed with her for a bit while he looked for a new apartment.

"You want to *crash* with me," she responded.

"Don't worry about it," George said. "There are other people I can ask. I'm sure Cressida would let me stay in the extra room in her apartment."

Jenny told George that she was moving. She was tired of student housing. She was looking for a new apartment herself.

"Maybe we should look for one together," she proposed.

"It would save money," she added.

"Sure," George said after a pause.

"*Sure?*" Jenny repeated.

"I mean, yeah," he said. "Yes. That makes sense."

Jenny wanted to live in Carroll Gardens. George didn't know much about Carroll Gardens, but he would love it, Jenny assured him; it was quiet and charming and beautiful, with a low skyline and lots of trees. It was the best neighborhood in New York City.

One Saturday they went to go look at apartments. They took a G train from Greenpoint, where George was currently cat-sitting.

As they got off the subway, Jenny gripped George's wrist.

"It's Raj," she whispered, staring at the crowd ahead of them on the platform. "Green shirt."

Raj was Jenny's ex-boyfriend and the reason she was familiar with the neighborhood of Carroll Gardens. They'd dated during one of Jenny and George's breaks.

He was in school to be a chef. He'd loved cooking for her and giving unsolicited back massages and foot rubs. When casually referring to their time together to George, Jenny had managed to invoke these facts.

Their relationship had lasted only a few months, but this had been long enough for Raj to decide that Jenny was it for him. When she broke up with him, Raj lamented, "I'll never love anyone as much as I love you." Or maybe it was: "No one will ever love you as much as I love you." George couldn't remember which, only that Jenny relayed this to him during an argument, in the spirit of a threat.

"False alarm," Jenny said, getting a better look at the man in the green shirt as they reached the top of the subway steps.

"This way," Jenny said, as George started to walk the wrong direction down Smith Street.

"Maybe you should email Raj," George suggested, "let him know we're moving here, so it's not an awkward surprise to bump into each other."

Jenny shook her head. "It'll be awkward either way. But he'll get used to it. It's just the first time, him seeing me with you, could be a little punch to the gut."

They cut over to Court Street, where they passed a bakery, a bookstore, a butcher with a statue of a pig outside.

George could see the charm. "I feel like I'm in a Richard Scarry book."

Jenny smiled tentatively. "Who's he?" she asked.

"Are you kidding?" George said. "Richard Scarry? You really got through college without reading one of his novels?"

Jenny looked embarrassed.

"You're mean," she said when George told her that Richard Scarry was actually not a novelist but a children's book author.

It was a little mean. Jenny's sheepish awareness of her ignorance of certain cultural subjects (books, films, music made before 1980) had initially struck George as endearing, less so when he realized she wasn't motivated to do anything about it. That, and her shameless fluency in a few reality TV shows—it seemed to George there was a correlation between the two.

After a few blocks, they turned onto a residential street. The sidewalk was narrow and buckled in places from the root growth of large trees. The houses were set back from the street and had gated patios.

"This used to be an all-Italian neighborhood," Jenny said as they passed a Virgin Mary statue.

Glancing over her shoulder, she added, in a whisper, "Which is kind of nice, because it means we don't have to feel guilty about displacing minorities."

"Just working-class Catholics," George said.

They arrived at an owner-listed rental Jenny had found on Craigslist, a brownstone on Clinton. They rang the buzzer, and a middle-aged couple let them in. The husband introduced himself as Alex, and then the wife did, too. They were both named Alex, they explained with good cheer, as if after however many years of marriage they were still amused by the coincidence themselves.

The apartment was on the top floor, and the couple and their children occupied the rest of the house. On the way upstairs, George made inadvertent eye contact with their teenage daughter, whose bedroom door was ajar. She lay on the floor, talking on the phone. There was something provocative about her languid sprawl, the carefree sway of her upturned bare feet.

As they passed by she glanced up, her moody eyes latching onto George, lingering in a manner that felt experimentally assertive, as though brandishing her teenage beauty like a child in possession of contraband.

That George was no longer a teenager was a fact that occasionally caught him off guard, rendering him momentarily bewildered and bereft, but, in this instance, he was acutely aware of his status in her eyes as a full-fledged adult male, a potential perp, Humbert Humbert.

The apartment was clean and well-kept, with lots of light and a working fireplace. Jenny effused over the tiled ceiling, the wooden shutters, the old-fashioned double-basin kitchen sink, and the Alexes looked pleased that she noticed and appreciated these details, which were original to the house, which was built in 1901.

"We briefly worked with a broker who tried to talk us into a gut reno," volunteered the husband.

"We said *absolutely not*," said the wife.

"Maybe we shouldn't tell you this"—she smiled at Jenny—"but the last two couples who lived here both got pregnant within the year."

George groped for a witty response.

"Must be something in the water," the husband said.

"Does the rent include hot water?" George asked.

The couple shook their heads. Jenny glowered.

On the way back down, the door to the daughter's bedroom was shut, underscoring George's anxiety that he had given her the wrong impression by not immediately terminating their earlier eye contact. But he also felt unjustly baited—he was not a creep. He was not a sexual predator.

As soon as they were outside Jenny started berating him for asking about hot water.

"They were trying to show us the kind of people they are, that it's not just about money to them, that they relate to their tenants on a personal level, and you ask if they'll be paying for our hot water."

"It's a perfectly appropriate thing to ask your prospective landlord," George protested. "We're not at a dinner party, Jenny. It's a business transaction."

After a minute of sulking, Jenny said, "The apartment was beautiful, but I think it would be a little awkward to walk through their house to get upstairs."

"I agree," George said.

A broker was meeting them at the next apartment, but he called to say he was running late.

"No worries, Allen," Jenny assured him. "Take your time, we're happy to wait outside."

When they got to the building, they sat on the stoop.

Ten minutes passed—no Allen. The front door to the building opened, and a guy poked his head out, looking dazed.

Jenny stood and began apologizing for obstructing his exit, though it didn't appear he was going anywhere in his mesh shorts and slippers. "We're looking at an apartment in the building," she explained. "We're waiting for the broker."

"Yeah, he just called and said to let you in. So, uh . . . come in, I guess."

George and Jenny followed him up a flight of filthy stairs into an apartment that reeked of Lysol and takeout. It was sparsely furnished but cluttered with electronics. Entering the bedroom, George toppled a liter of Diet Coke on the floor next to a futon. Fortunately, it wasn't very full.

"Since the broker's not here, I'll be honest with you," the tenant said as George peered into the alcove kitchen. "There's a mouse problem."

"Have you tried traps?" Jenny asked.

The guy sighed and rubbed the back of his neck. "Glue traps, snap traps, poison, something called 'the jaws of death.' I started dating a vegan and she made me try a thing you plug into the wall that makes a sound they don't like, that's supposed to make them not want to enter your apartment in the first place . . ."

Jenny, always interested in the humane alternatives to such problems, nodded eagerly. "And what happened?"

The guy flashed a bitter smirk in George's direction. "She turned out to be borderline, like every woman I date."

"But did the sound deterrent work?" Jenny asked.

The guy shook his head. "Didn't seem to make a dent in the population."

Jenny's phone rang; Allen was downstairs.

"We'll come out and meet you," she said.

Allen was exactly how George had imagined: late sixties, receding hairline, baggy suit. Outer-borough Jewish accent, the kind you seldom heard anymore.

"What'd you think?" he asked as they descended the front steps.

"The tenant said there's a rodent problem," George told him.

Allen found this amusing. "Welcome to New York, kids."

The next apartment he took them to was vacant. It was on the top floor of the building, and George could easily touch the ceiling.

"I find low ceilings cozy," Jenny said when he called her attention to this. "But I'm not sure about living in a fourth-floor walk-up."

George was surprised she'd object to this. "But you like exercise. When there's an elevator, you always choose to take the stairs."

"It's not me I'm worried about," she said.

Their voices bellowed in the empty space.

"Oh, come on," George defended himself. "I can handle some stairs." He felt bad saying this in front of Allen, who had paused to catch his breath on the final landing.

"I know you," Jenny persisted. "You're going to act like it's a big deal to run down to the store. You're never going to leave."

She started talking about a week they'd spent in his cousin's walk-up on the Lower East Side a few years earlier. She'd needed a lemon for a soup she was making, and when she'd asked George to go get one, he tried to convince her that the soup would taste better without it.

The time they'd spent arguing about it was a fraction of the time it would've taken him to go to the bodega on the corner.

Allen made a coughing sound, as if to remind them of his presence. Jenny looked slightly embarrassed—perhaps aware of how she might be coming across—but rather than drop the matter, she attempted to spin it as an amusing anecdote.

"The most frustrating part"—she looked at Allen—"was that he wouldn't admit that he was too lazy to go to the store. Instead he tried to turn it into a debate about whether lemon juice even belongs in soup!"

George barely remembered any of this. He'd been very depressed that week. That was one way his mind functioned well: forgetting the really dark times. But he believed Jenny's account. Lemon juice didn't seem like something that should go in soup.

The third apartment was next to an empty lot surrounded by a chain-link fence.

"There used to be a building there," Allen volunteered, "but it fell down."

"As buildings do," George responded.

"It won't always be an empty lot," Allen said. "They'll put something new up. Shiny new condos."

George asked Allen if he thought the landlord would consider a rent deduction, given that they'd be signing up to live next to a construction site.

Allen laughed sardonically. "Let me tell you kids something about how the world works . . ."

Without directly answering George's question, he spoke at length about the brutish nature of humanity. "People are selfish," he concluded his sermon. "They'll take what they can get and no less."

After this they looked at a ground-floor apartment with access to a garden.

"We could get chickens," Jenny said brightly as they stepped outside.

"I was thinking sheep," George responded. "Our own little flock. I'm sure Dizart would hook us up."

"I was being serious," Jenny said. "Chickens don't require much space."

"You want to get chickens," George said. "Here. In Brooklyn."

Jenny nodded earnestly. "They're very low maintenance. And what little work is involved, I'll take care of."

"What about when you go away for the weekend?" George asked.

"I think you can handle it."

"Could they potentially carry diseases?"

"Of course, they could *potentially* carry diseases, George. As can dogs and cats and all living organisms."

"What about their poop?"

Jenny shook her head dismissively. "It's nothing. It's not the kind you have to clean up."

"So it just sits there, more of it every day, and no one ever cleans it up?"

George glanced at Allen, who appeared to be enjoying this.

"Where do you buy chicken food?" George asked.

"We'd order it. And the other perk of having chickens is they eat your leftovers. Even banana peels. We'd never have to throw food away."

"So after dinner, we just come outside and scrape our plates onto the ground?"

"I was thinking we'd keep a bucket on the kitchen counter and then bring it out at the end of the day."

"And you'll clean out the bucket?"

"*Yes*, George, I'll do the strenuous job of filling the bucket with hot water once in a while."

"What if we have chicken for dinner?"

Jenny shook her head. "I wouldn't feed them that."

"What about when it rains or gets cold?"

"They go in their hutch."

"Hutch?"

"It's a little house," Jenny explained.

"They need their own house?"

"It's tiny, it's not a big deal."

"Do we build it ourselves?"

"I'm sure you can get a kit," Jenny said.

"Are we going to need a drill? How much is this all going to cost?"

"I don't know, George." Jenny nodded wearily. "I'm sorry I don't have the exact answers for you at this exact moment."

Acknowledging her likely defeat, Jenny struck a maudlin tone. "It's always been my dream to have chickens."

George looked around at the space, which was not very large, and imagined it covered in feathers and bird shit, banana peels and pizza crusts. He suspected Jenny's fantasy involved a wicker basket full of eggs, herself in some kind of prairie dress and a pair of wool clogs. She nurtured childish longings by making George the adversary; she needed him to say no so that she didn't have to consider the impracticality of whatever it was she thought she wanted and realize it wasn't worth it.

"Okay," George said. "I won't stand between you and your dream. Let's get this apartment, and let's get chickens."

Allen waited until now to chime in. "The owner has a no-dogs policy. I'm not sure how he'd feel about livestock."

On the way to the next apartment, there was a second Raj scare. Allen nodded matter-of-factly as George explained why Jenny had disappeared into a CVS.

"I'm pretty sure it's not him." George squinted at the man walking his dog across the street, who did not look Indian.

When Jenny came back out, George asked, "Should we be moving into a neighborhood where you're going to be so skittish?"

Allen held up his hands and said, "Don't look at me! My ex-wife moved to a different borough!"

The final apartment Allen showed them was above a laundromat. It had been advertised as having laundry "in the building."

"That's a little misleading," Jenny said.

"Name of the game, kids," Allen said. "Name of the game." As he shook his head, a lock of his comb-over broke loose and drifted down his forehead like a defective windshield wiper.

After they parted ways, Jenny wanted to talk about Allen. She felt bad for him. How heartbreaking to lose his business and then have no choice but to go work for the enemy.

"What are you talking about?" George said.

"How he lost the lease on his copy shop because his landlord doubled the rent. And now he has to work in the industry that's responsible for this kind of thing happening all over the city."

"How do you know this?"

"Because he told us when we were walking between apartments.

"I guess you weren't paying attention," she said with a shrug, a passive indictment of what she called George's "George-problem."

"It might benefit your writing if you weren't so wrapped up in yourself," she'd told him recently. "If you made a conscious effort to listen to other people, to take more of the world in."

George knew he was preoccupied. In any case, he had no interest in talking about Allen or speculating about his life. Allen depressed him. He wanted to forget about Allen.

George was tired. He'd had enough of looking at apartments. He was hungry and he had to pee.

They approached a coffee shop on the way to the subway, and George went inside to use the bathroom. When he came back, Jenny was on the corner, talking to a man.

"This is George," she said, as George joined them. "George, this is Raj."

He had a kind, benevolent face and was taller than George had envisioned. He was very tall—George was surprised Jenny had never mentioned this fact—with the stooped shoulders and gentle grip of a tall man who is eager to renounce any authority or capital his height might engender.

And yet, as they shook hands, Raj's attempt to mitigate his stature only made George feel smaller.

The handshake went on too long, and when George finally initiated a withdrawal, Jenny spoke, her words tumbling out a little too fast. "Well, it was great seeing you, Raj! Congratulations! Good luck with everything!"

"He's about to move to Buffalo to go to nursing school," Jenny said when they were out of earshot.

George was confused. "I thought he wanted to be a chef."

"He quit," Jenny said. "He just wasn't cut out for it. It's a stressful atmosphere, a restaurant, especially the kitchen. There's a lot of yelling that goes on, a lot of public berating . . ."

"You don't have to tell me," George reminded her. "I couldn't even hack it as a waiter. But isn't a hospital even more stressful than a restaurant?"

"What are you suggesting?" Jenny asked. "That he's going to fail?"

George said nothing, but Jenny continued to look at him interrogatingly.

"Anyway, he's not planning on working at a hospital. He wants to work at a nursing home."

"Oh. Wow." George couldn't think of a more depressing job.

"He'll be very good at it," Jenny said. "He's a natural caretaker."

"He seems like a very nice guy," George said as they waited to cross the street. They were two blocks from the subway.

Jenny took George's hand as the light turned. "I think we should go with the first apartment. It's so much nicer than everything else we saw."

"What about the awkwardness of walking through that family's home?"

"They seemed really nice. I think it would be okay.

"It's not a *forever* home," she said. "It's just for now, this particular stage in our life. It might even be kind of nice. Sort of homey."

"I'm sorry," George said. "But I'm not moving into that apartment. I can't live like that. Walking by some family every time I leave the apartment."

"Which one would you choose?" Jenny asked.

They approached a massive sycamore whose base had breached the square of dirt it had been allotted. A lattice of swollen roots ruptured a portion of the sidewalk. A man pushing a stroller was headed in the opposite direction, and as they converged upon the narrow passage, Jenny tugged George toward the curb, inviting the man to go first. But the man refused her courtesy, gesturing for them to proceed. Now both parties were stalled.

To end the standoff, George advanced, and Jenny followed.

"I guess I could do the one with the low ceilings," George said. "The fourth-floor walk-up."

Jenny said nothing, just stared.

"The one on Henry Street," he added.

"You could *do* it," she repeated. There was a mocking, bitter edge to her voice. But her expression was a little crestfallen.

"Yeah," George said. "I could do that one."

8. ZOMBIE HUT

George, 29

Rarely did it snow anymore, *really snow*, and so George was disappointed but not surprised when, after all the fuss and anticipation—the excessive salting of sidewalks, the fleets of sanitation trucks outfitted with plows, the Soviet-style lines at grocery stores as people panic-bought beer and bread and toilet paper, the overstimulated weathermen gesticulating at pixelated maps—what was supposed to have been a major blizzard turned out to be just rain. A fierce, slanted rain that brought down what remained of the leaves, which should've all been gone a month earlier, Jenny pointed out.

"When I was a kid," George said, standing beneath the sheltered part of the stoop as he smoked his first cigarette of the day, "I was pretty worried about global warming, but it seemed like acid rain, or the hole in the ozone layer, was kind of an abstract thing. But here it is, I guess . . ."

"Don't worry," said Larry, who was also a smoker. "Nature will have a chance to recuperate once humans kill themselves off."

Larry was in his late sixties and the most cynical person George had ever encountered. His cynicism did not mask a tender heart, and there was nothing performative about it. He was the real deal, a genuine misanthrope who could exist only in New York City, and George took a certain pride in living above him, though it also made him a little nervous—from various comments Larry had made to George in the year they'd lived in the fourth-floor walk-up on Henry Street, it was obvious that he could hear much of what went on in their apartment.

George finished his cigarette, but Larry had no qualms keeping him there as he rattled off his usual litany of complaints: the rising cost of the neighborhood, yuppies, parents who called their toddler "buddy," the word *super* used as an adverb, bike lanes, a new kind of shoe people were wearing that had toes, the national obsession with gadgets and fitness.

When George returned to the apartment, Jenny was on the phone in the bedroom. It was Saturday, and she would be home all day. A shrill, escalating tremor in her voice carried through the closed door, over the thrum of rain, the hiss and spit of the radiator.

George reclined on the couch, which was strewn with knitting materials. Jenny was making scarves and hats for the friends she'd made at Occupy Wall Street. This was her new project now that it was colder, and she was going to Zuccotti Park less frequently herself—something she felt guilty about, which was ridiculous considering how remarkable it was she'd made the time to go at all while juggling her law school workload and shifts at the immigration clinic.

There was a brisk breeze as the bedroom door was flung open.

"That was my mom," Jenny announced. "I told her we're not going there for Christmas anymore."

George sat up. He was surprised to hear this. Surprised, and a little irritated.

In the past, he and Jenny had spent Christmas with their respective families. But this year, Jenny had asked him to join her family for Christmas. It was hard for George to imagine not waking up in his childhood home on Christmas morning—he told Jenny he'd have to check with his mother. He'd assumed that Ellen would object to his absence on Christmas, might even forbid it, but she'd been fine with it. She'd made plans to spend a week visiting a friend in Milan. She was flying there now.

"What happened?" George asked.

"She invited Sadie's parents."

"Oh." George was confused as to the problem. Sadie was Jenny's sister's girlfriend—or fiancée. Now that it was legal, they were getting married.

Jenny's face gleamed with righteous indignation. "We've been together for half a decade and she's never even had your mom over for dinner. They've been together for barely a year and my mom's inviting Sadie's parents to *Christmas*?"

It wasn't in George's best interest to point out that he and Jenny were not engaged.

"Maybe it's because they're gay," George said. "Maybe it's to show her support."

"That has nothing to do with it," Jenny insisted. "She's never taken our relationship seriously. Even though we live together. Even though she knows I'm supporting you . . ."

Jenny looked at him nervously. "I didn't mean that."

"That's okay," George said. "It's true."

Jenny was paying his portion of the rent from a small family trust she had access to.

George was surprised she'd mentioned their arrangement to her mother. Jenny didn't like to talk about money. He wondered if she'd volunteered this information, or if Jenny's mom had asked how George was paying rent without a paying job.

In either case, George understood Jenny's mother's ambivalence about him. He saw himself through her eyes. It was unfortunate that he'd called her by the wrong name this past summer (Suzie, when her name was Cindy). At least she'd laughed about it: "George, you've known me for how long?"

"So, what's the plan now?" George asked. "Where're we going to go?"

Christmas was in less than a week; it was a little late for a change of plan.

George got up and walked to the window. They had a view of all the gardens on their block, though only some of them could actually be called gardens. You could tell who owned each property from what they did with the space: the synthetic grass carpets and cheap patio furniture of the remaining Italian-American households; the raised-bed vegetable gardens of the new young families who tenderly cultivated their snatch of earth; the sad, neglected lots attached to buildings like theirs, which had been divided up into rental units with high turnover.

"We won't go anywhere," Jenny said. "We'll have our own Christmas here."

* * *

Jenny woke George up at ten the next morning. She wanted to go get bagels. She liked to make a thing out of Sundays.

As they stepped outside, Larry was berating a passerby for depositing something in their building's private trash bin.

"Fuck you," he yelled as the offender strolled off. "And fuck your family!"

Seeing George and Jenny had witnessed this, Larry explained, "*Fuck you* doesn't have the impact it used to. Which is why I say, 'Fuck you, and fuck your *family*.'"

Larry winked at George. "You throw the family in there, that really gets them!"

The bagel shop on Smith was extremely popular on weekend mornings. As usual, there was a line out the door, and everyone on it was young and inscrutably stylish and radiated the nonchalance of people who never question their good fortune. George wondered if, to an outside eye, he blended in. He certainly didn't feel it. The couple ahead of them had a Bernese mountain dog. When they got to the part of the line where you could step inside, an employee approached to say the dog had to wait outside.

"But he's an emotional support animal." The woman spoke coolly, placing a slender hand on the man's back. "He was in a terrorist attack."

The employee didn't question the claim, but George suspected he shared his skepticism.

"Which terrorist attack?" George wanted to ask.

When it was finally their turn to order, they were out of every-thing bagels.

"I guess I'll take an onion," George said after a pause.

"Cream cheese?"

George nodded.

"Toasted?"

George hesitated to answer; if the bagel had just come out of the oven and was hot, no. Otherwise, yes. He wondered if such a request would make him seem fussy and entitled.

"*George.*" Jenny looked exasperated. "Do you want your bagel toasted?"

"I guess."

Jenny ordered: "Poppy. Cream cheese. Not toasted. Thank you!"

They ate their bagels on a bench in the park, even though it was cold. Afterward Jenny wanted to go for a walk.

They headed down Court Street. As they approached Yesterday's News, their path was obstructed by furniture and people perusing folding tables of knickknacks.

George noticed a desk. An old mahogany desk with an embossed leather top supported by two columns of brass-knobbed drawers. It was a beautiful desk; he was surprised to see it was only one hundred fifty dollars.

"You could use a desk," Jenny said cheerfully.

George envisioned himself sitting at such a desk, and the image summoned a familiar despair. It had to do with his father, whose fetish for fancy things he'd come to see as evidence of a tragic defect in his character.

"I have a desk," George said.

"That diaper-changing table you found on the curb?"

"It's not a diaper-changing table," George said.

"Bar cart, whatever it is, it's not a real desk," Jenny protested as they moved on. "You deserve a *real* desk. A grown-up desk."

Jenny's attention was diverted by a black velvet cloak in the window of a vintage clothing store.

George followed her inside, where the sales clerk greeted her with a warmth that suggested she was in here often.

"Isn't that special?" the clerk said when Jenny inquired about the cloak. "It just came in today. As I was putting it up, I thought to myself, *I don't think this is going to last very long!*"

The clerk chuckled, and Jenny chuckled back—a chuckle that was part affirmative and part giddy, the release of something she'd been trying to restrain.

Jenny was a shopper. She loved buying things, especially clothes. She had a lot of them. George hadn't realized how many until they'd moved in together and began sharing a closet.

The clerk removed the cloak from the mannequin, and Jenny took off her coat and tried it on. Her arms protruded from the slits. "So soft," she crowed, stroking the material as she faced a full-length mirror.

"What do you think?" she asked George.

"It reminds me of something my sister would've worn in high school."

Jenny made a face. Nineties Goth was not the look she was going for.

"To me it looks Victorian," she said.

"Super Victorian," the clerk concurred.

"How much is it?" Jenny asked, fingering the tag in back of her neck.

Rather than announce the number, the clerk unfastened the tag and discreetly passed it to Jenny, who nodded solemnly.

"I'll think about it," she said.

George wondered how this scene might have played out differently had he not been present.

When they were back on the street, he asked how much the cloak was. She timidly revealed the number.

"Three hundred and eighty dollars!"

"*Re*-lax," Jenny said. "I'm not going to get it.

"It's not very practical," she added wistfully. "I don't know where I'd wear it."

"You could wear it to keep warm at Occupy Wall Street," George said.

"You're mean," Jenny said, and started walking at a prickly clip.

George fell behind, but after a block Jenny paused at a red light and he caught up.

"Some people go through life trying to build others up," she said, refusing to look at him. "You like to poke holes."

The light turned. Jenny's gaze remained fixed straight ahead as they crossed. "It makes you feel better about yourself."

George couldn't dispute this. He did not want to be such a person.

"I don't think you're a hypocrite for getting involved in Occupy Wall Street," he told her.

Jenny finished the thought. "Even though I have a trust fund whose value is directly tied to Wall Street."

"No," George said. "If anything, it makes your commitment to the cause all the more meaningful."

He should've left it at that. But as they approached their stoop, George couldn't resist saying something else:

"It's your money, it's your business how you spend it. I do sometimes wonder how you, who are so concerned about waste and land-fills, reconcile that with owning so many clothes."

"Yes, George, I *am* concerned about *waste* and landfills, which is why practically everything I own is consignment or vintage. Have you never noticed?"

George knew this was an exaggeration, but he struggled to challenge the claim by questioning specific purchases. He was not particularly observant when it came to the particulars of Jenny's wardrobe.

* * *

When Jenny first proposed paying the entirety of the rent so that George could write full-time, he'd balked. It was only after she'd disclosed the existence of her trust that he'd accepted the offer, and only after insisting he would pay her back upon selling his book, which he was confident would happen now that he'd abandoned his original novel and started a new, better one about two guys trying to retrace the steps of Jack Kerouac's *On the Road*. The idea had come to him upon overhearing two recent college graduates discussing their plan to do this in a bar on Smith Street. To beef up the word count and intellectualize the narrative, George was repurposing part of his college thesis on Schopenhauer, incorporating lengthy excerpts presented as the characters' stream of consciousness.

On a good day, when his writing was going well, George didn't worry about anything. Not the fact that he was smoking over a pack a day (which he felt walking up the four flights of stairs), the emails he'd neglected to respond to, the periodic pain in a back molar, his expired driver's license, or the money he owed Jenny. Life felt on pause until he finished his book, at which point he'd deal with all these things.

But it resumed as soon as he heard Jenny's key in the lock. However productive he'd felt during the day, her return triggered a feeling of panic, of time passing with nothing to show for it.

"Did you not see my text about defrosting the lasagna?" Jenny asked, flicking the kitchen light on.

"Shit," George apologized.

There was no room in the kitchen for the refrigerator, so it was in the living room. George rolled his chair over as Jenny fished through the produce drawer.

"We don't really have anything," she said. "I'll have to go to the store."

Jenny went back out. When she returned, she went straight to the kitchen and made scrambled eggs and salad. When she was done, she carried their plates to the couch, where they ate their meals.

George could tell she was still irritated about the lasagna. She was usually chatty at dinner, but tonight was silent. Her legs were propped up on the coffee table, and when George nuzzled his foot against her ankle, she pulled it away.

"Jenny," he said.

"What?"

"How could I stay mad at you?"

"You're an idiot." Jenny tried to repress a smile.

After eating, George did the dishes. That was the arrangement; Jenny cooked, George cleaned up. They did not have a dishwasher, so it was a production.

When George was done, Jenny stood looking out their bedroom window, which faced the street.

"We have to get a Christmas tree," she said.

"But Christmas is in four days," George pointed out. "Isn't it a little silly to get one so late in the season? Hauling it up four flights of stairs, just to drag it back down a few days later?"

"Are you really going to be like that?" Jenny looked at him forlornly. "Please don't be like that."

She went into the kitchen and started making a lot of noise. Something Jenny felt very strongly about was that every night, before they went to bed, all the pots and dishes and utensils had to be returned to their proper place. God forbid a spoon linger overnight on the drying rack!

After some thumping and bumping, she tromped out holding a glass. She brought it over to George, who was lying on the couch.

"Do you see that?" Her fingernail tapped the rim.

George lifted his head and squinted. He didn't see anything.

"That's grease," Jenny said.

"Oops," George said. "Leave it in the sink. I'll take care of it later."

Jenny's cheeks flushed.

"*George*, I just had to redo half the dishes. Half of them had food residue on them . . ."

George closed his eyes in weary exasperation.

"You say you're 'not good' at doing dishes," Jenny continued, "like it's a special talent, something certain people are predisposed to, but doing dishes is not like learning a foreign language, or playing the piano. It's about making the effort . . .

"You don't see the point in applying yourself to activities that you don't take pride in being good at it. Folding laundry, cleaning, cooking, taking out the trash and recycling, putting a new trash bag in the garbage pail, making the bed, wiping the sink down after you've shaved, making sure we don't run out of toilet paper—you think I *like* doing these things? You think I take pride in them?"

Jenny waited for him to dignify her monologue with a response, but George was not in the mood. He was tired of this. Fucking tired of it. What was the point of doing the dishes only to be reprimanded?

"Where are you going?" Jenny demanded as George stood up and put on his coat.

"For a walk," George said.

Discovering he was out of cigarettes, George walked to Food U Desire. As he entered he nearly bumped into Larry, who was hunched over the ice cream bin by the register. George's instinct was to turn around and exit the store, but it was too late, Larry had spotted him.

George nodded a curt hello.

"Pack of Marlboros, please," George asked the guy behind the counter.

"Wait," Larry told George as he pulled out his credit card. "I'll walk back with you."

George waited as Larry circulated the aisles—fortunately there were only three—ultimately concluding, "Nothing I want here. Nothing I desire."

Jenny was in bed with the lights off when George returned to the apartment. It was unclear if she was actually asleep, or sulking. Either way, she was unresponsive when George climbed in beside her and whispered, "Tomorrow, when you get home from work, let's get a tree."

* * *

When Jenny got home from work the next evening, he said it again:
"Let's get a tree."

Jenny shook her head. "It's impractical."

"Oh, come on. Don't be such a Grinch."

They walked to a stand on Smith Street, next to the subway stop.

After surveying the inventory, Jenny led George to her choice. It
was tiny, scraggly, the saddest little tree.

"*That* one?"

Jenny nodded earnestly.

"I think we can do a little better."

"That's the one I want," Jenny said.

A sales guy materialized. "Ten dollars," he said. "But I'll give it to
you for eight."

"We can spend more than that," George whispered.

"It's not about the money," Jenny said.

"You feel sorry for it," George said.

Jenny nodded and chewed her bottom lip. Christmas brought
out a childish, sentimental side of her.

George was susceptible to it, too. "It Came Upon a Midnight
Clear" was playing on an outdoor speaker. He felt himself welling up
as he watched the man bundle their pitiful little specimen in some
mesh netting.

They walked home holding hands, George clutching the tree
under his arm like a pet.

As they approached the entrance to their building, they were
accosted by Larry.

"You *bought* that?" He pointed his cigarette at their tree.

"It was only fifty dollars," George said. "What do you think?"

"I think they sold you a branch. A branch they pruned off another
tree."

Jenny shrugged. "If we didn't take it, who would?"

"Is that what you thought when you met me?" George asked.

Larry loved this. "Now you know the truth! The truth of why she married you!"

"We're not married," George clarified.

Larry, who never looked surprised, looked surprised. "So, the verdict's still out!"

* * *

"They're having a candlelight vigil at Zuccotti tomorrow tonight," Jenny told George the next morning.

"Oh," George said. "On Christmas Eve?"

"It'll be nice. Smaller than the typical event. More intimate."

George nodded.

"I could be wrong," Jenny acknowledged. "Maybe people who don't normally go will go because it's Christmas Eve and they want to be around other people. Maybe it'll be big."

Jenny's shoulders rose in a childlike affect. "Either way, it should be interesting . . .

"I'd like to go," she said.

"You should go," George told her.

"But then you'd be alone. *Alone* on Christmas Eve." Jenny gave George a pitiful look, and then, with a sudden false enthusiasm, as though the idea had just occurred to her, her face lit up. "You could come!"

"That's okay," George assured her. "I don't mind being alone."

* * *

It was actually for the best, Jenny's absence that evening, because George still hadn't gone Christmas shopping.

He wasn't the only one. Court Street was teeming with last-minute shoppers. Everyone was in a rush. Bodies collided in the narrow aisles of the little gift shops and overpriced boutiques that were normally so quiet George wondered how they survived. Maybe this was how. The panicked atmosphere rattled George, but mostly it depressed him.

The crass materialism, the myopic consumerism, the corporate greed behind it all—how antithetical to the circumstances of Christ's birth, to everything he supposedly stood for. George recognized these thoughts weren't the least bit insightful or profound. They were the kind of thoughts he would have had at fourteen, and that would have made him feel wise and enlightened and above it all. But today, here he was, one of the sheep.

George found himself in another home goods store, flustered by the choices: irregularly shaped beeswax candles, fiber-flecked soaps, large wooden spoons, small wooden bowls, maps of Brooklyn a hundred years ago, maps of the subway today, culinary-themed posters. George could see Jenny liking these things—he could also see her finding them stupid and impersonal. There was something about the faux-urban-rustic curation of the miscellany that rendered the individual items inauthentic.

George bought a poster of onions, but it wasn't enough. He thought he should get her something else. Something nice that she'd actually be excited about.

He walked to the vintage store with the cloak that Jenny liked. He struggled to open the door before realizing it was locked. It was just past six. Shops were shuttering. The sound of metal grates coming down gave George an anxious, existential feeling.

He continued down Court. He walked into the first store that was still open, which was CVS. By the entrance to the store, a set of risers featured a collection of decorative carolers, plastic-cast figures dressed in old-fashioned foppery, the size of small children, lips parted in song.

After some deliberation, George picked one up and got on line.

It was long. It would make sense to have an express aisle, George thought, noting many of the customers had baskets or even carts full of items. Of the six registers, only two were open, and the employees who manned them appeared in no particular rush.

Ten minutes passed, and then twenty, and George was still on line. His phone buzzed with a text from Jenny reminding him to pick up toilet paper.

He turned to the woman behind him. "Do you mind holding my spot while I run and get something?"

The woman looked like she did mind. "I guess," she said.

"I'll be quick," George assured her.

George dashed off in pursuit of toilet paper. After several minutes he asked for help.

"Lower level," an employee told George, and pointed to the stairs.

When George returned to the line, the woman he'd asked to hold his spot had just stepped up to the register.

After some hesitation, George assumed the position at what was now the front of the line.

No one said anything, but in case they'd noticed, George glanced over his shoulder and explained, "I was on the line, I just ran to get some toilet paper. I was behind her." He pointed to the woman at the register.

"You can't keep shopping while you're in line," someone protested.

"You gotta go back to the end of the line," another concurred.

George regretted saying anything. "Really? I only have two things." He held up the caroler and the toilet paper.

Surly faces stared back at him. George interpreted the collective silence as permission to stay where he was.

But then a tall, bearded white guy who looked around George's age, maybe younger, spoke up. George had noticed him earlier. His messenger bag was adorned with pins: ALLY. FEMINIST. OCCUPY.

"Classic," he said.

* * *

Christmas morning, Jenny gave George a green crewneck sweater similar to the one he'd shrunk in the dryer, a hat she'd knitted, some dark chocolate, a burlap sack of organic pistachios, and a first-edition copy of *Stoner*.

"I found it in a pile of books on a stoop," she claimed when George asked her where she'd got it.

George was touched. She was so thoughtful, his Jenny, she knew him so well, that she'd lie about acquiring it for free so that he wouldn't feel guilty about the cost.

"It's a poster of different kinds of onions," George said, as Jenny unfurled her present.

Jenny managed a smile. "Wow. I never knew there were so many different varieties . . ."

"I got you something else." George went and retrieved the caroler from under the bed.

"It's a caroler," he said, placing it next to the tree. "I didn't realize when I bought it, but it actually sings."

He pressed the button to make it sing.

Have yourself a merry little Christmas.
Let your heart be light.
Next year all our troubles will be out of sight . . .

Jenny looked like she was on the verge of tears. George pressed the button to make it stop.

Jenny made pancakes. They ate breakfast. George cleaned up the kitchen while Jenny took out the trash and recycling. They took turns in the bathroom, made more coffee, got dressed.

It was only noon, and they still had the whole day to fill.

"Let's go for a walk," Jenny said.

They put on shoes and coats and went downstairs.

The neighborhood felt deserted, and that exacerbated the sad feeling of emptiness and what-to-do. It was one of those times when New Yorkers who had somewhere else to go went there.

Zombie Hut was open. That was a surprise.

It was Jenny's idea to order vodka and Red Bulls. They were disgusting, but they got a nice little buzz on and so they kept ordering more.

For a while it was fun. They had silly, asinine exchanges, like two people who'd just met in a bar and were curious about each other:

"I don't feel like an adult."

"Me neither."

"Do you think you ever will?"

"No. I don't know."

"Me neither."

A series of faux intimate disclosures somehow led to a conversation about Shakespeare. George referred to Shakespeare as funny, and Jenny said, "But does he really make you laugh? Like have you ever actually laughed out loud reading Shakespeare?" George wanted to say yes; he was pretty sure he had. As he tried to think of examples of passages in Shakespeare that had made him laugh, Jenny confessed that she'd never laughed at Shakespeare, not reading his texts or watching them performed. She wondered if this made her a philistine.

"Do you think I'm a philistine?" she asked.

George shook his head.

"What do you think I am?" Jenny asked.

"What do I think you are?"

Jenny nodded. "How would you describe me?"

That was how it started. Jenny wanted George to describe her. And George obliged by coming up with a bunch of complimentary adjectives: kind, generous, idealistic, determined, humble, self-sacrificing, supportive, altruistic . . .

Jenny wasn't satisfied.

"Sometimes I feel like you don't really know me," she said. "Or you're not interested in getting to know the real me. You think I'm this simple person. I know you love me, but sometimes I wonder if you're *in* love with me . . .

"Are you in love with me?"

George didn't know the answer to this. He didn't know what it was to be in love. They'd had this conversation before.

Jenny, who claimed to have no memory of what followed, would later refer to the episode as "our *Leaving Las Vegas* night," as though it somehow didn't count, as though it were a darkly humorous anomaly. But George, who did remember it, or most of it, saw it as a pulling back of the curtain, a peek at the hysterical, broken child who'd hitched her wagon to his.

George couldn't tell Jenny the one thing she wanted to hear, needed to know, and that was how it started. All her fears and insecurities about their relationship came out in a torrent of tears and accusations, and there was nothing George could say or do to reassure her. It didn't help that many of her concerns were warranted or resonated with George as questions he'd asked himself. Was he just biding his time with her until he "figured shit out," did he consider her his "intellectual equal," was this a "healthy relationship"?

Jenny was too far gone to care that she was causing a scene, and George had to coax her to leave the bar. They were halfway home when George noticed she'd forgotten her purse. Jenny seemed indifferent to this fact, but George insisted they go back and retrieve it.

By the time they got back to the apartment, she was mostly incoherent, and very angry.

Here George's memory began to fray, but he remembered Jenny cornering him in the kitchen and that there was a physicality to her anger. She kept thrusting her face up in his, shouting, crying, spitting. She was trying to provoke him to hit her. That George remained calm seemed to enrage her further.

She picked up a glass and threw it. Had she been aiming for George? He would never know. It hit the wall and shattered.

Jenny was suddenly silent, and still. There was glass all over the floor. George was wearing shoes but Jenny was barefoot. He picked her up so she wouldn't cut herself.

As he carried her out of the kitchen and to the bedroom, there was knocking at the door.

"Everything okay in there?" boomed Larry's voice.

"Yep!" George answered. "We're good!"

George laid Jenny on the bed. She looked up at him with fear and confusion.

"Did I break that glass?" she asked.

George nodded. "You threw it.

"I think you were aiming at me," he added.

"I'm sorry," she said.

"That's okay," he told her.

He wasn't sure what else to say, so he leaned down and kissed her. Her lips were salty with tears and sweat.

He placed a hand on her breast. He could feel her heart beating.

Wordlessly, with a seamless grace, they transitioned into sex, George slipping inside of her with a tender but feral conviction, and sustaining his erection for longer than he could recall having managed in his post-Lexapro life.

Afterward, they lay nude and entwined.

Jenny quickly passed out.

"I do love you," George told her.

9. LEMON RICOTTA PANCAKES

George, 30

Ellen had never wanted to live in the suburbs. Denis promised it would grow on her, but it did not. If anything, she found more to loathe with each passing year: the four-way stops, the sinister drone of leaf blowers, the chemically enhanced lawns with their little yellow flags sprouting up each pesticide season like daffodils, the caravan of minivans at pick-up plastered with PROUD PARENT OF A ____ bumper stickers, the constant trips to nearby strip malls to buy this or that, the dearth of small businesses other than nail salons on Main Street, the five-way traffic light in the center of town where it was possible to spend up to six minutes idling—a source of collective frustration and a frequent subject of editorials in the local newspaper, whose fondness for hokey puns and folksy approach to journalism might have been less grating were it not for its utter lack of humanity when it came to the privacy of its citizens (if some poor soul was pulled over for a DUI, their name was featured in the police blotter, like a modern-day pillory). And then there were the people who lived in the suburbs—all they wanted to talk about were their kids, and their kids' academic/athletic triumphs and struggles. They were so boring, the other mothers! Ellen made no secret of the fact that as soon as George finished high school she planned to move back to Manhattan, where she'd lived her whole life before having children.

But when George left for college she stayed put. She'd become accustomed to the sound of crickets outside her window at night. She couldn't imagine giving up her garden. George was relieved when she begrudgingly admitted these things. The thought of losing his childhood home was deeply upsetting.

And then their town was featured on the front page of the *New York Times* Style section. The article touted its Hudson River views, yoga studio, and newly opened vegan bakery. It made an impression. Real estate values shot up as young Brooklyn couples flocked to open houses.

Ellen wasted no time putting their house on the market. *Cha-ching, cha-ching!* A single open house generated multiple offers, launching a bidding war that yielded a figure well over the asking price. Ellen found a two-bedroom on the Upper East Side.

She would be moving the last Sunday of September.

George would have to clear out his bedroom. He had all summer to do this, but kept putting it off.

The Thursday before the move, he drove out. A dumpster obstructed the driveway, so he parked on the street.

Cressida was there, too. As George opened the front door, he could hear her yelling upstairs. "How dare you? How *dare* you!"

"Oh, come on, Cress," Ellen defended herself. "Was I supposed to keep every last drawing of a *centaur*?"

George went into the kitchen.

"You're here," Ellen said, coming down the back stairs.

"Starving," George said, taking a seat at the table. "Is there anything to eat?"

Ellen made George a grilled cheese. After finishing it, he was still hungry, so she made him another.

After he finished that, she started talking to him about his room. It was his responsibility to figure out what to do with all the stuff in it, but if he wanted her advice, *When in doubt, throw it out.*

"George," she said, noticing he'd reclined on the window seat. "You've got a lot of work to do."

"I know," George said, closing his eyes. "Just taking a little rest before I get started."

The house had a chill, but the upholstered cushion absorbed the warmth of the sun. It felt very nice. George wondered how many hours of his life he'd spent doing this. Hundreds, maybe thousands.

When he woke up, George couldn't tell how much time had passed, because the clock had been removed from its spot on the wall above the door. The cushion beneath his cheek was damp with drool. Dust motes drifted across a shaft of late afternoon sunlight.

Ellen stood at the counter wrapping plates in newspaper. Her gestures were brisk and methodical. "I left an empty bin in your room for you to store anything you'd like to keep in my apartment. Special things like photographs, yearbooks, stuff you'll want to show your kids one day. That's all I have room for. Anything else you want to keep, you'll have to take back to your own apartment."

"I know. You said that already," George reminded her.

As he shuffled upstairs, Ellen called after him: "And anything you *don't* want can go in the dumpster!"

George walked into his bedroom. It was confusing to know where to begin. On the top of his bookshelf was a ceramic owl he'd made in third grade. George took it down to admire it. It was good; one of the best in the class, he recalled. The more he looked at it, the more impressed he was with his third-grade self for sculpting it. He blew the dust off its talons and put it in the bin of keepsakes to show his future children.

George began going through his books. There were two copies of his senior yearbook. He was dismayed to discover one belonged to Nadia Ostrosky—painfully shy, poor old Nadia, with her puffy, pimpled face and Disney sweatshirts. He remembered now that she'd approached him in the hall and asked if he'd sign it. George, unsure what to write (they'd never really interacted), had told her he'd take it home and return it to her the next day. What a terrible human being he was.

George came across a journal he'd kept in college. It was written in a way that suggested he anticipated it being read by others, and yet even with this agenda of posterity, he was completely unlikable. It was amazing he'd had any friends.

In the top drawer of his bureau George discovered his old fake ID, a copy of the *New York Times* from the day after 9/11, some college rejection letters, expired condoms, mixtapes, stray socks, and a pair of leather slippers.

George had never worn them, never even taken off the tag—HANDMADE IN ITALY. They'd been a Christmas present from his father. George was fourteen, old enough to be polite upon opening them but young enough to experience a private pang of indignation—how foolish of his father to think he'd be excited by a pair of leather slippers.

Under his bed George discovered a milk crate full of CDs and old electronics. He was surprised to discover his Game Boy still worked.

George was on level four of *Super Mario Bros.* when Ellen came in. She saw what he was doing but didn't say anything. There was a gentle breeze as she shut the door and went away.

"I'm almost done," George said when she poked her head in an hour later.

Ellen continued to check on him, and each time, George braced himself for her nagging. But she didn't say anything.

George didn't register the dark until Ellen came in and turned on the overhead light.

"I'm trying to get rid of everything in the freezer," she said, handing George a plate of pigs-in-a-blanket.

"Is there ketchup?" George asked.

Ellen went back down and returned with a bottle of ketchup.

George made it to the penultimate level with two lives left, which he lost in the first tunnel.

It was almost eleven. His neck was stiff from hunching over. George felt depressed. What a waste of eight hours of his life. He was simultaneously exhausted and wired. He needed a drink.

Cressida called out to him as he passed by her room.

"Remember this?" She was holding a tobacco pipe.

George smiled, recalling Cressida's pipe-smoking days.

At the time, he'd been embarrassed, but it seemed funny to him now—seventeen-year-old Cressida smoking a pipe, an image memorialized in her senior yearbook photo, much to the chagrin of their parents.

"Wow, you're almost done," he said, looking around her room. Nearly everything was in boxes.

"Yeah, well, Mom made it easier for me by throwing most of my shit away before I got here . . .

"Including my childhood artwork," she added.

George nodded. "I haven't even packed a single box," he confessed.

"What have you been doing all day?"

"Game Boy," he said.

"Ha!"

George told Cressida about finding his old journal from college. How painfully pretentious he was.

She looked intrigued. "Like what kind of stuff did you say?"

"I can't even talk about it." George shook his head. "If I met a version of myself back then now, I'd think, What an awful person, but maybe deep down he's a decent person. But peeling back the layers, I just got worse."

Cressida laughed. "If you kept a journal now, do you think you'd feel the same way in ten years?" she asked.

"I don't know. That's a depressing thought. I'm going to see what's in the liquor cabinet," George said. "Want me to bring you something?"

"Nah."

At four a.m., George found himself on the penultimate level again, this time with five lives.

Once more, he did not make it beyond the first tunnel.

* * *

"George." Ellen was sitting on the edge of his bed. "It's almost ten."

"I'm awake," George said.

"I think you should get up."

"I'm getting up."

Ellen disappeared and returned a few minutes later with a sandwich, which George ate in bed before getting up to retrieve his Game Boy from the corner, where he'd tossed it in the fever of defeat a few hours earlier.

This was the fifth time George had had to start from the very beginning. He breezed through the first few levels, his muscle memory enabling him to navigate each obstacle with an effortless dexterity that was deeply satisfying, calming, restorative.

He was on level seven when he became aware of someone standing in the doorway of his room.

It was Jenny.

"What are you doing here?" George pressed pause and slipped his Game Boy beneath his quilt.

"I hear you're having a little trouble," Jenny said, taking a seat on his bed. "Your mom called. She doesn't think you can do this on your own."

"Ellen called you and asked you to come help me pack up my room?"

Jenny nodded.

"But I thought you had to spend the weekend preparing for that trial."

"It's not until Wednesday," Jenny said. "And I'm actually in pretty good shape."

George felt guilty, and more than a little pathetic, though he suspected Jenny was secretly delighted to receive a call from his mother. She reveled in being a martyr, summoned from her legal work to help her unemployed boyfriend pack up his childhood bedroom.

"Okay, well, how do you want to go about doing this?" Jenny said, looking around the room.

George shrugged. "I defer to you."

Jenny chewed her lip in a deliberative manner. "I think the best way to tackle this is to make categories. *Throw away. Donate. Keep.*"

She got started on the drawers. George retreated to the other side of the bed, where he was out of her sight line.

"What are you doing over there?" Jenny asked after a few minutes.

"Just giving the ol' Game Boy a final whirl before it goes in the dumpster," he explained.

"It's not right," he called out to her an hour later. "You, packing up my room while I sit here doing this. Unfortunately, it's one of those things where I've invested so much time that I can't just quit now, or else all that time will have been wasted. The good news is I'm on level twelve with nineteen lives . . ."

George was on the final level with four lives when the battery died.

"I'm sorry, George," Jenny said, when he told her what happened. "But maybe it's for the best."

* * *

Ellen ordered pizza for dinner. The kitchen was mostly packed, so they ripped up pieces of the box it came in to use as plates.

"What happened to all the alcohol?" George asked, discovering the shelf was bare.

"You're going to have to do without it tonight," Ellen said.

George mimed shooting himself in the head.

"If you really want," Ellen said, "you can probably find the box." She pointed to a stack of boxes in the corner. "It's labeled 'liquor.' I think it's near the top."

George located the box and pulled out a bottle of bourbon. He took his usual spot in the middle of the window seat.

"Do you drink alcohol every night?" Ellen asked.

"Yup," George answered. "No more than a handle."

Ellen glanced at Jenny, who pursed her lips and nodded to indicate she shared her concern, which was hypocritical, since most nights she had a drink, too.

"Jenny." Ellen stood up and rustled through a shoebox on the counter.

"I thought you'd appreciate these," she said, returning to the table with a stack of photos. "When George was four, he had a tantrum and threatened to run away."

"Oh my god," Jenny said, laughing. "George. *Look*."

"No thanks." George was familiar with the photos. He was naked except for his Keds, standing on the front stoop crying and clutching a *Fraggle Rock* lunch box. Though he didn't remember the incident, he felt allied with his four-year-old self—the indignity of his mother's reception of his rage as adorable, worthy of getting out her camera.

"What was George like as a baby?" Jenny asked Ellen.

"George was a beautiful baby. Came out with a full head of hair. Thick, long eyelashes. He cried a lot. A *lot*."

Cressida strode into the kitchen wearing a pink gown, across the front of which was written, in bold black letters, *BEST NIGHT OF MY LIFE*.

"Your prom dress," Ellen said.

Jenny smiled. "That's funny," she said. "What you wrote on it.

"I assume the dress didn't come like that," she added, when Cressida refrained from validating her comment.

"It did not," Ellen responded. "That was her personalized touch."

"That's clever. Kind of mocking the whole thing." Jenny smiled at Cressida, who nodded stonily back.

"I hated my prom," Jenny volunteered. "I pretended to be really excited about it, but it made me really self-conscious and I hated it and couldn't wait for it to be over."

"Why did you pretend to be excited about it?" Cressida asked, in her cold, interrogating manner.

Jenny looked flustered by the question.

"Because she's *nice*," George said. "Because she wouldn't want to ridicule an event that for some kids, especially those from a working-class background, is a big deal."

"Okay, George, want to let her speak for herself?" Cressida looked at Jenny.

"I thought something was wrong with me . . ." Jenny took a sip of water. "The prom is supposed to be so much fun, the highlight of high school." She took another sip of water.

"You wanted to fit in," Ellen said.

Jenny nodded. "I wasn't a very critical thinker back then. I just wanted to be like everyone else. I wanted everyone to like me."

George reached over and mussed the top of her hair. Jenny finger-combed it back into place.

"It's really nice of you to help out like this, Jenny," Ellen said. "I don't know what George would do without you."

"Oh, I don't mind this kind of thing. I actually enjoy organizing." Jenny noticed Cressida's dubious expression.

"It's easier when it's not your stuff," she said quietly.

"Well, George is lucky to have you," Ellen continued. "You do a lot for him. He told me at home you make him dinner every night."

"What?" Cressida chewed angrily. "Shouldn't he be making *you* dinner, considering he's the one home all day?"

Jenny shrugged. "I wouldn't say I make him dinner *every* night." A wan smile, her attempt to disguise her discomfort, only rendered it more obvious.

"George doesn't know how to cook," Ellen said defensively. "He's never been good about feeding himself."

"I wonder how that happened," Cressida said.

"Do you ever worry that you're enabling him?" she asked Jenny, who looked at George imploringly.

They were all looking at him. George exaggerated his slouch and began chewing with his mouth open, a dead look in his eyes.

He reached for the bourbon, sipped straight from the bottle, and burped.

Ellen giggled. "Oh, *George*."

* * *

After dinner, Jenny picked up where she'd left off packing. George went to look for batteries. The drawer where they were normally kept was empty, but he found some in a box, which he carefully retaped and returned to the stack.

George was playing his Game Boy when Ellen came in carrying a duffel bag. "These were all things I found of George's in the attic," she said, placing it by Jenny's feet. "I should probably bring it straight to the dumpster, but just in case there's anything . . ."

"I'll take a look," Jenny said.

Ellen left.

George spoke up from across the room. "I'm not in the mood to feel sentimental. So unless there's something in there that looks valuable or something, just get rid of it."

"Copy that," Jenny said.

"Awww. Look what I found . . ."

George pressed pause. Jenny was holding his *Fraggle Rock* lunch box.

"You can put it in the give-away pile," he said.

"Really?"

"Did you hear what I said?" George said, resuming his game. "I can't get sentimental about every little thing."

"I know, but are you sure you don't want to keep this?" Jenny fondled the box wistfully. "Maybe you'll want to give it to your own kid one day . . ."

George decided to pretend he was too deeply absorbed in his game to hear this. But the silence still felt fraught. He was relieved when it was pierced by the sound of his mother screaming.

Ellen had discovered a dead mouse in the back of the linen closet.

"I *knew* I smelled something!" she said. "Either of my dear children feel like assisting me in this unpleasant task?"

No, they did not.

* * *

"I don't think Cressida likes me," Jenny said as they climbed into his twin bed a few hours later. "I try so hard with her. And the harder I try, the more I feel like I'm annoying her. I feel like she sees me as this meek, pathetic, jejune idiot of a girlfriend."

George was impressed by her use of the word *jejune*.

"My sister doesn't like very many people," he said. "Possibly no one."

Headlights swept across the ceiling, illuminating the light fixture, which resembled a breast with an erect nipple—or so George had once thought, masturbating to it as a boy.

When Jenny fell asleep, George reached for his Game Boy.

Worried about waking Jenny up, he relocated to the couch downstairs. After working his way back up to the final level and losing, George decided he would not play anymore. It was getting out of hand. He lay there listening to the first birds of the morning, trying to muster the energy to get up and return to his bed.

When he woke up, he was still on the couch, and it was almost noon. He could hear his mother and Jenny laughing as he headed upstairs.

They were sitting on his bed, poring over the contents of a manila folder.

"Look at this one," Ellen said, and began reading a poem George had written in middle school:

'Twas once a king named Bart
Known for his powerful farts
Loud as thunder
Stinky as a clam
The poor Queen, people said,
To live with such a man . . .

"Where'd you find that?" George asked.

Ellen looked up. "When you didn't show up all summer, I started to go through some of your things. You had several bins of papers.

Mostly homework assignments and other junk, but I found a few gems."

George reached for the folder. Inside were some copies of hand-written letters to various public figures, a few essays, a couple book reports.

"Where's everything else?" he asked. "The short stories I wrote, the plays, my poetry . . ."

Ellen sighed and removed her reading glasses. "Listen, George. I wasn't sure you were ever going to make it out here, and I was feeling overwhelmed by the prospect of packing up this house by myself . . ."

"Are you telling me you threw it all away?" George was incredulous.

"I didn't '*throw it all away*.'" Ellen spoke crisply, calmly. "As I said, I sifted through everything and saved the best things."

"Like that fart poem," George said bitterly. "That struck you as an example of my best work."

Ellen put her reading glasses back on and glanced at the piece of paper. "It's a clever poem, George."

"I want to hear the rest," Jenny piped up. "Will you read the rest?"

Ellen picked up where she'd left off.

Indeed her royal majesty
Was in constant agony
For all her jewels and palace so shiny
Was not worth the smell of his highness's hein—

George picked up the ceramic owl and pitched it against the wall. One of its talons fell off, but otherwise it remained intact, robbing the gesture of any catharsis. Ellen and Jenny exchanged nervous looks, wondering what unhinged, possibly violent, thing George would do next.

"I'm going for a walk," he said.

George went downstairs, out the front door, and proceeded

down Willard, past the Powers', the Feinsteins', and the Kelleys'—
who no longer lived there. He kept walking, down the hill, crossing
Broadway, to the other side of town, where the lots were smaller
and the houses more modest: ranch houses, brick row houses, faux
colonials painted Easter egg yellow and green. The majority of the
houses in this town were ugly, Ellen was fond of pointing out; even
the century-old sprawling Tudors with sweeping views of the Hudson River Palisades were not pleasing to look at, with their dreary
gray facades, undersize windows, and severe angles.

George knew what she meant, but her preoccupation with the
aesthetic felt sacrilegious. For him, having grown up here, each street
was laden with memories and visceral associations, most of which
he could trace to a specific resident or episode, but some he could
not, and felt of a mysterious, primordial nature.

George continued walking all the way to his elementary school,
where he cut across the empty parking lot and into the woods, eventually arriving at what was known as the Meadow, a clearing in the
woods where high school students congregated on Friday and Saturday nights. In the light of the day, it looked less like a meadow than
a scrappy patch of dirt, embedded with bottle caps and cigarette
butts and shards of broken glass.

George sat on a log and thought of a poem he'd written in high
school about homeostasis. He'd turned it into a metaphor about
life, people always wanting things, never being satisfied. It wasn't a
consciously ambitious endeavor, just something he'd dashed off in
the margins of his notebook as a means to pass the time in double-
period bio, but reviewing it afterward, he'd thought it might be
good. He'd typed it up and showed it to Mr. Cummings, who was
so impressed he'd made copies of the poem to share with the class.
Mr. Cummings hadn't told George he was doing this beforehand,
and George would never forget the dizzying thrill of looking down
at the handout and discovering his own words. For forty minutes
he'd sat, cheeks burning, while his classmates analyzed his work like
he was Robert Frost.

* * *

George helped Jenny carry the throw-away items outside.

After dumping the contents of several boxes into the dumpster, George surprised himself by hoisting himself into it.

Jenny stood in the driveway as George waded his way through the mess, picking things up and putting them back down: CDs he'd bought twelve for a dollar, or whatever that deal was. Books. Shoes. A plastic shopping bag of mutilated Barbies. Robbie—a stuffed anteater he'd slept with for the first decade of his life. There was something obscene about the sheer bulk of it, the entrails of his childhood, objects that once mattered, and this was how they ended up.

"So, this is it," he said quietly to himself. "This is it."

George heard the front door open; Ellen called his name.

"He's in the dumpster," Jenny told her.

"Be careful, George!" Ellen called out. "There might be broken glass!"

A patch of tan poked out of a bag. He picked up the slippers his father had gotten him for Christmas.

George held them over the side of the dumpster for Jenny to see. "What are these doing here?"

"You said you didn't want them," Jenny said matter-of-factly.

"I assumed you'd put them in the Goodwill pile, not the *garbage*. They still have the tag on them. *Handmade in Italy.* Did you even notice the tag?"

George waited for her defense, an apology, an explanation, but Jenny said nothing.

"For someone who calls herself an *environmentalist*, I thought you'd be a little more scrutinizing when it came to throwing stuff out . . ."

George continued to admonish Jenny, and she continued to stand there, a passive receptacle of his anger, which made George feel like a bully, a tyrant, an ugly, broken person—which made him angrier.

"I mean, when you think of all the people in this country who can't afford to feed themselves, or heat their homes, let alone buy a pair of slippers . . ."

"*George!*" Cressida leaned out her bedroom window. "It's a fucking pair of slippers! What's wrong with you?"

Back in the house, George felt terrible. "I'm a piece of shit," he said, apologizing to Jenny. "A fucking pathetic piece of shit. I hope you know I know that."

Jenny looked unmoved. "Do you know how demeaning it is to be spoken to like that? While I'm spending the weekend being your packing bitch?"

George nodded, marinating in shame and remorse. Unlike rage, there was no discharging it, no external release valve. It was just something you had to sit with.

Everything that could go in boxes was packed. The movers would be coming at eight o'clock the next morning to take care of the rest.

They ate dinner at the local diner. It was a solemn affair.

When they got back, George took a final lap through the house, the setting of his earliest memories, which felt charged with biblical significance. The floors upon which he'd taken his first steps, the walls that contained years of his life. His life! George felt bewildered and disoriented. Untethered. As though someone had cut a hole in those years and he'd slipped through.

The plan was to drive back to Brooklyn that night, but George asked Jenny if she'd mind if they left in the morning, and she sulkily acquiesced.

They'd already stripped George's bed, so they slept on perpendicular couches in the living room.

After Jenny fell asleep, George took out the Game Boy. A few minutes after three a.m., he beat the final level.

Music played—a sweet, sad little song that reminded George of an ice cream truck—as more text appeared, this time materializing as individual letters, as if someone were typing a message to George in real time:

Y-O-U-R Q-U-E-S-T I-S O-V-E-R

Mario and Daisy boarded a spaceship and took flight.

Braced for a postvictory crash, George looked over at Jenny. He got up and knelt on the floor beside her couch so that his face was level with hers. She looked vaguely ethereal, illuminated by the yolky glow of the streetlight that seeped through the curtains, hair splayed across the cushion, cheeks plump with sleep.

George tucked a wisp of hair behind her ear. She stirred but didn't wake up. He kissed her parted lips. "My Daisy," he whispered, stroking her shoulder.

Finally she opened her eyes.

"I won," he told her. "I beat the final level."

Jenny looked confused and mildly irritated as George proceeded to describe the end of the game: Mario and Daisy's reunion, the congratulatory text, the spaceship, the haunting melody that sounded like an ice cream truck. But it was difficult to convey the poignancy of it, and Jenny drifted back to sleep before George had a chance to tell her that he planned to put the Game Boy in the dumpster, which he knew would please her.

George returned to his couch, unsettled by a sudden troubling thought. With Jenny, there had been no quest. She was always there, always available. He'd never had to chase her. He'd certainly never rescued her.

George was the kind of exhausted where it was hard to fall asleep, especially knowing he'd be woken up in a few hours. He had an idea: he would surprise everyone by making breakfast. He would make lemon ricotta pancakes. Denis used to make them on Christmas.

The Food Emporium wasn't open yet, but Madaba Deli was. George bought pancake mix, syrup, eggs, milk, butter, orange juice, lemons. They even had ricotta.

Everyone was still asleep when George returned to the house. He had to open and unpack several boxes in the kitchen before locating everything he needed: plates, place mats, glasses, utensils, mixing bowl, cast-iron pan, spatula, measuring cups, measuring spoons, a whisk, a zester . . .

Cressida was the first to come downstairs. "What are you doing?"

"Making lemon ricotta pancakes," George said. "I thought we'd have a nice family breakfast."

"Are you kidding, George? It's moving day. Mom's going to kill you."

George heard Cressida intercept Ellen on the stairs to warn her.

"Jesus Christ, George," Ellen said, stepping into the kitchen. "The movers are getting here in forty-five minutes."

"Don't worry, I'll clean it all up," George assured her. "You just take a seat. Breakfast is almost ready. Do you want some OJ while you wait?"

"No, George. I don't want some *OJ*. What I want is for you to pour that batter straight down the sink and clean everything up. I want you to make this kitchen look like how it did when I went to bed." She looked around and exhaled with irritation. "Now I'll have to repack all these boxes. Wash all those things in the sink . . ."

"I told you I'll do all the cleanup," George said.

"How are you going to wash all those things without dish soap? Or sponges? Did that occur to you?" Ellen asked. "You know, I held my tongue all weekend, but sometimes it feels like you have absolutely no consideration for others. A complete blind spot when it comes to the burden you put on others."

George was bewildered. This was not the reaction he'd expected. Ellen had more to say.

"And that tantrum you threw in the bedroom yesterday, throwing the sculpture against the wall. And then berating Jenny like that, after she'd spent the entire weekend packing your things while you played video games and slept till noon? I can only hope that's not how you live your life in Brooklyn."

George shook his head.

"I honestly don't know what's happened to you," Ellen continued. "When you were little, you had all these interests. It was such a thrill, as your mother, to watch you doing your things, and imagine the person you'd grow up to be. And I'm not talking about being some hotshot success at the top of his field—just a person who was engaged in the world, who had a thing he was passionate about doing. I want that for you, George. I want you to wake up in the morning and be excited to get out of bed and do whatever it is that you're passionate about. Or at least get out of bed and do it, even on the days when you're not excited about it. I think you'd find there's a certain dignity in that, just getting up and doing what's expected of you, all the more so when it's not what you want to be doing, or what you expected out of life."

George nodded. He agreed with that point.

"Do you have anything to say?" Ellen asked.

George shook his head. "I'm sorry," he said.

"I was just trying to make a nice family breakfast," he added meekly.

Ellen frowned. "Did we even have family breakfasts? I don't remember that even being a thing."

"On Christmas," Cressida said.

George poured the batter down the sink and then started running hot water over everything. He felt kind of numb, but also a little keyed up. It was like the shock of falling off a bike, after the initial rush of endorphins, before the pain sets in. He wanted to finish the cleaning up before the feelings kicked in.

Jenny materialized and began assisting in the cleanup effort. George wondered how much of what had transpired she'd overheard.

Together they worked swiftly and silently. Soon they were finished. Everything was returned to its proper box. The kitchen was ready to go and George was free.

"You okay?" Jenny asked.

George nodded. He felt a swelling in his throat.

"Are you sure?" Jenny said.

George shrugged. "Just need some fresh air," he managed in a whisper, and stepped outside. Something deep within was rising, and he wanted to be alone when it surfaced.

But Jenny followed him. Out the door, down the steps, across the grass, to a secluded spot behind the tree where there was supposed to have been a tree house.

And once it started—crying didn't even seem like the right word for it, it felt more medical in its physicality, closer to vomiting, or a seizure—George was glad not to be alone.

Jenny sat with him on the grass as he recovered.

"Where'd you learn how to make lemon ricotta pancakes?" she asked.

George shrugged.

"I thought I'd look it up on the internet," he said.

10. THE RINGER

George, 31–32

In the shower, George made an upsetting discovery: a lump on the lip of his anus. It was irregularly shaped and had a strange texture. As soon as his fingers came across it, a veil descended. Terror, despair. Grim resignation. There was a sense that everything in his life had been leading up to this.

George turned off the water. Lacking the will to properly towel himself off, he shuffled out of the bathroom dripping and sat down on the bed. After a few minutes, he lay back. The way his body was positioned on the mattress, he felt like one of those deflated clocks in a Salvador Dalí painting.

He lay there like that for maybe an hour. And then he heard a key in the door. Jenny was home earlier than usual.

"What's wrong?" she asked, finding him on the bed nude, limp, stricken.

George told her about the growth.

That Jenny didn't look particularly concerned was both irritating and reassuring.

"Let me have a look," she said.

George rolled over and parted his butt cheeks. "It's at about five o'clock," he said.

"I see it," she said. "It looks like a tiny ball of toilet paper got trapped in your butt hair and became matted to your skin."

George flinched as she removed it.

"Feel better?" she asked, showing it to him.

George nodded. Of course, he was relieved.

But he was disappointed not to feel something more. The veil had lifted, but the world was merely restored to what it had been prior to the discovery. There was still a sense of boredom and dread.

George put on some clothes. As he sat down at his desk he remembered why Jenny was home early: it was the night of the screening of Jeremiah's documentary at the Tribeca Film Festival. George did not look forward to it. If the film was bad, he would be frustrated by the positive reception it was bound to get just based on its subject matter (foster kid, high school debate competition). If it was good, that would also be hard for George.

He wondered if he should skip the screening and stay home and write, to make up for the time he'd lost due to thinking he had cancer.

George was at the part of the writing of his book where he needed to figure out what it was about, in broader, more philosophical terms, which required a kind of abstract thinking that was hard to achieve in the sober light of day. A kind of dreamy contemplation best pursued alone, at night, nursing some whiskey. But the opportunity rarely presented itself, as Jenny was always home.

"We should leave in about five," Jenny said, emerging from the bedroom all dressed up and ready to go. She looked happy and pretty, but as George told her to go on without him, that he planned to stay home and write, her features sharpened.

"I don't see what the big deal is," George said. "There'll be a million people there. I'll watch it when it comes out on Netflix."

Jenny picked a piece of lint off the floor. "And when people ask where you are? I explain you decided to stay home and write?"

"IBS," George told her. "Tell them my IBS is acting up."

Jenny frowned. "Irritable bowel syndrome?"

George nodded.

"But you don't have IBS."

"Pretty sure I do." George leaned back in his chair and placed a palm on his belly. "Pretty sure it's not normal to spend the amount of time I do on the toilet. The constant bloating and gas. Constipation one day, diarrhea the next . . ."

"How about instead of diagnosing yourself on the internet, you see an actual gastroenterologist?"

George wished she hadn't said this. The idea of meeting with a specialist unnerved him. What if it was something more serious?

"You think it could be colon cancer?"

Jenny shook her head. "You can't have two cancer freakouts in one day. I'm not doing this. You need to see a *therapist*, George."

She went into the bedroom and emerged a moment later in sweat-pants, the vacuum cleaner trundling behind her like a loyal animal.

"You're not going?" George asked.

"Don't feel like lying," Jenny said. "It's juvenile to tell white lies all the time."

She began violently vacuuming the apartment. George lifted his feet as she inserted the hose in the space beneath his desk.

"Fuck it," George shouted over the noise. "Let's go."

* * *

Jenny was embarrassed to show up late, so George went by himself.

He took the subway. Across the aisle from where he sat was a poem containing the line *I used to think a leaf was just a leaf.* This was his obstacle to finishing his book. In order to produce art, one had to see a leaf as more than just a leaf.

George, having once thought of inspiration as being derived from an external force, a matter of paying attention to the world, now understood it as something more neurological; something that transpired on a cellular level. Or did not. George feared that he'd lost the capacity to feel moved.

He could appreciate that something was beautiful on an intellectual level, but it didn't affect him, or alter his mood—unless it was a piece of art he was particularly impressed by, in which case it evoked jealousy that he hadn't created it. Jealousy, and the reflexive shame and self-loathing of recognizing how pathetic this was.

By the time George arrived at the theater, the film was half over. He was told he couldn't go in.

"Really? I can't just slip in the back? I'm friends with the director," George added lamely.

The usher was unimpressed.

George was heading back to the subway when he remembered the after-party. He pulled out his phone to look up the address.

It was at a club in SoHo. George was the first person there, of course. He was over an hour early.

The hostess led him to a cordoned-off section in the back reserved for the party.

George ordered a whiskey at the private bar. When he took out his credit card, he was told it was an open bar. He wished he'd known this beforehand. He would've ordered something better than Maker's Mark.

Done with his drink, George had to pee. The bartender pointed him to the restroom, which was back in the main area.

In lieu of a traditional bathroom was a row of transparent glass stalls. When the door to a stall was shut, the glass automatically fogged, providing the occupant with privacy.

There was a line, and it was unisex.

When it was George's turn, he entered the stall, locked the door, and waited for the glass to fog up before doing anything else.

Sometimes George sat down to pee. He'd read it was a more efficient way to empty the bladder. The article claimed there were medical benefits, and that certain countries went as far as to launch public health campaigns encouraging their male citizens to pee sitting down as a way to avoid prostate issues. He'd also noticed a problem lately with a few drops of urine trickling out after he was done—"post-micturition dribbling" was the term, caused by the weakening of urethra muscles as men aged. "You're barely in your thirties," Jenny said when George had relayed this to her.

As George was in the middle of urinating, the glass suddenly became transparent. George jiggled the door to see if it would restore the fog.

It did not.

George saw the other people waiting in line to use the bathroom. And they saw him. He was too angry to feel embarrassed. What kind of idiot thought it was a good idea to replace regular bathroom stall doors with glass?

George pulled up his pants. Upon exiting the stall, he bypassed the sink, a blue-lit trough filled with stones, and strode to the front of the club.

The hostess must have read his expression. "Is everything okay?" she asked.

"I'd like to speak to your manager," George said.

He had never spoken these words before, and it made him uncomfortable.

"When you get a chance," he added.

Moments later George found himself face-to-face with a man who had the thickest neck he had ever seen. He was sucking a piece of candy, like a caricature of a con man. There was something sinister about the symmetry of his sharp features. Or maybe it was the girth of his neck—naked, pulsing, artificially orange—framed by the white sheen of his collar. He radiated a certain vintage, reptilian masculinity that suggested a foot in a criminal world.

"One of your bathroom doors just malfunctioned," George told him.

"You gotta lock it," the man said. "The glass won't frost until you lock it."

"Oh, I locked it. The glass frosted, and then a minute later it went clear on its own."

The guy said nothing. Just looked at George and sucked his candy.

"If you're going to have doors like that," George said, "you need to make sure they actually work."

"Can I get you a drink on the house?" the guy asked.

George gestured to the cordoned-off area and explained that he was part of the private party and there was an open bar.

How about food? Did George want anything to eat?

George was escorted to the main bar and handed a menu. He ordered filet mignon, calamari, truffle fries, olives, a side of sautéed spinach. As the dishes started to come out, he felt ashamed for spitefully ordering more than he could eat. He offered a couple to his left his calamari. They graciously declined.

When he could eat no more, George left a generous cash tip on the bar and went out for a cigarette.

When George returned, the cordoned-off area was full of people. Benji was there with a girl George recognized from screenshots Benji had texted of her OkCupid profile. She worked for PETA. *Is she worth going vegetarian for?* he'd written.

George was in the middle of telling them about his bathroom incident when Solly came over with his wife, whom he'd met on a Birthright Israel trip.

"That was quite a film," Solly said.

"He cried," his wife announced with obvious pride.

Solly nodded. "In the final round of the constitutional debate, when Logan recites the Fourth Amendment—"

"He cried, *too*!" Benji's girlfriend interrupted.

"I did not cry," Benji said.

George was eager to resume his bathroom story—he'd just gotten to the funny part—but the two couples continued to talk about the film. He went to the bar to get another drink. As he waited to get the bartender's attention, Jeremiah approached.

"To be honest, I found that completely exploitative," George told him.

Jeremiah turned to the woman standing next to him. "My friend, George, the comedian."

"Kylie," she said, extending her hand. "So great to finally meet you."

George muttered a similar sentiment, though he'd never heard her name—he couldn't keep up with Jeremiah's girlfriends.

"I missed the screening due to some gastrointestinal issues," George explained. "But I heard it was really great."

"Thank you," Jeremiah said. "I heard your diarrhea was beautiful, too. Really moving."

George had another drink, and then another. Though he didn't know most of the people there, the party was surprisingly fun. Throughout the night, whenever a conversation turned to the film, George shut it down by explaining he hadn't seen it yet—"No spoilers!"—and changed the topic to the bathroom stalls, which he warned were subject to malfunctioning.

When George described what happened, people clustered around him. They were sympathetic and outraged on his behalf. It affirmed their fears of ostentatious and unnecessary technology.

"I *hate* that kind of bathroom door!"

"I've always been scared that's going to happen to me!"

Everyone thought the story was funny, and it got even funnier with each telling, as George let go of his pride and lingered on the more humiliating details, such as the fact that he'd been sitting on the toilet seat. People were curious when he explained his reasons for doing this. They wanted to know more.

"Which countries try to make their men pee sitting?" a woman asked.

George couldn't remember; he thought maybe Sweden and Japan. "Google it," he said. "I'm not making this up."

People took out their phones.

"Yeah, it's a big thing in Japan," someone said.

"Germany."

"Taiwan."

People loved George's description of the manager as a man who looked like the face attached to a headline about a husband whose estranged wife turns up in a duffel bag on the side of the New Jersey Turnpike.

George was finishing up the story when he was interrupted by the clink of cutlery on glass. Jeremiah was giving a speech.

"I just got off the phone with Logan . . ."

It was hard for everyone to hear him over the music, but someone must have alerted the management because the speakers abruptly cut off.

"I just got off the phone with Logan," he began a second time. "As I mentioned at the Q and A, he wanted to be here tonight, but for various reasons he couldn't make it. He wanted to know how it went. I said, 'Logan, honestly, when I was young, I dreamed of nights like this, but now that I'm living it, I can tell you, it's not about this.'" Jeremiah gestured around the room. "'It's about the time we spent together. The honor of earning your trust . . .' I kept rambling on, but Logan cut me off. He said, 'Okay, Jerry. Go back out there, have some more champagne, but not too much. You've gotta wake up tomorrow and start working on your next movie, where I play Denzel Washington's better-looking younger brother."

Everyone laughed but George—Logan's dialogue sounded made up.

On his way out, George was approached by a woman who introduced herself as a casting agent who worked in advertising. She was currently working on a hidden-camera commercial for a budget airline company. The concept of the commercial was to simulate the discomfort of flying by putting three people in an office cubicle meant for one, similar to passengers squished into a row of coach seats. Two of the people were actors, and they were supposed to act like bad seatmates, annoying the person in the middle, who was not an actor but a regular person who'd responded to an ad on Craigslist for a temporary office gig and had no idea a secret camera was capturing their expressions to possibly be used in a commercial.

George was confused why she was telling him all this. And then she asked George if he would be in the commercial. She'd been in line when the bathroom stall door had malfunctioned.

"Your facial expression was priceless," she said. "If you can make that face on camera, you could make a couple thousand dollars, maybe more."

George took her card.

When he got home, he told Jenny about his night. She was

annoyed at him, he could tell, from her chilly reception to the bathroom stall incident. Normally she would have found that amusing.

But when George mentioned being scouted by a casting agent, she looked interested.

"Sounds like a painless way to make a little money," she said.

* * *

Two weeks later, George got off at the Bryant Park stop and arrived at the address Ashley, the woman with the commercial, had directed him to, a tall, sleek high-rise. She'd warned him ahead of time that he couldn't let on that he was "the ringer"; he was to act as if he were showing up for an office gig, not an ad with a hidden camera. On the eighteenth floor, a different woman came out and spoke his name.

"Thanks for your patience," she said with a frosty grin. "If you'll come with me, I can get you set up."

There was an unnatural bounce in her step as George followed her down a hall, past rows of empty cubicles.

"You can take a seat in the middle," she said, gesturing to a cubicle that was occupied by two people, a man and a woman, whose overly wrought mannerisms betrayed their profession. There was a satirical affect in the intensity of their typing, their glazed expressions, their flagrant disregard for George's physical space. He had to hug his arms to his sides to avoid touching them.

George was given a document of numbers he was supposed to enter into a Microsoft Excel spreadsheet. He furtively scanned the desk for a hidden camera. Wherever it was, they'd done a good job hiding it.

As George typed random numbers into the spreadsheet, the woman began elbowing him and the man coughed. They were having fun. They were acting. They had no idea George was in on the joke.

After a few minutes the man got a little carried away with his fake cough; George felt the spray of actual saliva. He assumed this was accidental, that the man recognized he'd taken his fake cough too far and was embarrassed.

George looked at the man, who was now scratching his scalp in a gerbil-like manner. Glancing at his lap, George saw a constellation of dandruff.

Then he did it again. *Ahem-ahem!* A fine mist.

This was more than George had signed up for. He pushed his chair back and stood up.

George's fake boss reappeared. Behind her were other people.

They looked excited. George played dumb as they explained what he already knew.

This was a hidden-camera commercial! Congratulations! George might be on TV!

A man introduced himself as the director. "You did great," he said, shaking George's hand. "That was fan*ta*stic."

Someone thrust a form in front of him. George signed the dotted line.

Ashley appeared and walked him to the elevator. When they were far away from everyone, she winked at him.

"You killed it," she whispered.

* * *

When several months passed and George didn't hear anything about the commercial, he figured they decided not to use his footage after all. Then one day Ashley called.

"Are you sitting down?" she asked. The executives were so pleased with George's footage that they decided to hold off on debuting it until the Super Bowl. George was going to be in a Super Bowl commercial. They would have to pay George accordingly.

"You seem pretty nonplussed," Ashley said.

Nonplussed meant the opposite of what she thought it meant, George was thinking.

"No, it's cool," he said.

"I mean, it's six figures for ten minutes of work," Ashley said.

George called Jenny at work, who laughed when he told her he was going to be in a Super Bowl commercial, and even more when he told her how much he was getting paid: two hundred and fifty thousand dollars.

"Before taxes," he added.

"George! That's ridiculous! You're rich!"

* * *

The Super Bowl was months away, but Ashley sent George a link to a private portal where he could preview the commercial after entering a code.

The commercial started with an exterior shot of the high-rise, and then footage of George being led down the hall by the woman who was supposed to be his boss. A brief shot of her directing him to enter numbers into a spreadsheet was followed by the main part of the commercial: George looking disgruntled.

He was disturbed by the expression on his face. A kind of petty, irritable misery. It was something he often felt, going through his day, like he was just on the brink of losing it over some trivial frustration. He hadn't known it was visible to others.

George was surprised, once again, that anyone could stand being around him.

If you wouldn't take it on the ground, why would you take it in the air?

That was the commercial's motto, along with a promise of ample legroom for passengers who flew this budget airline. It was pretty stupid. Another dumb ad for dumb American consumers.

When Jenny got home, she wanted to see it.

She thought it was very funny.

"*George*, this is hilarious! You're a really good actor!"

"I don't know if you could call it acting. I found the actors on either side of me genuinely irritating."

"Oh, come on. You knew what it was, you were *acting*."

They watched it again. And again, and again. Jenny continued to laugh each time, real laughter, and praise his performance. George began to see it differently. He began to consider the possibility that it was acting. That he was, as she vociferously proclaimed, in possession of a real talent.

Jenny got up to start dinner. When she mumbled something about being out of the good kind of olive oil, George volunteered to go get some.

While he was out, he picked up a bottle of wine and Jenny's favorite kind of cookies from the Italian bakery.

When he returned to the apartment Jenny was spinning lettuce. She laughed as George snuck up from behind and began humping her.

George's concerns about Lexapro's diminishing his libido were unwarranted that night.

* * *

The day of the Super Bowl, Jenny asked George if he would mind leaving the apartment for a few hours so she could do a deep clean. "I'm going to be moving furniture around, vacuuming every square inch; it's going to be noisy and disruptive."

"I was hoping to watch the game," he said. "Starts at six-thirty."

"You can come back for the Super Bowl," she said. "Just be gone from four to six-fifteen."

George took his laptop to a café on Henry. After about an hour, his battery died. He hadn't thought to bring his charger.

He went back to the apartment to get it.

The apartment was not only much cleaner than before, but Jenny had laid out spreads of crackers and cheese, chips and dips, and deviled eggs.

He could hear Jenny vacuuming behind the closed bedroom door.

George opened the fridge and noticed a cake. *SUPER GEORGE* was written in icing across the top.

"What's the deal with this cake?" he asked Jenny in the bedroom.

"You weren't supposed to see that," she said after she shut off the vacuum. "We're having a Super Bowl party. A 'Super George' party. To celebrate your commercial."

"Are you kidding?" George wasn't feeling particularly social.

Jenny shook her head. "It was supposed to be a surprise."

"How many people are coming and what time are they getting here?" George sat on the couch and helped himself to some chips.

"Could you just go out and come back at six-fifteen?" she asked. "I told everyone it was going to be a surprise."

"Why would they care?"

"Please, George. I worked so hard to put this together. It's not the same if you're here as they trickle in. Just go away and come back then.

"And call or text to let me know when you're a few minutes away," she said.

George went back to the café on Henry.

When he came back, he could hear the buzz of voices from downstairs. George felt dread seeing all the shoes in their hallway. He braced himself before opening the door.

The party was in full swing. The living room was hot with their collective mass. George slipped inside unnoticed, and then someone shouted, "He's here!"

The room got quiet.

"You were supposed to call," Jenny said.

"I'm sorry," George said. "I got a little distracted. I, uh . . . So, this is a little awkward, but I just found out the commercial got cut."

Everyone looked disappointed.

"Something to do with a last-minute change in the budget," he explained. "They said they might run it on a few local stations, they're not sure yet."

There was an uncomfortable silence.

"That was a joke," George said.

An eruption of laughter. Someone handed George a drink, which he really needed. Jenny had invited people from different chapters of his life: high school, college, friends he hadn't seen or checked in with in ages, all gathered in their little apartment.

It was overwhelming at first, but George was touched.

"We're proud of you!" Solly's wife greeted him with an effusive hug. Solly offered him a fist bump.

Benji and the PETA girl were there.

"I thought you were shooting something in New Orleans," George said to Jeremiah.

"I chartered a private plane to come back just for this."

"Seriously?"

"Of course not. I flew coach, with a fucking three-hour layover in Atlanta. But I expect a portion of the residuals, given the fact that this never would have happened were it not for the after-party of my—"

"My kid wants your autograph," someone interrupted.

"Clark!" George said. "How the hell are you, man?"

"I'm grand," he said in an Irish accent. "I'm fucking grand . . ."

George was talking to Reuven, a high school friend, when Jenny stood on the couch and clinked a glass.

"Before the game starts, I'd like to say a few words. Anyone who knows George knows he has this *face* . . . a *beautiful* face, but a face that's not good at hiding what he's feeling. When I first met George, we were working at a restaurant, and I'd sometimes catch him looking at difficult customers . . . with that look of . . . you know the one. I didn't know him well enough to say anything . . . but then we started dating and that changed. Like, *seriously*, George, when I'm introducing you to someone, could you maybe smile? Or at least not look like you're at the DMV, or a doctor's office waiting to get a colonoscopy . . ."

Jenny was drunk.

"I give him a hard time about it, but I love that face. And today that face will grace television screens across the—" Jenny paused. "Do people watch the Super Bowl in other countries?"

"Yes," someone said.

"Today that face will be seen by people across the world. How many people watch it in the US, with our commercials?" she asked. "Like a few million?"

"Over a hundred million," someone said. "One in three Americans."

Jenny's eyes widened. The whole thing was so stupid, so silly, and yet her excitement gave George a lift.

"And I just wanted to say," Jenny continued, "how lucky I feel, to see that face every day."

Cups were raised. "To George!"

The game started. George was bored by football and circulated around the room while keeping an eye on the screen. He had been told the commercial was airing sometime during the second quarter, but then the second quarter ended, and nothing.

At halftime he texted Ashley, *You're sure it was supposed to be the second quarter?*

That's what I was told, she texted back.

"Wouldn't it be funny if they really did cut it at the last minute," George said to Jenny. "I wonder if they'll make me give the money back."

"Of course they didn't cut it," Jenny said. "There's still lots of time left."

When the final quarter started, George went downstairs for a cigarette. When he came back up there were only eight minutes left in the game and the score was close. Those who'd actually been watching the game were rapt.

George texted a question mark to Ashley.

She texted a shrugging emoticon.

George opened another beer. He wished he could at least show everyone here the ad on his laptop, but the preview link no longer worked. He wondered if anyone would suspect he'd been lying about the whole thing. What a bizarre lie.

And then, after a solemn ad for a financial services company, it was happening.

George had a moment of anxiety as a hush settled upon the room and everyone turned toward the TV, wearing polite, expectant grins, but it wasn't long before the laughter began, and when the commercial ended, a standing ovation.

There was a second eruption of excitement in the room as the game was decided in the final two minutes. George was only mildly resentful of being upstaged by the Patriots. His phone began rattling with texts.

Ellen called, and when George didn't pick up she tried Jenny, who did.

"Your first-grade teacher just called your mom," she shouted across the room.

The game ended, people began to trickle out. Before leaving, they all made sure to tell George how good he'd been.

"It was probably funnier because I know you," Jeremiah said, "but even so, that was probably the funniest commercial I've ever seen."

"Thanks, man," said George.

"I mean it," Jeremiah said. "No one watching that couldn't have laughed. You made over a *hundred million people* laugh just now. Hardly anyone in the world gets to do something like that. You know how many people saw my documentary? Like ten thousand, tops."

"Your documentary's a lot more meaningful than a thirty-second ad for an airline," George said.

"Still," Jeremiah said. "These things don't happen often. Savor this moment."

"George . . ." Jenny handed him his phone.

It was Cressida.

"I'm not trying to build your confidence, George. But I think this could be the beginning of something. I think you could be an actor."

"It's a hidden-camera commercial," George reminded her.

"Yes, but millions of people just saw it. Maybe this will lead to something."

"It's a little hard to just *become an actor* in one's thirties."

"That doesn't mean these things can't happen. Maybe you could take an improv class or something. See where it goes."

When the last stragglers had left, Jenny collapsed on the couch.

"That was a success," she said. "Did you have fun?"

"I did," George said, joining her. "That was really nice of you. Thanks for making it happen."

"It was fun." Jenny looked pleased. She lay back and rested her feet on George's lap.

There was a gaiety to the apartment's trampled disarray, the helter-skelter of cans and cups and paper plates, deflated throw cushions, soiled napkins. Looking around, George thought of a younger version of himself taking in the tableau and being impressed by the evidence of a thriving, lively social life.

"I think someone's calling you," Jenny said.

George stood up and followed the sound of the buzz. By the time he located his phone, the call, from an unknown number, had gone to voicemail.

"Hello," said an unfamiliar elderly woman's voice. "George, this is your philosophy professor Carl's wife, Bernice. I've been meaning to get in touch to tell you that Carl has advanced Alzheimer's and has recently moved into an assisted living facility. It's a nice place, as far as these places go, and close enough that I'm able to visit him every day. We never watch the Super Bowl, but it was on the TV in the room he's in and we saw a commercial with a boy, a young man, with a striking resemblance to you. And Carl's face lit up as he pointed to the screen. And I let him think it was you. 'It's George!' I said. It was the happiest I'd seen him in a while. I just wanted to share that with you. He was always so fond of you. I hope all is well."

"What's wrong?" Jenny asked, searching his face. Her teeth were stained purple from the wine.

George shook his head.

"What if this is my moment?" he said.

Jenny's mouth narrowed in worried confusion. "What do you mean, *your moment?*"

George shrugged.

"You mean you want to turn this into a bigger thing? Like get an agent or whatever?"

"Not that kind of moment," he said. "I mean, what if this is *it*?"

"This wasn't even something you'd set out to accomplish, or longed for, this is just something lucky that happened. This is nothing."

"I know," George said. "That's what I'm saying. The biggest moment of my life, and it's a stupid Super Bowl commercial."

"There are other moments in life to look forward to," Jenny said quietly. "Things that aren't so public."

11. TEN THOUSAND HOURS

George, 33

There was a line to get onto the Brooklyn Queens Expressway, and it was moving very slowly. George kept his foot poised over the accelerator. Every time the car ahead moved up a few feet, he abruptly did the same. Jenny protested that the jerkiness was making her sick, but George had no choice; if he didn't immediately close the gap, another car might attempt to nose its way in and cut the line.

"Ten thousand hours," he marveled. "Roughly how many total hours of people's lives will be spent traveling to get to this wedding."

"That doesn't sound right," Jenny said. "I'm not great at math, but ten thousand hours sounds too high."

"A hundred guests, roughly ten hours for those traveling round-trip from New York . . ." George recognized some trouble with his calculation. "Maybe it's more like a thousand hours."

A bird shat on the windshield. George turned on the wipers and pressed the button that dispensed wiper fluid, but there wasn't any fluid left, so the wipers just smeared the bird shit around.

Once they were on the ramp, there was a complete standstill. George licked his finger and inserted it into the corners of his empty Sun Chip bag to extract the last of the crumbs.

"I should've gotten the bigger size," he said ruefully.

"Look at those cute little trees." Jenny pointed to a cluster of tiny evergreens on the litter-strewn spit of earth adjacent to the ramp. "Do you think someone planted them?"

George shrugged.

Across the East River, the skyscrapers of lower Manhattan loomed in a menacing cluster. An ever-expanding crop of metallic phalluses. A monument to hubris and greed.

"I wonder if they grew on their own," Jenny said dreamily. "It's possible the seeds could have blown in from New Jersey."

"This is a joke." George put the car in park. In ten minutes, they advanced maybe as many inches. "We should just get out and walk."

Jenny opened her door and got out.

"What are you doing?" George called after her.

She was climbing onto the meridian to get a closer look at the trees.

"Was that necessary?" George said when she returned. "What if the traffic had suddenly started moving?"

"Look what I found." In her palm was a tiny pine cone.

"Will Dominic be at the wedding?" she asked, putting her seat belt back on.

George didn't know who she was talking about. "Dominic?"

"You guys lived with him as sophomores. The nightmare roommate. Played video games all the time, ate all your food, would knock incessantly on your door when you were trying to sleep late."

"*Dominic*." George hadn't thought of Dominic in years. "Dominic wasn't a roommate. He was a kid who lived in the neighborhood."

"Dominic was a kid?"

"Yeah, he was probably nine, ten years old. There was a housing project down the block from our dorm. He just started coming by."

George smiled fondly recalling the sight of Dominic slouched on the futon in the common room playing *World of Warcraft*. Dominic in one of his oversize T-shirts, mouth ringed with orange powder, his white-knuckled grip on the console, which would also be covered in orange powder—or chocolate, or pizza grease, depending on what he'd pilfered from their filthy kitchen. Dominic, with his buzz cut and furrowed brow, like a boy from the 1950s, his beady little eyes locked on the screen. *The street urchin*, one of his roommates used to call him when he wasn't around.

"Did you ever meet his parents?" Jenny asked.

George shook his head.

"Did you know anything about his family or living situation?"

"Nope."

Jenny had more questions.

Didn't it seem strange that this kid spent all this time at their dorm?

Did anyone ever come looking for him?

Wonder why he wasn't in school?

Didn't they ever worry about him?

"Of course," George said. "Of course, we worried about him."

"We made a phone call," George told her. "I can't remember if it was CPS. It might have just been the local police department. But we made a call, and they said to hold him there, they'd be over in half an hour. It wasn't hard to make sure he stayed; Dominic never wanted to leave. We turned off the video game, and I remember we were just hanging out on the couch with him, asking him questions, and it was weird, I got the sense that he knew something was up. Then two people showed up. A man and a woman. As soon as they stepped inside, it was obvious that they recognized Dominic—and that Dominic recognized them. He ran into my room and shut the door. I got it open before he managed to lock it. He crawled under my bed. He was crying. I had to pull him out and carry him out to the people. He was kicking and screaming. He really didn't want to go with them."

George spared Jenny a detail that he'd also kept to himself at the time. While carrying Dominic out to the common room, Dominic had peed.

"It was upsetting," George said. "It was unclear if we were doing the right thing."

"And then what happened?" Jenny asked.

"They took him with them," George said. "That was the last we saw of him. He stopped coming around after that."

"I can't believe you never told me this," Jenny said.

They finally made it onto the BQE only to encounter more gridlock as they approached the section that went underneath the promenade, which George had recently read was in danger of collapsing. Wouldn't that put a damper on the wedding festivities, George thought. He wondered how they would handle it. He imagined guests would receive an email acknowledging that one of the groomsmen had been killed in transit but explaining that the wedding would still go on. Perhaps a request that people not bring up the tragedy at the wedding. (A few days earlier, guests had received an email asking everyone to refrain from discussing a certain presidential candidate during the weekend.)

"I think I'll take a nap," Jenny announced, as they finally made it out of the city.

"He'd be about twenty-two now." She yawned, putting her seat back.

George fell into a peaceful driving trance. He thought about the short story he was currently working on. He was pleased with it. When he was done, he'd have seven completed short stories, nearly enough for a collection. He wondered what order the stories should go in. What he should call it. How he should describe the collection in his query letter to agents. He was mulling over these things, which were fun to think about, when Jenny yawned lustily, cracked her knuckles, and plopped her feet on the dashboard.

She was awake. And though she didn't say anything, the mere fact of her consciousness put George on guard. That at any moment she might narrate some thought, interrupting his own, was profoundly irritating. Her ignorance of this fact exacerbated his resentment.

Jenny's feet drifted off the dashboard; she'd fallen back asleep.

George was alone again. But he struggled to pick up where he'd left off, thinking uplifting thoughts about his book. He was distracted by dark thoughts about Jenny. That her presence triggered such a visceral, irrational anger disturbed him. It frightened him.

How had it come to this?

George recalled the way he'd felt about her when they'd first encountered each other working at that awful restaurant all those years ago. When she had yet to see the ugly side of him, and he the needy, difficult side of her, when there existed between them a simple and pure affection.

Sometimes he thought of this and wished they'd left it at that.

George stopped at a gas station off the Taconic. After pumping, he went inside the store to get coffee. When he was at the counter, he asked for Marlboro Lights. He wasn't planning to, it just slipped out. "Pack-a Marlboro Lights, please."

When he got back in the car, Jenny was fully awake. He showed her the cigarettes, held them up like contraband. "For safety's sake. Helps keep me awake and alert."

"You'd almost made it to a year," Jenny said, looking especially wholesome in her Fair Isle sweater, her cheeks flushed from sleep.

"That's why it feels safe," George explained. "It's been long enough that my body is no longer addicted.

"I'll throw out what's left soon as we get to the hotel," he assured her.

"I'm going to wait until we cross the border until I have one," he added, as further evidence of his self-control.

George kept his word. The WELCOME TO VERMONT sign felt like a friendly green wink as it came into view. To underscore his restraint, he clocked an additional three miles before casually reaching for the pack. After he removed the cellophane wrapper, it clung to his hand with static electricity; as he attempted to shake it off, it flew out the two inches of open window. It was an accident. In the grand scheme of litter, a piddling contribution. Nonetheless, George felt Jenny's reproachful glare. In the Green Mountain State of all places, no doubt she was thinking.

As George drew his first puff, he experienced a momentary spell of vertigo, but this quickly subsided, and the experience was just as gratifying, if not more so, than he had anticipated.

They arrived at the inn shortly before five.

"So beautiful," Jenny said of the rambling colonial, grandly situated across from a village green.

A leather strap of bells on the front door jingled as they let themselves in, where they were greeted by a convivial man with a ponytail who introduced himself as Fritz.

"This is so nice," Jenny gushed as he led them to their room. "We're so happy to be here."

The carpeted steps creaked as they carried their bags up a second flight of stairs.

"You'll want to watch your head," Fritz warned George as he opened the door to their room, which had dramatically sloped eaves. A four-poster bed occupied the bulk of the inhabitable space of the room. The scent of citrus and cloves bordered on cloying. Chaotically floral wallpaper was interrupted by the prim sensibility of the white eyelet curtains.

Jenny literally squealed in delight. "So cozy!"

Fritz beamed. "Glad you like it."

The jingle of bells from the lobby sent him trundling back downstairs.

On top of the dresser was an itinerary of the weekend's events, with a special set of instructions for George highlighted in yellow.

At five-thirty, members of the wedding party were to attend a rehearsal at the church, which, according to the accompanying map, was a mile down the road from the hotel.

Jenny didn't need to be there but wanted to come with George. She proposed they walk.

There was no sidewalk, which meant they had to navigate a bank of densely packed snow that had been plowed off the road. The rest of the season's snow had melted. The landscape looked sharp and brittle and leached of whatever life force had once animated it.

"Who the hell gets married in March?" George asked.

"It was supposed to be in June," Jenny reminded him. "They rescheduled so Kylie's dad could be there."

"Oh, yeah," George said. "Forgot about that."

It was one of those weddings where the bride's father was dying.

As the church came into view, a car pulled over, a Tesla. Benji rolled down the window.

"Nice car for a chess teacher," George said to him.

"You could be driving one, too, if you just did what I told you to do," Benji said.

He wanted George to invest his Super Bowl money in something called cryptocurrencies. He'd been on his case for the past year.

"You still haven't explained what these things do," George said.

"Numerous blockchain use cases," Benji said.

"I don't know what that means," George said.

"You don't need to," Benji said. "Just listen to me. Or don't. It's your life. I gotta get to the rehearsal."

"Let me in," George said. "I'm going there, too."

"You're in the wedding?" Benji asked.

"Why is that surprising?" said George. "I'm possibly Jeremiah's favorite person."

"I'd like to keep walking," Jenny said as George waited for her to join him in the car. "I mean, we're practically there."

"Okay," George said. "See you at the church."

There was a taxidermied possum in the back seat. George had never seen a possum up close. It was just as demonic-looking as it appeared in the fleeting glare of a pair of headlights.

"That's Jeremiah's wedding present," Benji explained. "You didn't see it on the registry?"

He had recently broken up with his girlfriend and, after a brief period of heartbreak, appeared fully recovered. Everything was hilarious. Life was a joke.

After pulling into a far corner of the church parking lot, Benji procured a joint from the glove compartment.

"I thought you were worried about being late," George said.

"I'm not going to hot bake the car, just taking a few hits." Benji lit the joint and passed it to George.

A Subaru pulled up in front of the church entrance. Solly emerged, extracted a baby from the back seat, and walked up the church steps.

"Remember Canada?" Benji said, exhaling.

George nodded, spotting Jenny in the rearview mirror. "That was the best."

* * *

"Fuck me," George said when he and Jenny returned to their hotel room after the rehearsal dinner.

"I forgot one of the best lines in my toast," he told her. "I wrote everything down, but I intentionally didn't memorize it, because I didn't want it to sound too polished."

"I guess that's what you get." George shook his head sadly. "I guess that's what you get when you try to allow for a little spontaneity."

"It was a great toast, George," Jenny said, snapping on a lamp. "Everyone loved it."

She opened a dresser drawer and pulled her pajamas out. He didn't understand why she bothered unpacking her things when they were staying only two nights.

George picked up the chocolate coin on his pillow. "You think people liked it?"

"Oh, come on. Couldn't you tell from how hard they were laughing?"

George shrugged. "I had trouble gauging if it was actually funny or if people were just drunk. I mean, some of the other toasts they were laughing at . . ."

"People were definitely a little drunk," Jenny said.

"It was *great*, George," she said with emphasis, catching him looking at her. "The best toast of the night."

"Then why'd you say people were definitely drunk?"

Jenny groaned. "I didn't mean that had anything to do with their reception of your toast. It was a wonderful toast, the stories you told, your delivery—everything about it was great."

She mustered a weary smile. "You're a natural."

George ate the chocolate. It was good. Dark, minty. There was something crunchy in it. When he was done, he asked Jenny if he could have hers and she curtly obliged.

"What did you think of the bridesmaids' toast?" George asked—he couldn't resist. "The rhyming one?"

"I thought it was cute," Jenny said. "They clearly spent a lot of time on it."

"Yeah, I think that was actually part of the problem," he remarked. "With a bunch of the toasts, actually. They felt overly rehearsed. Overwrought."

Jenny extracted a piece of floss from her toiletry kit and got to work in front of the mirror on the bathroom door. She was a meticulous flosser. It was like watching a sushi chef or a concert pianist—the graceful alacrity of her fingers. In all their years together, George had never known her to skip a night, except when she was very drunk.

"The other thing I noticed," George continued, "is that people talk for way too long. It doesn't matter how funny or charming you are, after five minutes, wrap it up.

"*Wrap. It. Up,*" George repeated. He dumped the contents of his overnight bag onto their bed and began fishing through the rubble.

"The trick with toasts is to keep it simple," he reflected. "Don't try to get all sentimental, don't quote philosophers, don't deliver abstract theories on what marriage is, just tell a story . . ."

Jenny started brushing her teeth with her usual rigor—maybe a little more. She left the door ajar, but George had to speak louder to be heard over the faucet.

"Just tell a story," he bellowed. "A story that captures the person's essence. A simple story that nonetheless contains complexity."

Jenny closed the bathroom door.

"Slight change of plan," George told her when she emerged a few minutes later. "We're going to have to go back to the city tonight."

"What are you talking about?"

"I forgot my Lexapro," he said. "I've summoned Fritz to help us carry our bags downstairs."

Jenny removed her glasses and began wiping the lenses on the hem of her T-shirt.

"That's not funny," she said, squinting.

George had forgotten to pack his Lexapro when they'd traveled to Nova Scotia for her sister's wedding the previous summer. Over the course of the week, he'd endured insomnia, irritability, constipation, brain fog—it was not pleasant for either of them.

"The strange thing is, I distinctly remember packing it. Do you think Fritz took it? When he came in to leave us the chocolates?"

Jenny put her glasses back on. "Did you really forget your Lexapro, George?"

George shook his head. "Just my toothbrush."

He borrowed hers. It was made out of wood.

They got into bed. George was exhausted. The drive, the toast, the socializing with people he hadn't seen in years—it had all taken a lot out of him. He was on the verge of sleep when Jenny leaned over and thrust her phone in his face. On the screen was a photo of a man and an older woman under the headline "From Hardship to Hope: Area Man Pursues Military Career."

"Do you think it's him?" Jenny asked. "I mean, Dominic's not a very common name . . ."

George skimmed the accompanying article, which described the upward trajectory of a man named Dominic who'd been raised by his grandmother in a housing project in Middletown, Connecticut.

He got out of bed and put on pants.

"Where are you going with my phone?" Jenny asked.

"Be right back," he said.

Benji was staying across the hall. There was music playing through the door, and George had to knock loudly to be heard.

Benji opened the door holding a handle of cheap rum. "Look who's up past his bedtime!"

Two girls in their early twenties—cousins of the bride—sat on one of the queen beds. Solly was at a desk in the corner rolling a joint.

"Party-town fun time," George said, stepping in.

Benji's smug air of youthful irreverence was starting to embarrass him. He was planning to micro-dose on acid before the wedding.

"*Fucking A*," Benji said when George showed him the photo on Jenny's phone. "Hundred percent that's him."

Benji brought the phone over to Solly—"The street urchin!"—and then over to show the girls.

"We knew this guy when he was a kid," he told them. "He used to come over and bother us, eat our food, play our video games, and now he's a fucking soldier!"

The girls seemed unsure of how to respond.

"I liked your toast," one of them said to George.

She had exquisitely unblemished skin, and a pretty, plump little face framed by corkscrew curls.

"That makes one of you," he told her.

The girl looked surprised. "*Every*one liked it," she said.

"It was hilarious," the other concurred. She was also pretty, in a medieval maiden kind of way.

"So, you're an actor?" she asked George.

"Solly just showed them your commercial," Benji explained.

"That wasn't acting," George said. "I just forgot to take my Lexapro that morning."

The girls found this amusing.

It gave George a boost, a little charge, the way they were looking at him—which was not the way they looked at Benji, in spite of his shameless efforts (upon arriving at the rehearsal dinner, he'd reshuffled the name cards to sit next to these girls rather than George and Jenny). George hoped Benji recognized that any chance he had with either of these girls was predicated on George's unavailability. So long as he was present, their attention was his.

"My favorite part of the toast . . ." one of the girls began to say, before pausing to glance at the other, as if to seek her permission to continue. "We were actually talking about it just before you came in . . ."

George reached for a beer in the cooler on the floor and took a seat on the other bed.

When he returned to his and Jenny's room, the bedside lamp was still on, but Jenny's eyes were closed.

"You awake?" he whispered, climbing into bed. "Thank you for saying all those nice things about my toast before."

"It was really good," she said softly.

"You don't have to talk about it more," George said. "I wasn't fishing . . .

"I just want to make sure you know how much I appreciate you. And how supportive you are. You're the wind in my sails."

Jenny made a sound that was like a laugh.

"I mean it," George said. "I know I'm a lot. I don't know how you put up with me sometimes."

She made another sound, close to a grunt, which he took to mean that she didn't find him too unbearable.

They had sex. It had been a while.

"What are you thinking?" Jenny asked as they lay in bed after-ward.

George was thinking about how, years ago, Jenny had been repeatedly conned by a waiter at the restaurant they'd worked at. This asshole Connor. He needed help with a vet bill, his rent, some kind of medicine his insurance wouldn't cover, a train ticket to visit his mother who was in a psychiatric facility in New Jersey—he was always borrowing money from her, and also her phone. One day Jenny got a call from a man, someone from Connor's life (Connor must have called him from her phone, which is how he had her number) and they started talking and he told Jenny that Connor was a drug addict and to stop lending him money. Jenny was mor-tified. In retrospect, it was so obvious Connor was lying; she felt like an idiot, a dupe. Being Jenny, she also felt guilty that she'd unknowingly contributed to the problem.

What had triggered the memory, George couldn't say, but in recalling the episode he experienced a sudden swelling of tenderness, a kind of paternalistic desire to protect her from the Connors of the world. Jenny clearly saw it on his face, his love for her. There was a slightly affected innocence in her demeanor as she'd asked, "What are you thinking?" She was, for all her virtues, not above the desire to hear nice things about herself.

"I was thinking about your generous, trusting nature," George told her. "What a good person you are."

And Jenny nodded. Looking slightly disappointed, he thought.

In his old-school gangster voice, George said, "What's a boyd like you doin' with a crumb-bum like me?"

Jenny smiled a little.

"I was also thinking that you're pretty," George said.

Jenny looked surprised. Propped her head up. "You never say that."

"I don't?"

Jenny bit her bottom lip and shook her head. "Never."

"Well, I think it," he told her.

"I've always wished I had more delicate features," she said.

"Let me see." George took her face in his hands and cocked his head in theatrical scrutiny.

"Nope," he said. "I wouldn't change anything about you. Very pretty. A bonnie lass."

Jenny smiled bashfully. "Thank you," she said.

* * *

The wedding itself was a blur. George drank eight or nine drinks. Possibly more. Toward the end of the night, the band left, but someone hooked up a phone to the speakers and the dance party continued. When he woke up, George had a dim memory of people circled around clapping and laughing as he broke out his signature dance move, the overturned cockroach.

"I think I'm too hungover to drive," he told Jenny as she packed her things. "I think I might still be drunk."

Jenny drove. Lulled by the hum of the engine, the *tick-tick-tick* of the blinker as she shifted lanes, George fell asleep.

It was not restorative. When he woke up two hours later, he felt just as miserable, if not worse. It was flurrying. Large, irregularly shaped snowflakes drifted down like discs of dandruff. They were far apart and immediately melted upon contact with the windshield. Jenny had the wipers on the lowest setting; every thirty seconds or so they'd squawk to life, leaving a streaky residue.

They were on I-91, which was not the route they'd taken on the way up. George was familiar with I-91, because it cut through the town where he'd gone to college.

"You're awake," Jenny observed. "How are you feeling?"

"I'm alive," George said. "Why are we on I-91?"

"We're stopping at a Chinese restaurant," she responded with perky authority. "We're meeting Dominic and his grandmother for lunch."

"What?"

"I found his grandmother on Facebook. Last night at the reception. I sent her a message explaining that we'd just come across the article, and you'd known Dominic as a boy and wanted to reach out to him. She wrote back right away, and we ended up exchanging a few messages, and I told her that we'd be passing through Middletown tomorrow . . ."

Jenny glanced at him, expecting him to protest. But George felt like clay in the shape of a body.

"It's nice to reconnect with people, George." She reached over and touched his knee. "Who knows, maybe there's something we could do for him."

George yawned. "I get the impression he's doing pretty well for himself."

"Did you even read the article?" Jenny asked briskly. "He's living in Section 8 housing with his grandmother. Until recently, they were in a *shelter*."

George rested his socked feet on the dashboard. "I thought it said he was in the army."

"He's not *in* the army," Jenny said. "He fixes helicopters for the army."

George considered the technical skill and confidence required of such a job. It was beyond anything he could imagine doing.

"That's even more impressive," he said.

As they got off at the exit, the flurries turned to drizzle.

They approached the southern perimeter of George's college campus. Passing by a row of limestone and brick buildings, some of which had been the location of classes he'd taken, others he'd never set foot inside and yet walked by every day, he felt a pang of despair. Never again would life be so promising, so full of friends and intellectual pursuits. Never again.

Jenny parked in front of the Chinese restaurant where they were supposed to meet Dominic and his grandmother. It was next to a plaza, where speakers piped classical music to deter a subversive crowd from loitering. It worked; there were no people of any kind.

It was one-thirty, and the restaurant was nearly empty. From its perch in the front window, a mechanical cat waved at a desolate Main Street.

"There'll be four of us," Jenny told an employee.

He gestured for them to sit anywhere they liked. Jenny led George to a booth by the window.

Jenny took the seat across from him.

"Shouldn't we be on the same side, so we're both facing them?" George asked.

"You're right," she said, coming over to him.

"Whatever your expectations of this are, just a reminder that I'm extremely hungover. I wasn't even able to talk to my closest friends at the brunch this morning. So it might be a little difficult for me to 'reconnect' with a kid I used to play video games with a decade ago."

"I think you'll rise to the occasion, George," Jenny said.

She suddenly looked stricken. Something out the window caught her attention: a man walking down the street in a MAGA hat. He was with an older woman. They were approaching the restaurant. George suppressed a laugh—the article had not mentioned Dominic was a Trump supporter. Ha! His dread of the hour ahead was tempered by vindication. Whatever Jenny's fantasy of this reunion was, it would not be that.

Jenny manufactured a smile and waved as they entered. "Stand up," she whispered to George as they approached.

Like a puppet, George rose and extended his hand.

"Good to see you, man," he muttered.

There was nothing of the boy he remembered in the stony countenance beneath the red cap, and George interpreted Dominic's limp grip as a juvenile means of expressing his attitude toward this rendezvous. Not the handshake he imagined Dominic used in the world of the armed forces.

The grandmother was slow, heavyset. She had closely cropped bronze hair and a broad, toadlike face. As she lowered herself into the booth, the lenses of her glasses caught the light, obscuring her eyes.

A waiter brought menus. They were large and many laminated pages long. George appreciated this; it gave them something to hide their faces behind, something to do.

Eventually it was time to order, and the menus were taken away.

Jenny looked at Dominic. "It's so nice to meet you after hearing about you all of these years."

George wished Jenny hadn't said that. It suggested he talked about Dominic a lot. He had maybe mentioned Dominic in passing half a dozen times. She shouldn't have said that.

"You think he'll be our next president?" George asked, pointing to Dominic's hat.

Dominic shrugged.

Eager to change the topic, Jenny began extolling the natural beauty of Middletown. The rolling hills, the sky, the Connecticut River. Dominic and his grandmother listened neutrally.

"As we were driving in, I saw a *swan*," she announced with great excitement. "It was in the reservoir. Or maybe it's a lake. You know that body of water you pass right after you get off the highway?"

No, Dominic and his grandmother did not.

"Did you watch the last debate?" George asked. "He was something, wasn't he."

Both Dominic and his grandmother nodded.

George felt Jenny's glare as he continued to solicit their politics.

"She's a crook," the grandmother said as George pivoted to Hillary Clinton. "Got blood on her hands."

George grinned in spite of himself as she began to discuss the details of the death of a man named Vince Foster.

She hadn't gotten very far when Dominic cut her off.

"That's wack." He looked reproachfully at his grandmother. "Kind of talk makes you look batshit. Makes you sound stupid."

"So, Jeremiah got married this weekend," Jenny said, smiling at Dominic, as though this news would mean something to him.

"He's one of the guys who lived in the dorm," George explained. "You once killed him in *World of Warcraft*.

"You took a victory lap around the courtyard," George reminded him. "Benji carried you on his shoulders."

Dominic listened impassively.

Their dishes materialized. George regretted ordering seafood soup. There was a lot going on in his bowl. Shrimp. Scallops. Fish. Calamari. George tried not to envision each creature in its natural habitat. It seemed obscene that their fates intersected in this bowl.

Jenny attempted to draw Dominic out by asking him questions about his work. His monosyllabic answers led nowhere. His reticence struck George as hostile, as though he thought Jenny had some sort of agenda.

Which Jenny did, to some extent. She needed to prove something to George. That life was more than a series of random encounters. Or that, taken all together, these random encounters added up to more than the sum of their parts. There was meaning to the way people's lives brushed up against other lives. Nothing was for naught.

George was unnecessarily skeptical and guarded—that was the main lesson.

As Jenny asked Dominic about his second year of community college—she remembered every detail of the article—his grandmother interrupted to ask George what he did for a living.

George felt uncomfortable telling these people he was currently working on a collection of short stories, having no need for a job on account of appearing in a sixty-second hidden-camera commercial.

Jenny spoke up: "George recently discovered he has a talent for comedic acting."

She was in the middle of the story of George's commercial when Dominic's grandmother interrupted again. "When he was little, Dominic wanted to be in the Life cereal commercials. The kid on the box."

"What are you talking about?" Dominic's tone was scornful.

"You wanted to be Mikey," she said. "The new one.

"The real Mikey was getting too old," she told Jenny and George. "On the back of the box, it said they were looking for a new Mikey. Alls you had to do was send a photo."

Wherever this story was going, Dominic appeared mortified by it. In the petulant flush of his cheeks, George saw a trace of the kid he'd known.

"I says, Okay, Dominic, and we send his school photo." Dominic's grandmother smiled. "He was a cute kid. Blond hair, freckles. Cute kid."

Jenny nodded and smiled encouragingly.

"Every time we go to the Stop & Shop, Dominic runs to the cereal aisle. But it's still the old Mikey. *Grandma, Grandma, when's it gonna be me on the box!* I says, Dominic, it could be any boy in America. We have to wait to see who they pick."

Jaw clenched, Dominic shook his head.

"He wanted to be Mikey so bad, he started telling people that's his name. One day his teacher calls . . ." Dominic's grandmother looked directly at Jenny. "Starts talking about a kid named Mikey. I can't remember what he did that day. Teachers was always calling. I says, Mikey? I says, You mean Dominic?"

"What the fuck are you talking about?" Dominic's face was red. There was a sudden appearance of a purple vein on his temple. "Why do you make *shit* up?"

Dominic's grandmother raised her eyebrows and pursed her lips. There was something provocative in her cool reaction to his outburst.

"He doesn't remember anything from when he was a kid," she said matter-of-factly, taking the last bite of her egg roll.

"I remember coming home from school and you in the kitchen," Dominic said, "sucking *dick* for *dope*."

Maintaining her placid composure, Dominic's grandmother finished chewing. Upon swallowing, a single tear materialized in the corner of one of her eyes. It lingered for a moment, like a bead of dew, before descending down her cheek, leaving a trail of mascara in its wake.

Dominic draped an arm around her shoulder. His free hand squeezed the rim of his cap, reinforcing its slope, deepening the shadow it cast over his eyes, which gazed, with tender despondency, out the window.

"Sorry," he said under his breath.

George's discomfort eclipsed his earlier vindication. Though there was some solace in the thought of Jenny's inevitable apology for orchestrating this reunion.

Jenny quietly asked, "Did they ever choose a new Mikey?"

The grandmother nodded. "A girl," she managed in a whisper.

The waiter came to clear their dishes.

"You can just run this," Jenny said, passing him her credit card. "No need to bring us the bill first."

When it was time to leave, Dominic helped his grandmother out of the booth. Once she was on her feet, he helped her put her coat on. He rested a hand on her back as she shuffled toward the exit, pausing by the door to pluck a mint from a dish.

He did not hold the door for George and Jenny, who were a few paces behind.

It was no longer precipitating. The sky remained overcast, but stepping out of the dim restaurant, the light felt shrill. A mechanical chirping indicated it was safe for visually impaired pedestrians to cross Main Street, but there was no one waiting.

"I'm glad we did that," Jenny said when they were in the car. "Even if it was a little awkward at times, I think it was a nice thing to do.

"It was a nice thing to do," she repeated with quiet resolve.

"He obviously felt shy around you," she added, looking at George.

"You think that was it?" he asked.

She pretended not to register his facetious tone. "Oh, yeah. Definitely. You didn't notice he could barely look you in the eye?"

"Oh, I noticed," George said.

Jenny smiled a little. "I thought I was going to cry when he put his arm around her. You could tell how much he loves her. In spite of everything, he *loves* her."

In the beginning, George had been touched by Jenny's inclination to see things a certain way—or at least profess to. She'd once teared up over a commercial that showed a couple aging into senior citizens. Her declaration of such mawkish sentiments now left him cold. It made her seem simple. Stupid and simple.

But she was neither of these things, because there was an element of provocation in such declarations. She was baiting George to respond in the opposite fashion. It was a way of pathologizing his disposition, as if he needed that.

"I think you're smarter than that," he told her as Jenny pulled out. "I think you saw their relationship for what it was, but you'd prefer to put a bow on it and move on.

"I'd like to think I'm not overestimating your social-emotional

204 • The Book of George

intelligence, or whatever you want to call it, to believe you recognize that the little reunion back there was not such a *nice thing*. More than awkward, it was upsetting. A shitty experience for all parties. One that never needed to happen.

"Do you think it's cute?" George asked. "The whole dopey Pollyanna thing. Is that why you do it?"

Jenny was silent. George felt guilty. He wrestled with the instinct to go further, say something even more hurtful, inciting her to retaliate with a barb of her own, to settle the score.

Finally, she spoke. "Sometimes I think you forget that when I was eight, I saw my dad carried out of our house in a body bag."

Jenny had waited until a few months into their relationship before telling George about her father's suicide. She told him the whole story, as she remembered it, as well as details she was too young to have known or understood at the time, which she would learn later from her mom. George was impressed by her plainspoken candor. He assumed it was something she discussed freely and often. But that would be the most she ever spoke of it with him.

It was something she'd wanted to get out of the way, he later concluded, so that there would be nothing left for him to ask about later. George understood. There were few things more off-putting than other people's attempts to elicit the details of your personal tragedy—the gingerly probing questions, the awkward platitudes when those failed. Jenny loathed being the object of others' sympathy.

"I don't think you're a dopey Pollyanna," George said. "I didn't mean that.

"You're resilient and brave.

"I love you," he told her.

She refused to say it back. She was sitting unnaturally erect, gripping the wheel like it was the helm of a ship.

"Do you ever think what it's like to be around you all the time?" she said bitterly. "Your moods—*your* energy?"

A lance of silver light punctured the cloud cover.

"I'm sorry," George said.

* * *

He woke up as they were crossing the Brooklyn Bridge. It was dusk. Lights twinkled above, from behind, and up ahead. The dashboard also glowed with lights.

Physically, George felt a little better.

"Thanks for driving," he said.

Jenny turned her podcast off. "What?"

"I said, *thanks for driving*."

Jenny nodded.

"I love you," George told her.

"Your tree," he said as they got off the bridge. "Plucky little guy. Do you think someone planted it, or it grew on its own?"

"That's a different tree," Jenny coldly informed him. "The tree you're referring to is off the ramp to get onto the BQE, not the bridge."

After crossing Atlantic, they hit a streak of green lights. Jenny slipped through a few yellows but stopped at the final light before their block.

There was a spot right in front of their building. Another car got to it first. An SUV.

"It's not going to fit," George said, as it struggled to back in. "Let's just wait until it gives up."

Jenny pulled up behind the spot and put on her blinkers. The vehicle pulled out and tried again.

"Make that twelve hundred hours." George glanced at Jenny. "I forgot to include time spent looking for parking upon returning to the city in my estimate."

"They better not get divorced," Jenny said dryly. "Wouldn't that be embarrassing for them? Knowing we're all thinking of the hours we spent traveling to and from their wedding."

206 • *The Book of George*

The vehicle pulled in and out, in and out.

"Air smells good," George said, opening the window. "Faint odor of spring." He sniffed again. "Those bulbs you helped plant in the park, they should be coming up soon."

Jenny shrugged.

"Next year I'd like to be part of that," he said. "I don't care how early you have to get up, I'm there. Give me one of those green jerseys, put me to work." Jenny was focused on the parking spot. "You think I'm all talk," he said. "I mean it. Sign me up.

"Make some new friends while I'm at it. Some older people. Actual grown-ups."

"Good for you, George," Jenny said.

"How's Linda?" he asked.

Jenny shook her head.

"Barbara?"

"I have no idea who you're talking about," she said.

"That friend you made on the volunteer crew. The older woman you used to talk about. The one who knew all about birds. Who calls the weeds, or whatever, 'this charmer.'"

"Carol," Jenny said.

"How is she? Have you checked in on her? She doing okay?"

Jenny shook her head wearily. "I don't know, George. I assume so."

"That was cool what she told you about how pigeons breastfeed. Never heard that before."

"Fucker," Jenny said, as the SUV finally managed to wedge in.

"That's pretty impressive," George said. "I didn't think it was possible."

"Can I have a cigarette?" Jenny asked as they looped back down Clinton.

"They're gone," he told her. "I threw them away when we got to the hotel."

Jenny looked at his lap. "I'm supposed to believe that's a deck of cards in your pocket?"

George took out the pack. There were only two left.

"I might as well have the last one," he said, extracting both.

They lapped the block again. And again. Jenny gradually expanded the radius of their search. There were no parking garages in Carroll Gardens. There was one in Cobble Hill, but you had to be a member.

"Let's try those sketchy little streets by the Gowanus," George proposed.

"Did you know this is the oldest retractable wooden drawbridge in America?" he asked as they crossed the canal.

"I did," Jenny responded curtly. "I was actually the one who told you that."

"So, Benji thinks I should invest in cryptocurrency," George said. "He thinks I should put all my Super Bowl money in . . .

"Thoughts?"

Jenny shrugged. "It's your money."

"It's amazing what New Yorkers endure," George reflected as they circled back, having found nothing. "Can you imagine people from another part of the country putting up with something like this?"

Jenny pulled up in front of a bodega and asked George to get her a Snickers.

"It's on me," he said as she started to give him cash.

George bought two Snickers, potato chips, a Gatorade, and a bouquet of carnations.

"And it's not even Valentine's Day," he said, handing her the flowers.

Jenny smiled sardonically. "You shouldn't have."

When another forty minutes had passed, she double-parked in front of their building.

"There's no need for us both to suffer through this," she told George. "You can go in."

"That's very nice of you," he said.

Before getting out of the car, George reached across the console and took Jenny's hand.

"I love you," he told her, once again, unprompted, which she was always complaining he never did.

Jenny's fingers remained limp. She sat quietly, looking straight ahead. "Okay," she finally said. "What are you going to do about it?"

12. SWASTIKA

George, 35

Jeremiah owned an apartment in a prewar building across the
street from Washington Square Park. It had a balcony, a kitchen
that was big enough for a real table, a dining room, two bedrooms,
and a living room that was easily twice the size of George's studio
sublet above a psychic parlor on Smith Street. By New York stan-
dards, the apartment was huge.

It was about to get even bigger.

When Kylie got pregnant with twins, the apartment next door
went on the market. What the heck, they thought, and bought it.
They were a social couple. Wouldn't it be fun, they decided, to invite
their friends to come over and paint the walls before they got knocked
down to combine the two apartments into one?

Food and drinks would be served.

George did not covet Jeremiah's money, or anything about the
way his life looked on paper. What he envied—which was also the
source of his contempt—was Jeremiah's comfort in the world. His
lack of self-consciousness that enabled him to throw a party that
was essentially a celebration of how rich he was.

The party was in full swing when George arrived. People had
brought their kids. Solly was there but couldn't socialize, because
Ira, who was now two, was having a tantrum—or, as Solly put it,
"having some very big feelings."

The energy was shrill, chaotic. George poured himself a drink at
the serve-yourself bar, picked up a paintbrush and a Dixie cup of
red paint that had been left out on a tray, walked down the hall into

one of the bedrooms where no one was, and painted a swastika on the bare wall.

He wasn't sure where the impulse had come from. George wasn't anti-Semitic. He was half Jewish.

It had been a difficult day. George had been fired from his job as a book club facilitator. A book club facilitator! The club had met earlier that week. They had read Louis Auchincloss's *The Rector of Justin*. In preparation, George had read the book extremely carefully, making notes in the margins, which he'd later typed up and synthesized into a series of discussion points. The book tackled a lot of themes—religion, tradition, class, gender, sexuality, patriarchy, the point of education—and the document ended up being eight pages single-spaced. Suspecting he wouldn't be able to get to it all in the course of an hour, George arrived with copies for each member of the group to take home.

The book club, which consisted of a group of eleven friends, all women in their fifties, had existed for over a decade, but George was a recent addition. They wanted a facilitator to help keep the conversation on topic—"to prevent us from talking about our kids," it was explained. It was only the second time he'd attended a meeting, and George thought it had gone well. But that morning he'd gotten a call from the founder of the book club—the woman who had hired him. The members had been "disappointed" by the discussion. They felt George had done too much of the talking, and spent too much time explaining the book to them and not enough asking them questions. They would like him to ask them more questions. Questions such as *Who was your favorite character and why?* Perhaps George could google "how to be a book club facilitator."

George turned the swastika into four connected cubes and colored these in. He added a triangle on top of the box, so that it looked like a house. Next to the house he painted a stick-figure family: parents, kids, dog. Then he rejoined the party in the living room and helped himself to another scotch.

Good for you, Jerry, George thought, surveying the premises.

Jeremiah, who had never been quite in the thick of things in college, had managed to cultivate a social universe in which he was now a player. The people he surrounded himself with reinforced his image of himself and his lifestyle. They were almost all couples. People rarely used the term *yuppie* anymore, but that's what they were.

It was a pretty boring crowd, but George surprised himself by having a good time, drifting around the room, amusing people by being a benign asshole.

Benji and his new girlfriend showed up but only stayed for one drink. George knew a few other guests from college, and other gatherings Jeremiah had hosted, but there were also a lot of new people, which meant introductions.

"And this is Homer," a woman said, holding up a toddler.

"Goochy-goochy-goo," George said dryly, and wiggled his finger.

When the child recoiled, the mom looked embarrassed.

"He's normally the friendliest guy," she insisted, and started telling a story about how on the way over, he'd smiled and waved to everyone they passed on the street, including a homeless man.

"I think he's hangry," the child's father interrupted, offering the child a paper plate of smoked salmon.

"Come back in a few," the mom told George. "He'll be his sweet self again."

"Too late," George responded. "The impression has been made."

Other people had been watching the interaction, and there were chuckles as he walked away.

George had been feeling like a loser recently. It was nice to be reminded that he could be good company. A fun, irreverent presence.

As evening became night, people with kids began to peel off, and those that remained were more interested in drinking than painting. Jeremiah turned the music up.

Carrie Michaels appeared.

George hadn't seen Carrie Michaels in years.

"Carrie Michaels!" he said when they crossed paths at the bar table. They'd never been particularly close, but he felt a swell of affection for her now in her ridiculous fur-collared coat and red cowboy boots.

She returned his warm greeting. "George!" Her eyelids were covered in glitter. "Do you know if there's any more ice?"

George needed some, too. They went into the kitchen. A circle of women was gathered in front of the refrigerator. Not wanting to interrupt, George and Carrie paused, waiting for them to notice they were in the way and move aside.

It seemed like it might be a while. Kylie was carrying on about how hard it was going to be to be "homeless" while the renovation took place. It was estimated to take six to nine months, during which time they'd be renting an apartment in Gramercy.

"Knowing contractors, that means a year," someone said.

"And co-op boards," another said. "We had the biggest asshole on ours. An architect who liked to throw his power around."

The subject changed to the food preferences of toddlers.

"If it were up to him, he would eat cookies all day, given the choice," one of the women lamented of her child.

"You don't need to say that," Carrie Michaels said, addressing the speaker. "You already said it was 'up to him,' so you don't need to add 'given the choice.'"

There was a frosty silence as the women looked at Carrie.

"Sorry, I'm a copy editor," she said.

"For the *New Yorker*," she added quietly as the women continued to stare at her.

"We forgot to get ice," George said as the two of them stepped back into the living room.

Carrie shrugged and put a cigarette in her mouth.

"I'm not sure you should do that in here," George said as she procured a lighter.

Carrie smiled defiantly. "Isn't the point of the party you can do whatever you want, make a mess, it doesn't matter, it's all getting redone?" The cigarette bobbed in her lips. "Like if I wanted to, I could just pop a squat right in the middle of the floor?"

"You know how people get about cigarette smoke," George said.

The music suddenly cut off.

"Folks." Jeremiah's voice cut through the din. "Folks," he repeated in a louder voice.

Carrie looked at George and rolled her eyes. He assumed she was thinking the same thing he was—since when did Jeremiah call people "folks"?

"Just a quick announcement, folks," Jeremiah said. "We're only painting the walls in this room, where the drop cloth has been laid out."

There was some murmuring.

Someone painted in their bedroom.

Who would do that?

It got on their rug.

"Let's go out to the terrace," George said to Carrie. "We can smoke out there."

"Don't you have your own?" Carrie said when George asked for one of hers.

George explained his new rule: he couldn't buy cigarettes, but he was allowed to accept them from other people.

"But I didn't offer you one." Carrie passed him her pack. "You're actively soliciting."

"I know," George said. "Which means now I have to make small talk . . ."

George was surprised to hear that Carrie also lived in Carroll Gardens.

"I would've guessed Williamsburg," he told her.

"Please." Carrie made a face. "That place is for kids."

"Do you ever forget how old you are?" George asked.

"Yeah," Carrie said. "Like I think I'm thirty-five, but I might be thirty-six? It's not an automatic thing I know anymore. I have to pause and think about it."

Jeremiah stepped outside. "Don't tell Kylie," he said, taking a drag of Carrie's cigarette.

Carrie smirked. "Do you remember how you used to inhale cigarettes like you were taking a hit of a bong?"

"I don't know what you're talking about," Jeremiah said.

"I taught him how to smoke," Carrie told George. Glancing back at Jeremiah, she added, with a little wink, "Among other things."

"You guys slept together?" George asked.

Carrie nodded and Jeremiah promptly went back inside.

"He was a virgin," Carrie said proudly. "I took his virginity."

"I never knew this," George said. "When we were freshmen?"

"Just once. It was right after winter break, you and Solly hadn't gotten back yet and we were hanging out one night . . . Why do you look so shocked?"

"I dunno," George said. "You don't seem like each other's type."

"You don't think I was his *type*?" Carrie feigned indignation.

"You know what I mean," George said. "It's a compliment. He has a history of more basic girls."

"Are you trying to say that if I was a little more J.Crew, all *this* could've been mine? As if I'd fucking want, like, a suburban house in Manhattan?"

George wondered out loud how much the apartment had cost.

"Two-point-one," Carrie said. "For this one. The other one, the one they just bought, was one-point-eight. And I wasn't Googlestalking. I was just trying to look up the directions to get here, and a real estate listing popped up."

"Okay," George said. "So we're basically talking four million before the renovation."

"And that's not including maintenance," Carrie added.

"It's amazing how much being a documentary filmmaker pays," George said.

Carrie looked confused. "You know he has family money . . ."

"Oh." She smiled. "You were being facetious."

Carrie's gaze drifted toward the skyline. "If I had this kind of money, I wouldn't buy this apartment. I'd get a brownstone with a garden."

"It would be nice to just step outside and feel the earth beneath your feet," George agreed.

"You must have made a nice chunk of change in that Super Bowl commercial," Carrie said. "I didn't see it, someone just told me about it. They said you were really funny."

"I was okay."

"What about the money? How much was it?"

George shook his head.

"Oh, *come on*. Everyone used to talk about their salaries, and now all of a sudden we're in our thirties, it's gauche . . ."

"Don't like talking about it," George said.

"Why? It's gone? You spent it all on shoes?" Carrie gestured to George's ratty New Balances.

"Crypto," George said. "Benji convinced me to invest it all in crypto. He was on my case about it as soon as I got the check. It took him a year and a half to convince me to do it, and when prices started going crazy I did it, and then as soon as I joined the party, it crashed. Story of my life."

Carrie laughed.

"I'm sorry," she said. "I always laugh at bad things. It's not funny. Carrie's face turned serious. "My dog died," she said.

"The one you had in college that you used to bring everywhere?"

Eyes glistening, Carrie nodded. "Frankie."

"So, he lived a long life," George said.

"Very long. He'd have been seventeen last week.

"This is embarrassing," she said, wiping a tear from her cheek. "It's been almost three months and I still can't really talk about it without crying."

"It's not embarrassing," George said. "It's a totally normal reaction. I don't think I ever got over losing Freckles."

"Was that your childhood dog?"

"Yep."

The windows of Jeremiah's multimillion-dollar apartment buzzed as the remaining revelers shouted along to the chorus of "Come On Eileen." George had an involuntary image of himself picking up a stone flowerpot and hurling it through the French doors.

"To be honest," George said, "I don't know if having a dog is worth it, having to go through that."

This made Carrie laugh. "Oh, George, then what's the point of anything?"

"That's the question, isn't it." George sighed.

"You used to do this funny thing," Carrie said. "I can't remember exactly, but it had something to do with a penis in an airport?"

George nodded. "You want to see my impression of a clinically depressed penis going through security at an airport?"

Carrie's face brightened. "Yeah."

"Okay," George said. "It's been a few years. I might need another drink."

They went back in and refilled their cups. George did his impression of a clinically depressed penis going through security at an airport.

Others watched.

"This was his party trick in college," Jeremiah explained to his new friends who didn't know George.

George could tell he was embarrassed. There were some polite smiles, but it didn't land the way it had in the early 2000s.

But Carrie thought it was funny. She laughed so hard that she started coughing. It was the cough of a smoker. Thick, deep, wet; a whiff of decay and mortality.

George felt a twinge of contempt, that she would cough like that in the company of strangers, even though he had, on many occasions, prior to cutting back.

"You should get that checked out," someone said.

"S'okay," Carrie rasped, blinking back tears. "Just a lil' tickle."

She smiled meekly as Jeremiah handed her a cup of water.

After she recovered, Carrie served herself a vodka tonic and started painting something on the wall. George's contempt passed. There was

something plucky and incorrigible about her, and it was sort of adorable.

"What *is* that?" George asked.

"A llama," Carrie told him.

"Are you kidding?" he said. "That's terrible. Are you sure you're a
righty? Do you want to try again with your other hand?"

Carrie giggled as he insulted her other attempts at various animals. Beneath her silly makeup, she was pretty with her gap-tooth
smile and freckles.

They went out for another cigarette, came back in to refill their
cups, and went back out.

George was about to kiss Carrie Michaels when the door opened
and Jeremiah said, "Hey, kids, we're closing up shop."

Suspicious timing, George thought.

As they rode the subway back to Carroll Gardens, George asked,
"What's up with the two dots over the second vowel?"

Carrie yawned, looking confused.

"In words that have two of the same vowel next to each other,
like *cooperate*, why do they put two dots over the second *o*?"

When it was obvious that Carrie didn't know what he was talking
about, George said, "You're not really a copy editor for the *New Yorker*."

Carrie looked at her lap. "*Women's Wear Daily*," she said quietly.

By the time they made it back to his apartment, they were both
too tired to do much of anything.

"I'm sorry," Carrie said.

"It's okay," George told her, and confessed that it was probably
for the best because he had a patch of eczema on his penis and he
was worried that sex might irritate it.

"It's not funny," he said when Carrie burst into giggles. "It's actually pretty demoralizing."

They fell asleep spooning but when George woke up the next
morning, he was alone. Carrie must have slipped out. He was relieved.
There was never a time when George missed Jenny more than waking
up in bed next to a person who was not her. The effort it required

to get through whatever this person's expectations of the morning were—brunch, coffee, even a simple walk to the subway station—was taxing, fraught with awkwardness, fatigue, and weak attempts to maintain the impression his more charming, animated drunken self had made the previous night. George had yet to pursue a second date with any of the women he'd met over the dating apps, though he'd slept with a few, maybe half a dozen, he'd lost track. There was no denying the excitement of sex with a new person, but the comfort of the familiar—that was something George had taken for granted, among other things about Jenny.

After getting home from Jeremiah's wedding, Jenny had given him an ultimatum. She refused to call it that, but that's what it was: she didn't care about a wedding, but she wanted to have a child, and if George couldn't commit to that, she was out. George wasn't against the idea of having children—he'd always imagined he would—but he couldn't fathom trying to start the process immediately, when there were still many things he hadn't done. But Jenny insisted it had to happen in the next couple of years, as she was almost thirty-five and didn't want to take any chances.

George didn't want to string her along and hurt her chances of having a baby.

They both agreed it would be easier not to keep in touch. They didn't have any mutual friends, so George didn't know what Jenny was up to or anything about her life, but he thought of her often. She'd been the most consistent person in his life for over a decade, and now, suddenly, she wasn't in it at all.

George couldn't drink like that anymore. The cigarettes exacerbated his hangover. He felt disgusting, exhausted, depleted—physically and spiritually on the verge of collapse. Seeing it was only ten, he tried to fall back asleep, but a few minutes later his phone rang.

It was Carrie, telling him she was *running behind.*

George was confused. "Running behind?"

He had promised to meet her in the diamond district at noon, she reminded him. She had to sell a necklace she'd inherited from her godmother and needed George to accompany her so that she didn't get ripped off.

George drank water, took Advil, brushed his teeth, started to get dressed, ran back to the bathroom, vomited in the toilet, took some more Advil, brushed his teeth again, and headed out the door.

They met on the corner of Forty-Seventh and Sixth.

Carrie looked surprisingly kempt. She was wearing glasses and a navy peacoat and had done something different with her hair. The contrast to how she normally presented herself was striking.

"I like your hair," George said.

"It's a wig. I'm supposed to look like a basic bitch.

"You're my husband," she announced, holding up her hand to show George the ring on her ring finger.

"You've really never been here before?" Carrie said as they reached the corner of West Forty-Seventh Street.

"Not that I recall," George said.

"Let me explain how it works. The men standing outside the storefronts are mind readers. If you're just passing through trying to get to Sixth Avenue, they ignore you. But if you're here for a reason, they pick up on that and they'll start competing for your business.

"I'll show you," she said. "Walk a few paces behind me, but don't make it obvious that we're together."

Carrie began walking. No one took note of her until the end of the block, when a man said, "You selling?"

Carrie whipped her head around to make sure George had caught this. "What did I tell you?" She grinned. "Mind readers."

"But why did you ignore him?" George asked as they waited to cross to the other side of the street. "I thought we were here so you could sell a necklace."

"You don't go with the first person who tries to get your business," Carrie explained with an air of condescension.

They crossed the street, and this time George walked beside Carrie as they strolled down the block. They caught the attention of a Hasidic man. "Looking for a ring?" he asked.

"We're already married." Carrie flashed her fake wedding ring. "My mother died. We're looking to get a quote on a necklace she left me. I need cash so we can pay for a proper burial."

"I'll take you to my father." The man gestured for them to follow him. "He'll give you best price."

George had assumed they would be entering a store, dealing with someone across a counter, but that was not how things worked in the diamond district. They were led through a discreet entrance of a nondescript building, where they were subjected to a security check. After passing through a metal detector, they rode an elevator to the eighth floor. Like cattle being led to the slaughterhouse, George thought, as they gamely followed the man down a long, narrow hall.

"This is my father," the man said, opening the door to an office.

An older, fatter version of the man sat at a desk. Above him a sign on the wall read: IN GOD WE TRUST, EVERYONE ELSE PAYS CASH.

Carrie took the necklace out of her purse and handed it to the older man.

The son spoke to his father in Yiddish.

"Did you tell him what the money's for?" Carrie asked the son.

"*Aleha ha-shalom*," the father said.

"That means 'rest in peace,'" the son translated.

"Thank you," Carrie said.

The father put the necklace on a scale and pulled out a calculator.

"Two hundred fifty-one dollars," he said.

Carrie looked at George. "That barely covers the price of her coffin," she said, and stood up to leave.

Variations of this scene played out in three more back rooms. George started to get annoyed. Carrie was clearly enjoying this, it was a game to her, but he had better things to do.

"I don't understand what you're holding out for," George whispered when she received a fifth offer, once again, for two hundred fifty-one dollars. "The price of gold fluctuates on a daily basis, that's why they're all quoting the same price. It's a mathematical equation. You're not going to do better."

Carrie begrudgingly accepted the offer.

"It's just so unfair," she complained as they stepped outside. "That they get to sell it in their store for so much more."

"That's what middlemen do," George said. "That's how they earn a living."

As they walked through Times Square, Carrie pulled out the cash and began fanning herself. "Do you know how much coke I can buy with this?"

"What are you doing?" George said. "Put it away."

Carrie laughed and put the money away.

"For the record, I was just kidding," she said as they descended the steps of the subway. "It's to help pay my rent."

After they got off at Carroll Street, Carrie tried to give George one of the bills. "Your commission," she said. "Just take it."

When George refused, she insisted that he at least come back to her apartment and let her make him a sandwich.

George had had enough of Carrie Michaels for one day, but he didn't know how to say no to her. And it had been a while since someone had made him a sandwich.

She lived on Hicks Street, right next to the Brooklyn Queens Expressway. Her apartment was on the first floor, which meant there were bars over the windows. It was even tinier than George's, sparsely but cozily furnished. Everything looked delicate and was arranged in a way that looked very deliberate: love seat, armchair, record player.

George felt oversize and clumsy. "Is that the bathroom?" he asked, pointing to a door.

Carrie nodded. "You have to hold the flush down for several seconds for it to work. If it doesn't work, wait at least a minute till you try it again."

"I'm just peeing," he felt obligated to say.

When George emerged, Carrie was standing at the counter making lunch.

"Let me tell you how to make egg salad," she said in a funny voice. "Listen up, I've got a really good recipe. First you boil some eggs. Then you peel off the shells. If pieces of shell get stuck, don't fret, just hold the egg under some running water. Eventually, it'll flake off. Then you take a fork and mash the eggs. If you like, you can use a potato masher. Add a scoop of mayonnaise, a dash of salt, a sprinkle of pepper . . ."

She turned her head to look at George.

"Shelley Duvall," she explained. "From Robert Altman's *3 Women*."

"Oh." Looking down, George could see the track marks of a vacuum on the rug. "I don't think I remember that scene."

He wandered over to the bookshelf, which was a bunch of wooden milk crates stacked on top of one another. The books were arranged alphabetically by author. The hardcovers were in dust jackets. George was impressed to see a copy of Anne Carson's *Autobiography of Red*.

"Thank you," George said as Carrie handed him a plate and a paper napkin folded in a triangle.

"You can sit," she told him when he started to eat the sandwich standing up.

Carrie was on the love seat.

George took the armchair. This tidy little apartment depressed him. It altered his sense of Carrie being a wild and free person, not caring what others thought.

After taking a bite, Carrie dabbed the corners of her mouth with her napkin. "Can you believe we're almost in our late thirties?"

"Fucking depressing," George said.

"It feels like no one's growing up," Carrie said. "Like we'll always just be a bunch of kids.

"And not in a fun, 'young at heart' kind of way," she added. "In a self-obsessed, spiritually immature way."

"Jeremiah seems kind of adult," George said.

Carrie raised her eyebrows as she finished chewing. "Superficially, maybe. Emotionally, he'll always be an eighteen-year-old virgin whose mother shops for him.

"Our generation sucks," she declared. "For a while I thought it was the internet. Facebook. Google. Never having real debates because you just google the answer to whatever it is you disagree about. But I've been thinking about it more, and I think it's also that we've never had any real hardships as a society. Wars, famines—"

"We've had wars," George said. "And the 2008 financial crisis."

"It's not the same," Carrie said. "I'm talking about *real* hardships. Something that affects the entire country, rich people, too. A dictator, a plague, that kind of thing."

"We had 9/11," George said.

"Oh, please." Carrie scoffed. "I remember after 9/11 all the guys in our dorm put down their bongs and video games and began pacing the hall whining about being drafted. At first I was annoyed— thousands of people had just died, and they were trying to make it about themselves—but then I got kind of excited. I kept thinking of you all in uniforms standing on a tarmac, and I'm not going to lie, it was a good look. You were suddenly men. It was romantic.

"I wrote a poem about it," Carrie said, carrying their empty plates to the sink.

George had forgotten Carrie was part of the poetry scene in college. He had a vague memory of attending a reading she participated in, in a basement somewhere, and being impressed by whatever it was she'd read.

Returning to the love seat, she pulled her wig off and ran her fingers through her real hair, which seemed thin and dull in comparison. "I actually just found out it's getting published in the *Paris Review*."

"Wow," George said. "Congratulations."

"Not really," Carrie said. "But Omega took another poem I wrote."

"What?"

"Small press you've never heard of." Carrie stood up and pulled a booklet off the bookshelf.

"I've got extra copies," she said. "Read it when you get home."

She went to the bathroom.

George read the poem. It was about her dead dog.

In the poem the dog was alive, liberated from the suffering of old age, a puppy again, gamboling through the fields of Prospect Park. It made George think of Freckles, her salty puppy breath, her staring into George's eyes, her excitement upon waking up in the morning and finding herself in the company of the boy whose bed she'd fallen asleep in, as though it were some miracle. Together! Another day!

Carrie returned. George was aware of her scrutinizing his face.

When it was clear he wasn't going to confess to having read her poem, she asked, "If you could've been our age in another decade, which one would you choose?"

"Not this one," George said. He had given this a lot of thought over the years. "Maybe the seventies. Early seventies."

Carrie looked at him expectantly. "Now you're supposed to ask me, *Carrie, what decade would you choose to be born in?*"

"I see you thriving in the twenties," George said.

Carrie looked pleased. "Really?"

George nodded. "You'd be cool," he said. "Like Dorothy Parker."

Carrie pursed her lips. It looked like she might tear up. "Did you know she's my hero?"

George shook his head.

"Dorothy Parker is my *hero*."

The silence amplified the sound of the BQE. George wanted to leave.

"Do you ever make an inventory of your assets and think, It doesn't add up?" Carrie twisted the fake wedding ring off her finger and placed it on the table.

George shrugged. He wasn't in the mood to have this conversation.

"Like I know I'm funny," Carrie said, "but I'm not as funny as . . . Well, a bunch of people I know are funnier than I am. I know some things, but I'm not the smartest person in the room. In fact, there are huge holes in my education because I was too fucking self-absorbed to take advantage of what I should've learned in college. I'm definitely not accomplished. As far as looks go"—she sat up a little straighter—"I'd say I'm slightly above average for New York, depending on the day, depending on the neighborhood . . ."

She looked at George, as though inviting him to weigh in.

"I've got some things going on, but when I put them all together, it doesn't add up . . ."

George felt something sharp on the armrest. It was the needle of a feather. As he pulled it out, the down of another feather now protruded from the same spot. He pulled that out, too.

"Sorry," he said, noticing Carrie staring at him. "I'll stop."

"I guess that's part of growing up," Carrie continued. "Coming to terms with your mediocrity.

"Unless, of course, you're Jeremiah . . ."

"Jeremiah's a hack," George said.

Carrie looked a little shocked and a bit thrilled.

"I mean, on a technical level, he's very competent. He has good instincts when it comes to subject matter. But I wouldn't call him an artist."

"I didn't." Carrie bit back a conspiratorial smile. "I've actually always thought his films are overrated . . ."

George tried to think of a way to extricate himself.

"I'm glad I went to the party last night," Carrie said. "I thought it was going to be stupid, I almost wasn't going to go." She rested a socked foot on the armchair, allowing her toe to graze his thigh. "But then I wouldn't have bumped into you."

Now George really felt trapped. He picked up a small round throw pillow and tried to balance it on his index finger like a basketball.

And then he farted.

He waited for Carrie to laugh—it made quite an impressive sound—but she did not. She avoided his gaze, her cheeks darkened.

It took a moment for the odor to register.

"*Well.*" George sighed, putting the pillow down. "I should probably get going."

Carrie withdrew her leg. "I'll walk you out," she said.

As they reached the bottom of the stoop, she procured two cigarettes and offered one to George, who shook his head, then said, "Eh, actually, maybe I'll take one for later."

Carrie raised her eyebrows. "You want me to give you one for *later*?"

"Sure." George held out his hand. "If you don't mind."

"Dude," she said, dropping it in his palm. "You've got to work on your manners."

"Merci beaucoup," George said, tucking it behind his ear.

"You're welcome," she said crisply.

"*Well*," George said. "Nice catching up. I'm sure we'll run into each other in the neighborhood."

Carrie laughed dryly. She was miffed. George worried he'd hurt her feelings.

"Keep writing poems," he said, in what was intended to be a friendly, morale-boosting tone.

"Keep facilitating book clubs," she responded.

George raised a hand in a limp wave and turned to go. He could not walk fast enough. He was conscious that with every step he took, he was that much farther away from her, and it was a relief.

Two blocks later, George surprised himself by turning around.

Carrie was sitting on the stoop where they'd parted, still smoking, head bowed as she scrolled through her phone. The cigarette was long. It must have been her second.

"Carrie," George said, summoning her attention. "That was kind of a fucked up thing to say. *Keep facilitating book clubs.*"

"Oh, come on, George. I was being playful. It was a joke."

"It was a fucked up thing to say," George repeated.

Carrie shrugged and took a drag. "Well, that fart was kind of fucked up."

"What?"

"You pissed me off with that fart." She spoke with the smoke in her mouth and then gracefully exhaled.

"You're upset that I *farted*?" George laughed in disbelief. "Pardon me for having a little gas after a night of heavy drinking."

"That wasn't 'a little gas,' George. That wasn't an *oops, I farted* fart. That was a protracted, theatrically loud, shotgun, illegal-fireworks-from-Chinatown kind of fart. It was the kind of fart you do when you're all alone. To make sure you're still alive. To reassure yourself that you actually exist."

George was impressed by her riff on the fart. In another mood he might tell her that she should write it down, maybe a poem would come out of it.

Carrie took a drag. "You don't fart like that in front of someone you shared a bed with the night before."

"I think my ex-girlfriend would testify otherwise."

"That's different. We're not in a *relationship*." Carrie looked at the ground as she ashed. "When you fart like that, it's saying, I don't see you as a woman . . ."

Now George understood why the fart had offended her. He felt bad.

"It was a gross fart. I'm sorry it happened in your apartment.

"I have a delicate stomach," he added.

Carrie looked amused. "A delicate stomach?"

"It's true," George said. "But I should've tried to hold it in. I'm sorry."

Carrie nodded. "Thank you."

George waited for her to apologize.

"Your turn," he said.

"My turn?"

"To apologize for the book club comment."

Carrie shook her head. "I was being sincere. I think you should keep on being a book club facilitator. It's a decent job. Don't give up so easily."

"That's not what you meant by it and you know it."

"Who are you to tell me the intention behind my words?" Carrie said.

George should've left then; she was playing games, she was in a mood, but he felt compelled to reason with her.

"You know, in case it's not obvious, I feel pretty shitty about myself. Because I don't have much going on right now, I took that book club job really seriously. I spent a lot of time preparing for that meeting. If I can't do that—if I'm not good enough to be a *fucking book club facilitator* . . ."

"George." Carrie briefly closed her eyes. "You not being a good match for that book club is not a referendum on your intellect. From what you told me, it sounds like you were too smart for their purposes. You didn't even get fired. They gave you some feedback about what they want, and you *quit*."

Carrie stomped out her cigarette and stood up.

"You want my advice? Go back and be what they want. Ask dumb questions, nod when they answer. *Humor* them. They're paying you to make them feel smart, not impress them with your own insights.

"Listen, I get it, it's frustrating not to be able to flex your own brilliance. You should see the *shit* they give me to edit. You think I've never been tempted to rewrite the articles completely so that they reflect my level of education and critical-thinking skills? To make them something I'd be proud to be associated with? Or at least not hugely embarrassed? Well, guess what? I wouldn't have a job if I did that. I know what's expected of me, and I deliver.

"You need to get over yourself, George. You have this Eeyore affect going on, you act all pathetic and self-loathing, but you're actually extremely egotistical. You think you're too good to be anything short of exceptional, and maybe you could've been exceptional, if you'd had the humility and discipline to commit to whatever it was you decided to do, and really go for it, which is scary, because what if you were just okay, or merely competent. That would be worse, in your eyes, than not even making it at all. Just being average."

"I don't know where this is coming from," George said. "You

don't even know me. You have no idea what I've been through. You know nothing about me."

"Oh, please, I know you. I know *exactly* who you are . . ." Carrie's voice trilled over the traffic. "You're a privileged white guy who grew up thinking you were God's gift. No one ever told you your shit stinks. Now you're bitter about the fact that for the first time in history, being a privileged white guy is not going to get you all the things."

"Wow," George said. "I don't even know how to respond."

He was aware that he was grinning. Jenny had called his attention to this; when he was really angry, he grinned. She said it scared her. That he looked like Jack Nicholson in *The Shining*.

Carrie didn't look scared. She looked smug.

George spoke in a measured tone. "I come back here, to tell you that you hurt my feelings, to show you I'm a vulnerable person, a person with feelings, and *this* is how you respond? Pigeonholing me? As if you're not a *privileged white girl* yourself?"

He searched Carrie's face for remorse. She gave him a cool little shrug.

George was halfway down the block when he heard her call out to him. Her voice was muffled in the rush of the BQE, but it sounded like she said:

"It's never too late to change!"

Or maybe it was *Don't ever change!*, like what people write in yearbooks.

13. BAD MEN

George, 36

While a visiting professor at a liberal arts college, George's first cousin once removed, the Shakespeare scholar of the late-night voicemail from long ago, made an off-color joke about the conversion of a copy room into a lactation room. The previous winter he'd propositioned a young editor at a journal that was publishing an essay he'd written. At a party for the launch of his most recent book, he'd tried to engage a publicist in a conversation about anal sex.

George was not close to this relative, and none of these events would have impacted his life had they not shared both first and last names, which appeared on an online spreadsheet featuring allegations of sexual misconduct attributed to various male figures in the media world.

The document went viral.

George was living at his mother's apartment. He had moved in after letting his lease expire on a studio that had a mold problem, which he'd concluded was the reason for his eczema. The rash started on his wrists and forearms, and then cropped up other places: armpits, back, face, groin, legs, penis. A doctor at a walk-in clinic prescribed steroids in addition to the Benadryl he took each night to sleep.

George assumed the eczema would go away after moving into Ellen's, but that did not seem to be happening. Isolated islands of rash met up with each other, colonizing vast swathes of his body. George had never realized eczema, which sounded like the punchline of a joke, could be so debilitating.

The extra bedroom in Ellen's apartment was wide enough to fit a pair of twin beds separated by about half a foot. There was no room for a dresser or any other furniture. The wallpaper—courtesy of the previous owners—depicted bucolic scenes of early American life. Men in knickers fetched water from wells, young maidens communed on mossy logs on the banks of gurgling brooks. Inches from George's pillow, a boy milked a cow.

The light that came in from the shafted window was perpetually gray, making it impossible to tell what time of day it was or if it was sunny or overcast.

George might have felt claustrophobic were it not for a twelve-foot ceiling, which gave the room the feeling of a tomb rather than a coffin.

A few days after George arrived, Cressida showed up. She was seven months pregnant and supposed to be on bed rest—something to do with her cervix. Her roommate/boyfriend/unborn child's father worked from home, and she discovered that she could not tolerate being trapped in an apartment with him. Things about him that had never been an issue were suddenly a problem. She couldn't stand his smell. His beard. The sound of his voice. His puns.

Cressida confided all this to George their first night as roommates. They lay in their beds talking for nearly an hour. Or Cressida talked while George mostly listened. He was curious what had inspired her to keep the baby, but it seemed like an insensitive question.

"Do you mind if we turn off the light?" Cressida asked George.

George got up to do this. He assumed this meant Cressida wanted to sleep and took out his Kindle, but then she picked up where she'd left off.

"The worst thing is he isn't a bad guy. He's actually a really good person, just not someone I want to spend the rest of my life with. Or even another day with."

"That's a tough situation," George said.

It wasn't as awkward as George would've imagined it—sharing

a tiny room with his pregnant sister. It was actually kind of nice to have company. Both he and Cressida spent much of the day in bed, Cressida watching movies on her laptop, George editing student essays.

He was working remotely for a company that helped foreign students apply to colleges in the United States. The students were predominantly Chinese, the children of wealthy businessmen. George didn't correspond with the students directly; everything was coordinated through the company, which sent him personal statements to edit.

George pitied kids whose parents were so invested in sending them halfway across the world—with the expectation that they pursue MBAs upon graduating from college, and then return to China, or Japan or South Korea, and make lots of money—but he also resented them. He resented having to squander his creative energy laboring over ways to inject a bit of humanity into their one-dimensional narratives, which were riddled with grammatical errors and comically awkward syntax and were excruciatingly boring. There was a shocking deficit of critical thinking, introspection, or intellectual curiosity. George didn't think it was racist to make such observations; he was confident he'd find the personal statements of the children of the American one percent similarly lacking, if not worse.

A few days after Cressida moved in, George was surprised to discover the name of an old classmate in his inbox.

And I always thought you were one of the decent ones, was all the email said.

George was confused.

And then he clicked on the link below the message, which brought him to a Google spreadsheet featuring the names of men accused of various transgressions against women, ranging from the trivial (creepy emails) to the criminal (rape).

There were some impressive names on it, writers and journalists with high-profile bylines. George was surprised that his relative was included; he wasn't aware of his having achieved a level of success that would translate to notoriety.

George responded to his classmate with a lighthearted *ha-ha, not me*, and immediately received an apology.

A few hours later, he received another email regarding the document from someone he'd gone to high school with. By the end of the day, he'd received three more messages, two from strangers, all castigating him for these indiscretions committed by this cousin he barely knew.

George wasn't planning on mentioning the spreadsheet to his mother or sister, but the next day Cressida came upon it on her own. She brought it up as they ate dinner with Ellen. Their mother was not versed in the language of the internet and had a contrarian impulse when it came to the gender politics of the day. Her initial confusion became outrage on behalf of the other George, her dead ex-husband's cousin, whom she saw as the victim in all this.

"The few times I met him, I found him pretty insufferable," she admitted, "but I just don't understand—if what you're telling me is true—why his career is over because he made a few inappropriate comments. How can a person be 'canceled'? I don't like it. The whole thing feels very puritanical to me."

"Why was he insufferable?" Cressida asked.

Ellen frowned. "Loves hearing himself talk. Will carry on about some subject you know more about than he does. Never asks you a single question. Not one."

George refrained from telling her there was a word for the kind of man who did that.

"Didn't he once call and leave you a not-very-nice voicemail?" Ellen asked George. "Something about *don't bother being a writer, you'll never succeed*?"

"Why would he do that?" Cressida asked.

George shrugged; he didn't feel like talking about it.

"I told you," Ellen said, "he's kind of a jerk."

"Dad thought so, too," she added.

"What did you think of Dad when you first met him?" Cressida asked.

"What did I *think* of him?" Ellen repeated the question.

"Like what did you see in him?"

After a thoughtful silence, Ellen said, "He was unlike the type of men I'd grown up with. He was sensitive and observant. A good listener. But, actually, it was something he was wearing that caught my attention. We were at this party, and he'd taken off his jacket, and I noticed that he was wearing suspenders, the kind men used to wear when I was a child. It's a good look on a man, suspenders—I remember thinking how unfortunate that they went out of fashion and how debonair of him to wear them anyway."

"He was *debonair*," Cressida said with a little smile. And Ellen smiled back, wistfully.

George left the table as the conversation continued. For him, this kind of talk was only painful.

* * *

The spreadsheet was created in a way that people could add to the list of bad things each man had done. The box next to George's name kept growing. Cressida kept them apprised of the latest developments.

Made a pun about balls. Weird fixation on inviting me to "break-
fast."

Complimented my post-pregnancy weight loss.

"Give me a break," Ellen scoffed. "How is that a crime?"

Men whose indiscretions were deemed violent were highlighted in red.

"At least the world doesn't think I'm violent," George reflected.

"You're taking this surprisingly well," Cressida said. "I'm really impressed. A lot of guys wouldn't be handling this with such . . . What's the word for when a person takes something in stride?"

"Sangfroid," George answered.

The physical discomfort of George's condition only left so much room for mental anguish, he supposed. But there was also something else.

George noticed a pattern. Each time he began reading a hostile message from a stranger who'd seen his name on the list, he was possessed by an unbearable itch. To avoid scratching himself to bloodiness, George kept his fingernails extremely short, which meant that when the itch struck, he had to find other ways to deal with it: rough textiles, stiff-bristled hairbrushes, the metal thing his mother used to clean cast-iron pans.

Eventually, editing the spreadsheet was disabled so that no one could add any additional information, but that didn't stop it from making the rounds.

There was an article about it in the *Times*. Other news sources covered it after them, and George received more hate mail. Most were from women he didn't know who'd found him on Facebook.

Some of the messages called for George's castration or some other genital disfigurement; others reveled in his humiliation: *May your mother read this!* More than one contained a link to sign up for unemployment. *I hope you've had a fulfilling professional/romantic/ sex/social life because the truth is out and you're DONE.*

Cressida remained sympathetic.

"I'm sorry, George," she kept saying. "You don't deserve this."

She offered to screen George's email so he didn't have to read any more, but George wanted to see the messages.

George had done many things he was ashamed of, but when it came to sex and relationships with women, he had always been respectful, bordering on timid. To be the recipient of such undeserved vitriol felt oddly anointing, on a spiritual level. It was as though he were being tested, and he was passing the test by handling it with such equanimity, such sangfroid. It was a feeling he remembered experiencing as a boy, of being in communion with some higher power. Of being chosen.

But the messages affected him physiologically. Whenever he read one, he immediately started scratching.

* * *

One afternoon, George stood shirtless in front of the full-length mirror in the hall, sweeping a hairbrush across the right side of his torso.

Cressida came out of the kitchen eating ricotta cheese straight from the carton like it was ice cream. "What are you doing?"

George explained that one of the eczema chat rooms said you could soothe an itch without further irritating the skin by looking in the mirror while scratching the opposite side of wherever the itch was on your body, which would trick your brain into thinking you were scratching the actual site of the itch.

"That sounds like utter bullshit," Cressida said, but as she watched, she looked intrigued. "Is it working?"

"Shhh," George said. "I need to focus."

"It's okay that you used my hairbrush without asking," Cressida said, "but you're going to have to sterilize it afterwards by boiling it in a pot of hot water."

The rattle of the elevator stopping on their floor sent them both back to their room. Whenever they heard their mother returning to the apartment, they always made a point of being in bed. George wasn't sure why—it was an instinctual thing. They never discussed it.

As the front door opened, Cressida rested the empty carton of ricotta on the windowsill and pulled up the covers. George rolled over on his side, facing the boy milking a cow.

As she walked down the hall, Ellen poked her head into the room.

"There was an article about it in the *Times*," she told them.

"The list," she clarified.

"We know, Mom," said Cressida. "It came out a week ago."

"Well, I only just got to it.

"Poor George." She sighed. "He probably thinks everyone believes it. He's probably sitting there thinking his reputation is ruined."

"What about *me*?" George sat up. "What about me and my reputation?"

"Yeah," Cressida chimed in. "What about George!"

Ellen made a dismissive gesture. "Anyone who knows George will know it's not him."

"That doesn't help when someone who doesn't know me googles my name," George said. "That'll be a fun icebreaker on a first date. 'I'm not the guy who's on that list—but I'm related to him!'"

"What's Jenny up to these days?" Ellen asked as they sat down to dinner that night.

George shrugged. "Still a lawyer, I assume."

"You never hear from her?"

George shook his head.

"What about on your birthday?"

"Nope."

"Really? She was so invested in you. You'd think she'd check in."

"She doesn't owe me anything," George said, detecting a hint of criticism in his mother's tone and feeling defensive.

"So, it sounds like it's really over this time," Ellen said ruefully.

"Thank God!" Cressida said.

Looking at Ellen, she said, "Come on, Mom, George can do better. I don't mean find a person better than Jenny, but a better relationship."

"George *loved* Jenny," Ellen said.

"I'm not saying he didn't. It just didn't seem totally . . . balanced. It was obvious they met when they were too young and got stuck in this holding pattern. I'm sorry, George, but it was painful to watch. More for her sake."

"Can we not talk about this?" George asked. He resented their relationship being summed up so tritely. So blithely.

* * *

George developed a new patch of eczema on his scalp. He was troubled by the memory of an article about itching in the *New Yorker*. If there was any scientific information in the article, George had forgotten it. But an anecdotal detail remained. There was a man who couldn't stop scratching an itch on his scalp. One day he was scratching and felt something wet. He looked at his fingers, expecting to see blood, but the liquid was clear. It turned out to be from his brain.

Instead of a walk-in clinic, George went to an actual dermatologist, who assured him his brain was not leaking but noted that some of his eczema patches looked "a little angry."

"Could be an infection," she said.

Lab results confirmed George had streptococcus.

Ellen returned from the pharmacy with George's antibiotics and a package of Pepperidge Farm chocolate chip cookies.

"They were out of the soft-baked kind," she said, handing them to George.

"Maybe your eczema would get better if you didn't eat so much crap," Cressida said.

"It has nothing to do with diet," George countered, repeating what the doctor had told him. "It has to do with a breakdown of the skin's barrier."

"Oh, George." Cressida shook her head sadly. "It's all connected."

* * *

The news cycle moved on, and George's hate mail slowed down. Other, more mundane sources of anxiety and conflict cropped up.

George often worried about going too far with his "edits," but his supervisor praised his work and kept giving him more. It was a morally compromising job.

One evening George put dish soap in the dishwasher (apparently there was a difference between dish *soap* and dish *detergent*), resulting in a mess that took hours to clean.

Two days later, Cressida overloaded the washing machine and it broke.

Ellen was pissed.

"I've told you repeatedly, this is not an industrial machine in a laundromat," she said. "You have to be careful how much you put in."

A man came over to fix it. As Ellen led him down the hall, she said, "My adult children are both living at home at the moment," and shut the door to their bedroom.

"She's embarrassed of us," Cressida said.

George agreed. There was a sneer in her tone. *Adult children.*

Later that week, a technician came over to give Ellen a tutorial on how to navigate her new TV. After he left, George asked how much it had cost and why she hadn't asked one of them for help.

"I love my TV guy," Ellen said, ignoring the questions. "He used to be part of something called the Geek Squad, but now he has his own business. He's twenty-seven and he never went to college. Grew up in Staten Island. Brilliant.

"I mean, I think he might be a genius," she added.

"Why are you ashamed of us?" Cressida asked.

"I don't know what you're talking about," Ellen responded.

"You're ashamed of us for not being whatever your definition of 'adult' is." Cressida used air quotes. "You think we're spoiled and never grew up. For not being the kind of people who could run their own business. Or even be in the Geek Squad."

"I never said that," Ellen countered. "You're the one saying this. And so what if you couldn't be in the Geek Squad?"

"It's obvious it's how you feel." Cressida looked at George, who declined to weigh in.

"You know, your generation made things really difficult for ours, Mom. Have you considered how impossible it is for us to achieve basic things your generation took for granted? Such as home ownership?"

Ellen nodded coolly.

"That reminds me," she said. "I'm hosting a co-op board meeting tomorrow night. It starts at seven and shouldn't be more than an hour. Would you mind staying in your bedroom?"

"Okay," George said.

"What if I go into labor?" Cressida asked. "Am I allowed to come out then?"

* * *

"I haven't felt the baby move in a long time," Cressida announced, shuffling into the kitchen for breakfast one morning.

Hearing this made George nervous, but Ellen said, "I'm sure it's fine."

Cressida called her doctor's office. A nurse told her to drink orange juice and wait an hour. If the baby still hadn't moved, she should call back.

Cressida lay in bed waiting to feel something.

An hour later she called her doctor's office a second time.

"About forty-five minutes by subway, twenty by cab," George heard her say.

After getting off the phone, she went to find Ellen, who was still in the kitchen reading the *New York Times* and drinking her tea.

"They want me to come in," she announced.

"Oh. I'm supposed to meet my friend Joan for lunch . . ."

Cressida looked irritated. "I wasn't asking you to come with me, I'm just informing you, they're concerned, and they want to do an emergency ultrasound.

"To make sure the baby's still alive," she added bitterly.

"I'm sure it's fine, darling," Ellen said. "Babies sleep. That's what they do."

"I can go with you," George offered.

Cressida stood on the corner while George stepped out into the street to hail a cab. One of those minivan ones immediately pulled up. George struggled to manually open the door, and then it happened automatically.

After climbing inside, they couldn't figure out how to turn the TV off. The traffic was stop and go. After a little bit of news, a commercial came on for Jimmy Fallon's late-night show. Then a weather forecast. Then the same commercial again for Jimmy Fallon.

"Can't stand that guy," Cressida said when the commercial aired for the third time in ten blocks. "Thinks he's so funny."

His shtick was stupid, but George felt sorry for Jimmy Fallon. The more the commercial aired, the needier he seemed. A certain kind of neediness particular to entertainers, especially comedians. A neediness that the laughter of the live studio audience could never fill.

George suspected that after working his whole life to get to where he was, Jimmy Fallon resented having to traffic in the kinds of jokes that constituted comedy on a major network; that the kind of people laughing at him weren't the kind of people whose approval he coveted. He was considered a success, he'd landed the most plum gig in the industry, and yet he went to bed hating himself.

Or maybe Jimmy Fallon wasn't that complicated. In that case, good for him.

Most of the other women in the waiting room of Cressida's ob-gyn were Hasidic Jews. George wondered why this was.

Cressida jumped up when her name was called. The nurse noticed George remained seated. "You coming, Dad?"

"Brother," they said in unison.

"He's the uncle," Cressida clarified.

"Uncles are welcome," the nurse said.

"Don't worry," Cressida whispered to George as they followed the nurse down a hall. "It's just a sonogram, it's not like I'm getting undressed or anything."

"I don't want to know the gender," Cressida told the ultrasound technician. "In case you see something."

"I say nothing," the technician promised. She was older. Her accent sounded Russian.

The room was dark, illuminated by the lights of various screens and electronic devices. Cressida got on the reclining exam chair and pulled her shirt up. The technician squirted jelly on her exposed belly, then pulled out a contraption that she began sliding across her skin.

George was nervous. He kept looking at the technician's face for clues. Her steely Soviet stare revealed nothing, but from her silence, George suspected that something was wrong.

Finally, she spoke. "Come on, baby," she urged.

"Is everything all right?" George asked.

"Wake up, baby," the technician said. "Wakey-wakey."

"It's napping," George said. "Isn't that pretty normal?"

George looked at Cressida. If she was scared, it didn't show. Cressida never appeared scared. George wondered why that was. She wasn't a repressed person, she experienced a full range of emotions that she exhibited quite freely, but fear wasn't one of them.

"Good morning, baby." The technician smiled.

"It woke up?" George said. "It's awake?"

The baby was fine.

"How's your writing going?" Cressida asked as they took a subway home.

George shook his head. "It's not."

Cressida looked sad to hear this. "You're not writing anymore?"

"Not at the moment."

"You mean all that time you spend on your computer, you're just editing student essays?"

George nodded.

"Do you get any fulfillment out of it?"

"It pays well," George said.

"What about all that money you made for the Super Bowl commercial?"

"It's gone."

"*What?* But you don't spend shit. How is that even possible?"

"Bad investment." George shook his head. "I don't feel like talking about it."

"You should keep writing," Cressida said.

* * *

George continued to take Benadryl each night before bed, but his body was becoming accustomed to it. Instead of knocking him out, it delivered him into a stupor. Part of the problem was that Cressida went to bed later than he did, and it was difficult to fall asleep with the light on. One night he took twice the recommended dose. As he lay there waiting to be taken, he noticed a subtle movement on the wallpaper. A dog was running in place. Its body remained static, but its legs were going this way and that. A few inches to the left, a couple do-si-doed. A willow tree trembled in the breeze. The boy milking the cow was laughing.

And then Cressida snapped the lamp off and everything went black.

George slept deeply. When he woke up, it was almost ten. He felt groggy but peaceful. He reached for his phone and checked his email. There was an unfamiliar name in his inbox. He assumed it had to do with the list. He asked Cressida to open it for him and delete it. He wasn't in the mood.

He handed her his phone and walked to the bathroom.

He was brushing his teeth when he heard Cressida shout from the bedroom, "George! It's an agent! She really likes your book!"

It had been over a year since George had queried agents and many months since he'd received his last rejection. He'd assumed it was over.

A colleague of mine passed the manuscript of All for Naught *my way*, the email began.

Two gushing paragraphs later, it concluded, *Your manuscript has much going for it. I'll be honest with you, if this were fifteen or even ten years ago, I think you'd have a shot. Unfortunately, short story collections are increasingly a tough sell, and I'm not seeing a market for young white male authors at this time.*

George started itching. Itching, itching, itching. It was unbearable. He went into the living room, stripped down to his boxers, and began writhing around on the oriental rug, generating a warm friction. It went beyond relief of the itch. It was blissful. Almost like an orgasm.

But then came the pain. It felt like his body was on fire. Patches of inflamed pink skin flashed red like demented Christmas lights. Unlike the itch, there was nothing to be done for the pain.

As he lay there enduring—enduring, enduring, another test from God—George could hear his mother on the phone in the kitchen. She was telling someone about his eczema.

"An oatmeal bath," she was saying in her calm, sensible way. "Really? It just went away? How good to know. I'll tell George to take an oatmeal bath."

When the pain subsided, George put his clothes back on.

"*George*," Ellen called out as he passed by the kitchen. "Apparently, an oatmeal bath is good for eczema . . ."

George walked out the door, down the stairs, and headed to the nearest store that sold cigarettes, a bodega on the corner of Ninety-First and Madison. It had been over a year since he'd last smoked, one of the longest stretches of no smoking since he started his senior year of high school. He didn't feel like a pathetic failure, however, because he was going to smoke only two.

George planned to offer the rest of the cigarettes to a homeless person, but when he didn't pass any on the way back, he tossed the almost-full pack in the trash on the corner.

He waited until he was on his mother's stoop before lighting up. His mother's street was not the kind of place where people smoked on stoops, or even sat on them. George reveled in violating this aesthetic.

The town house directly across the street from his mother's building was a very expensive nursery school that specialized in teaching toddlers classical music. During the morning hours there was a row of high-end strollers parked on the sidewalk out front. Cressida, who was in the market for a stroller, claimed they cost four figures. She had pointed out that none of them was chained up, as was almost always done when leaving strollers outside in Manhattan.

There was nothing stopping anyone from walking off with one. Someone could throw the entire load into the back of a truck and sell them online.

But that never happened. It was that kind of block. There was a sense of being insulated from the rest of the city.

It was street-cleaning day, and all the cars on the north side of the street were occupied by drivers poised to pull out at the sign of a traffic cop. This was a common sight in New York, where parking spots were scarce. Drivers would wait in their cars until a traffic cop or street cleaner materialized, moving only when they were at risk of getting a ticket.

As George lit his second cigarette, a traffic cop rounded the corner. George was confused when none of the cars moved. Maybe they didn't see him.

The cop rapped on the passenger-side window of the first car he approached.

When the driver didn't budge, the cop spoke through the glass, "Time to move."

The car stayed put.

"If you don't move, I'll give you a ticket," the cop said.

He was Asian. Small. George wondered if it was a coincidence he'd been assigned traffic duty.

The driver was not intimidated. George waited for the cop to write him up, but instead he moved on to the next car, where a similar scene played out. And then again, with the next two cars.

As the cop passed by George, he looked up and shook his head. He continued to knock on windows, issuing threats he did not follow through on.

Before disappearing around the corner, he shouted, "Next time everybody gets tickets. I mean it!"

George walked to the corner to fish a third cigarette out of the trash. On his way back to the stoop he heard the rumble of a street cleaner. It was on the other end of the next block, headed in their direction. Now the cars would have to move.

246 • *The Book of George*

George lingered as the street cleaner advanced. He wanted to see the cars scatter like frightened insects, but the drivers showed no signs of moving.

George knocked on the passenger-side window of a BMW SUV parked directly in front of his mother's building.

The glass rolled down. The driver looked to be in his fifties and was wearing exercise clothes. The loose folds of his pink neck were accentuated by the smooth contours of his sweat-wicking jersey. He was listening to the Rolling Stones and had to lower the volume to understand what George was saying.

"The street cleaner's coming," George repeated.

The man nodded. "Thanks for the heads-up." The window closed.

George stood there for a moment and, seeing the guy had no intention of moving, knocked on the window again.

"The street cleaner has to be able access the curb," George said as the window rolled back down. "You have to move your car so it can clean the street."

They looked at each other, this man and George, in a mutually appraising manner. George had the self-awareness to recognize how he came across to a man like this: sleepy, unkempt, not a power player. But a man like this had no idea how he looked to George.

He wore an Apple watch and had done something weird to his hair. Put some kind of product in it to make it stand up a bit in front, to disguise the fact that it was thinning. He had no idea what a fool he looked like. What an asshole. He was the type of guy who went through life completely oblivious.

"I'm not worried about it," he said. "The super takes care of it."

"The super?" George repeated.

"My super," the man said. "I live here." He gestured to George's mother's building.

The window started to roll back up, but George stuck his hand in the gap.

"I see," he said. "You live here, so you get to decide how the street gets clean. Don't feel like being inconvenienced into allowing the street cleaner to do its job, no problem, the super will take care of it . . .

"*Mike*," George added, remembering the super's name. "Because he doesn't have enough to do."

The guy gave George a curious look.

"Yeah, I know Mike," George said. "I live here, too."

The man looked dubious. "Number nineteen?"

"Three F," George said.

The man smirked. "Is that right? Because I know the woman who lives there. I was at her apartment just last week for a board meeting."

"I'm her son." George had to shout to be heard above the street cleaner, which was unable to access the curb as it crawled by. None of the cars on the block moved.

"Aren't you a little old to be living with your mother?" the guy asked when the vehicle had passed and the noise subsided.

George grinned. "Nice one."

The window started to roll up but stopped when George's hand didn't move.

"Please take your hands off my car," the guy said.

"Fair enough," George said, withdrawing his arm. "But one more thing—"

The man waited.

"Fuck you," George told him. "And *fuck* your family."

"Okay, buddy." The man grinned. "Have a lovely day." The Rolling Stones resumed, the window closed, and George, who'd been holding the key to his mother's apartment, dragged it along the side of the passenger door, turned, and entered the building.

* * *

A few days later, George was woken up by Ellen coming into his room.

"Nick from upstairs just dropped off an invoice from an auto body shop." She reached over and tugged the cord of the shade. It snapped up violently, and a dull gray light filled the room. "He said you vandalized his car."

George looked at his mother, who stood, arms crossed, in the narrow space between the twin beds. Cressida materialized in the doorway, hands clasped around her belly, looking intrigued.

"Do you have any idea what he's talking about, George?"

George nodded. In the immediate wake of the episode, he'd felt a little thrill, but that was gone.

"I keyed his car," he said.

"You *what* his car?"

"I keyed it," he repeated quietly.

Ellen frowned.

"That's when you drag a key along the side of a car and it leaves a mark," Cressida explained.

Ellen looked bewildered. "Why would you do something like that?"

"He refused to move his car for alternate street parking, we had a little exchange, and I lost my temper."

For a moment, Ellen looked on the verge of laughter, but she was far from amused. "George, I don't even know what to say . . . *Vandalizing* a car? A car that belongs to one of my neighbors?"

"Whatever it is," George said, "I'll pay for it."

"You'll certainly pay for it, but the money is almost beside the point," she said. "This is someone I have to see on a regular basis, ride the elevator with, deal with at board meetings. Did you consider how uncomfortable this makes things for me?"

The room felt especially narrow as George lay in his bed blinking, his mother looming over him.

"I just don't understand what got into you," Ellen went on. "What the hell possessed you to do such a thing? What if he'd decided to press charges? Did you want to add a misdemeanor to your résumé? It's just so *stupid*, George—so utterly stupid and reckless and juvenile."

"Wait—how'd he know it was you?" Cressida asked. "Was he in the car when you did it?"

George nodded.

"That's bold," Cressida said.

"I didn't think he'd notice," George explained. "It was after he'd closed the window. He was listening to music."

"I don't know what to make of this," Ellen said. "But it makes me worry about you. It makes me think that maybe I don't really know you." She spoke with a chilly composure. The initial rush of her anger had subsided, and now she was disturbed—disturbed and disappointed by what George's actions revealed about him.

As she looked at him in a probing way, George felt a particular kind of leaden remorse he associated with being reprimanded for doing something bad as a child. A sinking, paralyzing conviction that he was an inherently bad person—selfish, dishonest, weak, beyond repentance.

"Have you ever done anything like this before?" Ellen asked.

George shook his head. "I've lost my temper, but not like this."

"What do you think it was about this guy, or this particular situation, that set you off?" Cressida asked.

George thought about this. "I didn't like the way he treated the traffic cop."

As he described the scene with the cop, Cressida interrupted. "But I don't understand—why didn't he just start giving everyone tickets?"

"He just couldn't do it," George said. "Maybe he felt outnumbered and intimidated, or maybe he felt like a fraud, like he couldn't take himself seriously as an authority figure. For whatever reason, he just couldn't do it. And the drivers must've known it, or else they would've moved, and he knew they knew it."

It was unclear if Ellen was following.

George spoke after a silence. "I'm sorry, Mom. I'm sorry to make things weird with your neighbor."

"To be honest," she said with a sigh, "I always thought he was an asshole."

"So you're proud of George," Cressida said.

"Proud?" Ellen raised her eyebrows. "No, I wouldn't say I'm proud of him for defacing someone's car."

"Well, I'm proud of him," Cressida said. "He could've just been a bystander, and instead he decided to get involved. To confront the bully. And that's admirable."

"It wasn't like that." George shook his head. "I'm not proud of what I did. I'm ashamed."

"Oh, George." Ellen's face softened. George sensed she appreciated the depth of his contrition. "I don't want you to be ashamed . . ." She took a seat on the edge of his bed. "I just want you to be okay. Are you *okay*, George?"

He nodded, but Ellen's gaze lingered, tender, worried, pained.

"I'm okay, Mom," he said.

She patted his knee beneath the covers. She was not a toucher, his mother, and when she did attempt some gesture of physical affection, it felt forced. It had been Cressida who'd pointed this out to George; she did a funny impression of it. But today it didn't seem funny. Nor did it seem forced so much as tentative, as though Ellen was braced for rejection. It made George sad that his mother was this way— sad for her, sad for him.

George reached down to squeeze his mother's hand, but before he could make contact, she withdrew.

"Did I . . ." Ellen had trouble finishing her sentence. "Was I an all right mother? Sometimes I blame myself for . . ."

"You think you fucked up with George?" Cressida cut in. "What about me? I'm about to have the child of a dude I met on Craigslist. Not even Missed Encounters—Room Wanted."

Ellen laughed. A full, deep laugh that filled the room. Cressida looked pleased with herself; it was not often their mother laughed like that—George couldn't remember the last time he'd heard it. It made him happy. He wanted it to go on and on.

"Well," Ellen said, wiping her eyes as she composed herself. "We should get on with the day."

George sat up. "How much is the invoice for?" he asked.

"I can't remember," Ellen said. "I left it on the kitchen table."

George shuffled into the kitchen in his boxers. Cressida followed.

"Fuck me," he said, looking at the figure.

"Fuck me," he repeated.

"George!" Cressida pointed at his nearly naked body. "Your eczema!"

"What about it?" he asked.

"It's gone!" she said.

14. THE SMELL

Jenny, almost 40

A cold front had passed through earlier. The wind swept the sidewalks clean. On the west side of the street, the curb was lined with tidy little nests of litter and dried leaves. The air felt fresh, imported.

And then Jenny got in her car and there was the smell of rot and decay. She'd first noticed it on Tuesday, when she'd moved the car for alternate side parking. Today it was worse. Even driving with her mask on and the windows open.

At a light, she fished through her bag for a second mask. Fortunately, she was on her way to get the car inspected. Whatever it was, they would handle it.

The garage was on the other side of the Gowanus Canal, in the industrial hinterland between Carroll Gardens and Park Slope. The only other business on the block was a coffin factory. Even so, there were no parking spots, and so Jenny double-parked, put her blinkers on, and went into the office. She was still wearing two masks, and she was glad of this, because the man behind the desk was not wearing any. On the wall behind him was a poster of a bald eagle set against an American flag and an expired swimsuit calendar.

She told him her name and that she had an appointment for an inspection. He scanned a clipboard.

"Don't see you." His mustache was so thick you couldn't see his lips move as he spoke.

"I called yesterday to confirm," Jenny told him.

He glanced at the clipboard again and shook his head with provocative indifference.

Jenny felt a pang of righteous frustration. She was a single mother of a toddler during a pandemic. For her to get out and do things was not easy.

"Is there any way you could squeeze me in?" she asked.

The man stared at her in a cold, appraising manner, his mustache sloped down like a frown. Jenny wished she wasn't wearing her pussy-hat. In her rush out the door, she couldn't find a normal one.

He sighed and picked up a pen. "Year, make, and model?"

"Honda. I can't remember the exact year, maybe 2012? Sometime around then."

"What kind of Honda?"

"It's a, um . . ." Jenny's cheeks burned beneath the masks. She was wearing a hat with ears and had forgotten the word for what her car was. She wanted to explain that it was a recently acquired car—a hand-me-down from a relative.

"Hybrid?" the man guessed.

Jenny nodded.

"Should be about forty minutes," he said as she handed him the keys.

Jenny thanked him and turned to leave.

She paused at the door. "There's a funky smell," she told him. "In the car. I just noticed it driving over here."

"Where's it coming from?"

"I don't know. But it got worse when I opened the vents."

"It's coming from the engine," the man said with weary authority. "Before you go, let me take a look."

They stepped outside.

"Pull in," he said, seeing she had double-parked.

Jenny got in the car and gingerly nosed onto the sidewalk—she couldn't see if any pedestrians were coming. The man stood in the entrance to the garage brusquely beckoning her to proceed. *More-more-more-more*, then he abruptly flashed a palm. Jenny braked with amateur gusto.

"Pop the hood," he ordered.

"Pop the hood," Jenny repeated to herself.

Somewhere in the vicinity of her knee was a lever to make this happen; she knew that much.

When it was obvious she couldn't find it, the man gestured for her to get out.

Jenny got out, he leaned in, pop went the hood.

Before opening it, he held his hands over the top, fingers splayed, as though warming himself by a fire. There was a subtle bouncing in his body, as though he was counting to ten. When he finally reached his fingers under the hood to lift it up, he did so with stoic resolve, as though bracing himself for something unpleasant.

"Oh, boy," he said, taking a step back. "This is no good. No good at all."

He pulled a handkerchief out of his pocket and covered his nose as he leaned over the engine. Then he reached into another pocket and pulled out a flashlight. After scanning the light this way and that, he found what he was looking for.

"It's a squirrel," he said.

Jenny drew a hand to her masked mouth.

"Not your fault," he told her. "Happens this time of year, when it gets colder. After you park, the engine is warm, they climb up, take a little nap, you get back in the car, turn the ignition on, things heat up real fast.

"Not your fault," he repeated.

Jenny nodded grimly.

"I can't have my guys work on this car," the man told her. "It's unsanitary."

"Of course," Jenny said, though this surprised her. She'd thought they'd be equipped to deal with this sort of thing.

The man put the hood back down. "When do you need the inspection by?"

"It expires tomorrow," Jenny said quietly.

The man looked resentfully compassionate. "You'll get a ticket if you leave it on the street. Do you have a driveway where you can park it?"

Jenny shook her head. "My fault for leaving it to the last minute," she said.

"Here's what you do," the man said. "Take it to the car wash on Fourth. Explain the situation and tell them you need them to clean it up. They say no, you ask to speak to the manager."

Jenny nodded.

"You tell him, *Look, I'm in a pickle . . .*"

Jenny nodded again.

"Bring it back here soon as it's taken care of. We're open till six."

"Thank you," Jenny said.

"My name's Charlie." The corners of his mustache rose ever so slightly. "I'm the owner."

Jenny called the babysitter to let her know it was going to take longer than she'd thought.

She drove to the car wash.

She parked and went into the office. She explained to the woman at the front desk that she didn't need a traditional car cleaning, she was there because there was a dead squirrel in her engine. Would it be possible for them to remove it?

No. The answer was no.

Jenny went back outside. Standing beside her car, she called a few other local auto body shops.

No one would help her, or even propose a solution, though one of the mechanics she spoke to asked if she had any "bad blood" with anyone and suggested she file a police report.

"You mean you think someone put it there on purpose?" Jenny almost laughed. "I don't know anyone who would do that."

"You think you know someone," the man said. "You'd be surprised. I had an ex-girlfriend smear dog shit all over my car. Windows, inside the door handles. Dog shit everywhere. She didn't even have a dog."

Jenny got back in the car, her frustration becoming self-pity. No one would help her. She was completely on her own.

She drove back up Fourth Avenue and made a left on President Street with the intention of crossing the Carroll Street Bridge, forgetting that it was eastbound only. By the time she realized her error she was already on the bridge, and there was a police car coming the opposite direction. She pulled over to make the officer's job easier. She would cry as he issued her a ticket. She would tell him there was a dead squirrel in her engine, that her inspection was about to expire, and she didn't know what to do. She would cry and he would help her.

It was not a police car. Jenny decided to linger for a bit, in case one did come along—though there wasn't much traffic on this bridge.

She turned the car off and stepped out. The canal was still and green, and if you didn't know what toxins lurked within it, you might even think it looked lovely, framed by the terra-cotta ruins of old factories beneath a brooding gray sky.

There was a novelty to standing alone, on a wooden drawbridge, in New York City.

Jenny became aware of a person advancing in her direction. A man wheeling a small piece of luggage, which made an excessive amount of noise. There was something loose and unwieldy about his gait, which reminded her of George, who, when walking down a hill, used to swing his arms in an exaggerated manner, as if enlisting gravity to do more of the work. His reluctance to exert energy doing anything he found tedious or inconsequential—dishes, bed-making, handwriting, small talk—was supremely irritating. More than indolence, it felt like a specific kind of male arrogance, a disregard for the impression this made on others, because anyone who cared about such things wasn't worth impressing. By the end of their years together, this was how Jenny was inclined to see it—though, of course, depression also played a role.

Funnily, in the beginning, before she knew what to make of it, she had found it charming.

One afternoon, as a new hire in the restaurant where she'd worked, George had dropped a tray of cocktails. He'd been carrying it across the room in his casual, lackadaisical way when his wrist went slack and everything drifted off. Jenny had laughed. There was something inherently comic about George's haplessness, his delayed reaction to what had just occurred—he'd looked confused as he noted the empty tray, still in his hand, and then the mess on the floor, which Jenny had helped him clean up. At the end of his shift, he tried to give her the sum of his tips from the day. For a terrible waiter, he pocketed a lot of cash. Especially during the lunch shifts, which were mostly women.

Women liked George. He was fun to look at. Boyishly handsome. Jenny had never quite grasped if he was indifferent or oblivious to this fact, but it didn't seem to figure into his sense of himself.

It was other aspects of his personhood that preoccupied him.

Jenny sometimes conjured George up on figures from a distance, only to discover, as they crossed paths, that the men looked nothing like George. But today, as the man who walked like George approached where she stood, he stopped and took off his mask, and it was him.

It was George.

She hadn't seen him in nearly four and a half years. The last she'd heard, he was living at his mother's apartment on the Upper East Side. He was not on Facebook, and she didn't keep up with any of his friends. It was sort of like he'd died. But now here he was, standing before her, alive.

She sensed the moment was just as flustering for him. He stared at her with the unwavering intensity of a child, but there was something bashful, sheepish, even, in his expression.

He had gained some weight. His features looked smaller in the doughy expansion of his cheeks, which had an oily pubescent gleam.

"I guess we shouldn't hug," Jenny said, extending an elbow in his direction. It took George a moment to register that she was waiting for him to do the same.

They touched elbows. George's smile melted into something more rueful, and he pursed his lips, a hint of a tremor in his chin.

Jenny said, "'What people call fate is mostly their own stupidity.'"

George looked amused. "You've been reading Schopenhauer? The philosopher of pessimism?"

Jenny nodded. "He's interesting. I can see how he'd appeal to you."

She pointed to his bag. "On your way to the airport?"

"Those are tools," George said. "I'm headed to the library on Henry to fix some voting machines."

Jenny was surprised. "Is it a volunteer thing?"

"It's a job," George said. "Howie set me up with it."

"Howie?"

"Cressida's husband. It's his uncle's company."

It took Jenny a moment to sort through what he'd just said.

"Cressida has a husband named *Howie*?"

"And a baby girl. I guess she's technically a toddler now . . ."

"Oh," Jenny said. "Wow. I can't quite picture her as a wife and mother."

She immediately felt bad for saying this, but George nodded knowingly. "I had a hard time imagining it, too. But she's a good mom. And Howie's a great guy. She gives him a hard time, but I actually think they're pretty happy. He's a woodworker. Very calm, takes it all in stride."

"That's wonderful," Jenny said. "Good for Cressida."

She asked if he had any photos of the little girl.

"Screen's a little cracked," George said, taking out his phone.

Jenny was relieved that the child did not look like George. It would be difficult, for her, to see a child that looked like George.

"She's cute," Jenny said.

George glanced at the screen and smiled.

"Too cute for her own good."

He was smitten with this little girl; it was obvious from the subsequent photos he showed her. In one, the little girl was sitting on George's lap as he blew out candles on a cake. Jenny felt a little sting of jealousy.

"It was just your birthday," Jenny remembered.

George slipped his phone back in his pocket and glanced forlornly in the distance. "Yes," he said with a rueful sigh. "Thirty-eight."

"I'm almost *forty*," Jenny pointed out.

George looked unimpressed. "But you're a woman."

"What does that have to do with it?"

"Women live longer than men."

Jenny laughed. "Oh, George."

"It's true," he said glumly.

"That's my car," Jenny said, remembering what she was doing here. She explained the situation.

"I'm in a pickle," she added.

George's expression conveyed sympathy, but he did not offer to help. Many men in this situation would offer to help. Not George. It wouldn't even occur to him.

"Where are you living these days?" Jenny asked.

"Cortelyou Road," he said.

"*Ditmas*," Jenny said. "I love Ditmas. All the trees and beautiful old houses . . .

"Do you live in one of those beautiful old houses?"

After a delay, George nodded. "In one of the more ramshackle ones. It's Cressida's place. I mean, technically, it's her in-laws'."

Jenny did her best to maintain a neutral expression as George matter-of-factly explained his situation: he was sleeping on a couch in Cressida and Howie's apartment, which was on the top floor of Howie's parents' house. He didn't volunteer how long this had been going on, or how the circumstances had come about, and Jenny didn't probe, though she was curious. She was surprised Cressida would tolerate the arrangement.

"How's your mom?" Jenny asked.

George flinched. There was a look of wounded surprise on his face.

"She died," he told her. "This past March. I guess I forgot to put you on the email . . ."

"Oh, George," Jenny said.

George's eyes pooled as he nodded. He turned to face the water.

"Covid?" Jenny asked after a silence.

"The official cause was pneumonia." He cleared his throat. "She had ovarian cancer. She wasn't doing well, but she qualified to take part in an experimental therapy, but there was all this bureaucratic bullshit, and they kept on delaying the start date, and then she got pneumonia."

He turned back around and kicked a shard of concrete into the road. "Cress thinks it was actually Covid—it could've been Covid.

"The official cause was pneumonia," he repeated with a shrug.

"Oh, George. That's so sad. I'm so sorry." Jenny's words felt woefully inadequate.

She wanted to say more, something less trite, but George's demeanor turned shifty. He patted his pockets—a habit from his smoking days—pursed his lips, and nodded rapidly. He was trying not to cry.

"Is that a pussyhat?" George pointed to Jenny's head.

Jenny pulled it off. "I was in a rush out the door."

"Put it back on. It's cute."

"Cute?" Jenny repeated.

George nodded. "Looks cute on you."

Jenny put the hat back on. "I would have thought you'd have a problem with these," she said. "You could be a little cynical about . . . *performative activism*, I believe was your term for it."

"I was a jerk," George said. "You deserve a trophy for putting up with me for as long as you did."

Jenny wondered if he could see through her attempt at a smile.

Recently she'd gone on a walk with a friend, and they'd passed a couple on a bench. It was hard to tell how young they were, but they were quite young, maybe even teenagers. The boy was cupping the girl's masked chin and kissing her through her mask. The friend had called her attention to them: "Look, isn't that a beautiful love? That's a beautiful young love." And Jenny pretended to feel similarly, though the sight had not brought her joy.

It had made her think of George, and how in love she had been with him. Deeply, irrationally so. It was not something she could justify or explain, this love, but for many years it had been the organizing principle of her life. But he had not felt that way about her. He had loved her, but he had not been *in* love with her. And that was a confusing and painful truth to reckon with, because growing up, Jenny had nurtured assumptions about love. She assumed it was a given that she would meet her person, fall in love, have children, and live cozily ever after. And whatever storms life brought would be weathered together. It would almost be easier to have concluded the whole thing was a myth, but looking around, you could see it happened that way for some, even many, people. It was something some people got to experience, and others didn't.

"I had a baby," she told him.

George looked surprised.

"Freddie. He'll be two in January."

"A boy," George said.

"A boy," Jenny repeated, hoping to convey that she was not disappointed.

It was true she'd had mixed feelings upon learning the gender during the anatomy scan. All her life she'd imagined having a daughter.

And then he'd arrived, her baby boy, and they placed him in her arms, this pruned, purple lump of a person, and to her horror and astonishment, what everyone said would happen—the instantaneous attachment, the love that was supposed to go off like a bomb in your heart—didn't happen. Fatigue, postpartum—there were explanations, but as the days became weeks, a full month, and then two, there lingered the question of whether this would be the case had Freddie been a girl.

It was a gradual process, but at around seven months, Jenny no longer entertained such thoughts, and by the time he was a year old, she couldn't imagine ever having them. He was it for her, he was Freddie. She couldn't imagine any other child.

It complicated Jenny's feelings toward men, this love for Freddie. It forced an awareness that all men, even the most remote, the most insufferable, had once upon a time been little boys. Soft, guileless, wide-eyed little boys, with their little boy voices and little boy preoccupations: *Dog! Ball! Loader!* The simplicity of their joy, their earnest pursuits—it made her heart thump.

Jenny showed George some pictures of Freddie. He didn't ask; she just took out her phone.

"What's he into?" George asked as Jenny scrolled through her photos.

"Oh, you know," Jenny said. "The usual stuff. Animals. Loaders . . ."

"And you're married?" George interjected, a bit awkwardly.

Jenny shook her head. "It's just the two of us. I used a donor."

"You want to hear something wild," George said after a moment. "In one of the last conversations I had with my mom, when she was still lucid, she told me that Dizart was probably my father. My biological father."

"Wow," Jenny said. "That is . . . a surprise."

George nodded.

"And Cressida?"

"Just me," he said.

Jenny was shocked. Though it also made a little sense. She wanted to know more—she wanted to know everything—but George was clearly eager to change the subject.

"Does he like dinosaurs?" George asked.

"Freddie? Um . . ." Jenny considered this. "You know, I'm not sure he knows about them."

"What?"

"He doesn't watch TV yet, and I don't think he has any toy dinosaurs. We read a lot, but I can't think if any of the books have dinosaurs in them . . ." Jenny wondered if this was an oversight on her part.

"He's not even two," she said defensively. "I don't want to scare him. How would I explain extinction?"

George looked at her fondly. "As soon as we all get the vaccine, Uncle George will take Freddie to the museum. We'll see some dinosaur bones, I'll explain the whole thing."

Jenny was confused—George and Freddie did not belong in the same sentence, and now this image of the two of them walking hand in hand up the steps of the museum?

"Is that a *man bun*?" Jenny asked.

George touched the knot of hair at the back of his neck. "Haven't gotten my hair cut in a while."

She wanted to ask him to take it out so she could see what it looked like long, but George was funny about his hair. He didn't like it when people complimented it, which happened often, as it was a certain kind of brown that caught the light, thick and healthy-looking. It was nice hair.

"That's an important job," Jenny said. "Fixing voting machines."

George shrugged. "A lot of people are voting by mail this year, so it's not as important as it might have been during normal times."

"Every vote counts," Jenny said. "You never know how close the election will be."

"Won't be close in New York," George said.

"Pop the hood," George said, slapping the hood. "Old George is going to get this dead squirrel out of your car."

"You don't have to do that."

"Pop the hood!"

Jenny opened the door and found the lever.

"You're going to want to wear a mask to block the smell," she said as George lifted the hood.

"*Jesus Christ*," he said, holding a hand over his face.

George put on his mask.

"You might need a flashlight," Jenny said as he peered into the engine.

George took out his phone and turned on the flashlight function.

"I believe it's on the right side," Jenny said. "Maybe towards the back?"

George directed the flashlight as instructed, then turned and walked away from the car and began dry heaving. He bent over, hands on knees.

When he recovered, George unzipped his bag of tools and took out a pair of disposable latex gloves.

"You're just going to reach in and get it?" Jenny asked, impressed. "Do you need me to hold the flashlight?"

"Nope."

George leaned over the engine. Jenny turned around so she didn't have to see.

"I need a stick," he called out after a few minutes.

"A stick?"

George nodded. "It's pretty far down, which makes it difficult to reach. But if I could poke it down even farther, I think it would just fall out the bottom."

There was an empty lot adjacent to the bridge. Jenny untethered a dead vine from the chain-link fence.

"Here," she said, bringing it to him.

George tossed it over the side of the bridge.

"Too flimsy," he said. "I need something more substantial. Like a broom handle."

"What about that thing you use to scrape ice off the windshield?" Jenny said. "An ice scraper?"

She opened the trunk. "Or what about this?" She pulled out an umbrella. It was the tall, Mary Poppins kind.

"This could work," George said, taking it from her.

A cluster of clouds disbanded, and the resulting light felt cloying.

Jenny squinted at George, who looked possessed, brandishing the umbrella as he hunched over the engine.

After a few minutes of poking, he paused to take off his jacket.

His T-shirt had little holes in the armpits. It was too short, and as he resumed his position leaning over the engine, it rode up his torso. His lower back was softer and hairier than Jenny remembered. As he continued toiling, the hairs, which were long and fine, wilted and became matted to his clammy skin, resembling a gently used lint roller.

Jenny felt guilty, standing there making a mental inventory of his physical imperfections while he did this favor for her.

"Any plans for after the election?" she asked. "I assume the job ends then."

"It continues," George said. "There are other small elections, we do periodic testing, firmware upgrades, preventative maintenance, training sessions. I'm part of the core crew. We work year-round.

"But I'm actually thinking of going back to school for a master's in education."

"To be a teacher?"

"High school English," George said.

"*George!* That's wonderful!"

George shook his head, and Jenny said no more. She understood why he'd find her gushing approval of such a practical decision patronizing. And yet she felt a little bitten, as she always had when he'd recoiled in response to her enthusiasm about something he had mixed feelings about.

She should have known better. *You'll make a great teacher, George.* She should've just said that.

But would he be a good teacher? George loved reading, could be fiercely opinionated about books, but being a high school teacher required patience and humility, and lots of grading of papers.

"And what about you?" George asked. "Are you still lawyering?"

"Yup. I'm working at housing court. I represent tenants."

"You like it?"

Jenny shrugged. "Depends on the day. It's a tough job. You have a lot of clients. You lose a certain number of cases. There's only so much you can do, and it's kind of crushing."

"I bet they really appreciate it," George said. "The people you represent."

"Eh, some do. But there's actually a distrust of free lawyers."

"Really? But you chose to do good work. You're the most decent ones in the field."

"Not everyone sees it that way. Some people think you're just a shitty lawyer who couldn't get a higher-paying job."

George looked disturbed by this.

"I get it," Jenny said, defending her more difficult clients. "I can understand how they might have that impression."

She took a seat on the curb. "But a lot of clients are grateful. Last week, one of my clients, this older woman, Ms. Williams, sent me this nice text out of nowhere. It was sort of like a pep talk. I try to project confidence, but she must have picked up on my impostor syndrome, or whatever you want to call it . . .

"Wanna hear it?" Jenny asked.

"Sure," George said.

"If you insist." Jenny took out her phone. "Okay, here it is—

"'You're a phenomenal lawyer. Don't get down when you lose a case. Take deep breaths. Breathe in these words until you feel it. Everyone thinks a knight in shining armor comes in the form of a man. But for me it came in the form of a Jenny.'"

Jenny was embarrassed. Reading the text out loud, it sounded a little over the top, a bit immodest, but George looked touched. He'd stopped working on the car and was looking at her, lips inverted, his forehead etched with feeling. A breeze plastered his shirt against his torso, revealing a sweet little paunch.

"I'm sure it's true," he said.

Jenny shrugged and slipped the phone back in her pocket.

George resumed working on the car, then stood back and shook his head. "I don't know if I can do this. I'll spare you the details, but it's really wedged in there. And rigor mortis isn't helping."

Jenny grimaced. "Thanks, George, I really appreciate you trying."

"Don't thank me," he said with a sigh of defeat. "I actually might've made things worse."

George rested the umbrella against the side of the car. He removed his mask and his gloves.

"It was a valiant effort," Jenny said.

George reached into his pocket and pulled out a pack of cigarettes. He was still smoking.

"Which of his books did you read?" His cigarette bobbed in his lips as he procured a lighter.

"*The World as Will and Representation*? *On the Freedom of the Will*?"

Jenny shook her head.

"*The Art of Being Right*?" He took a seat beside her on the curb.

"I didn't really read Schopenhauer," she admitted. "I just read your college thesis."

George made a point of turning his head away from her as he exhaled.

"I found a copy in your mom's house," Jenny explained. "That weekend we spent cleaning out your bedroom before she moved. I didn't tell you. I was afraid you'd insist on throwing it away, so I just took it. And then I hid it somewhere and forgot about it. A few months ago, I found it in an old box of papers."

"And you *read* it?"

Jenny nodded. "I skimmed parts. I never took philosophy in college, so I couldn't quite follow everything."

"Not versed in the jargon," George said.

"Yeah. But the parts I understood were really interesting."

George looked intrigued. "Which parts?"

"I liked your criticism of his argument about happiness," Jenny said.

George nodded, inviting her to elaborate.

"In response to his theory that there's no such thing as happiness, just relief from bad feelings, you pointed out how this ignores instances of unexpected joy," she said. "Like when nice things happen that you weren't anticipating."

He nodded some more.

"You wrote about taking a walk at night," she went on. "And seeing this thing floating above you. This mysterious, ethereal mass, you had no idea what it was, but it was beautiful, and it felt like a private, spiritual moment. The next day you found out it was a giant soap bubble. Someone had poured laundry detergent into a fountain or something. But even knowing that, in recalling your experience of the moment, you were able to access the joy and awe you felt at the time."

George looked moved.

"And then you talked about the fallacy of equating desiring with suffering. How anticipation in itself can be pleasurable. How it's fun to look forward to things, even if they don't happen."

An ice cream truck trundled across the bridge and made a left into the lot adjacent to the canal, where food service trucks parked when they were not in service.

George rose to his feet. "Back to it," he said.

"I thought it was impossible," Jenny said, as George reached for the umbrella.

"Just give me a little longer," he said. "I think I can get it."

"George," Jenny said, after a few minutes. "I really appreciate this, but I've got to get back."

"Just let me finish." There was an edge to his voice. "I know I can do this."

Jenny had to pee. She didn't know how much longer she could hold it.

"I have to pee," she said.

"Go for it," George said. "No one's looking."

"I'm a woman, George. It's not so easy."

"Is there somewhere you could go on Smith Street?"

Jenny sighed. "I guess that's my best bet."

"Leave me the key," George said. "In case I need to move the car."

Jenny gave George the key and walked to the Starbucks on Smith. Their restroom was out of order, and so she trekked to the one on Court.

By the time she headed back, the light was going going gone.

As she approached the Carroll Street Bridge, Jenny saw George standing, looking out over the canal, smoking another cigarette—but no car.

"I'm so sorry," George said as she approached.

"What happened?"

"I thought it might be easier to get out if I turned the engine on . . ." George put out his cigarette. "That it would heat up the muscles and get rid of the rigor mortis. So I turned it on and started poking under the hood again. And I must have absentmindedly put the car in drive, and put the parking brake off, because it started moving.

"Fortunately, I'd left the door open and it wasn't going very fast, so I was able to hop in it before it crashed into anything, but there was a cop car down the street, saw the whole thing. Me, driving a car the wrong way down a one-way street with the hood popped. And, of course, my license is expired."

"Where's the car?" Jenny asked.

"They impounded it." George shook his head sadly. "I'm so sorry. I'm such a dunce. I'll pay for it."

Jenny didn't want to betray her frustration and self-pity. She didn't want to make George feel any worse. "It's not your fault," she told him. "You were just trying to help. And you don't have to pay for it.

"Do you know where they took it?" she asked.

George shook his head. "They wouldn't tell me. Said you had to call 311. They were such assholes."

Jenny took out her phone to call 311. George's hand intercepted her. His ungloved fingers took her fingers and squeezed them.

"It's getting inspected," he said. "I drove it to the auto body shop on Union. They're about to close but said they'd do it first thing in the morning. It's in their garage, so you don't have to worry about it getting a ticket."

"You *did* it? You got the squirrel out?"

George folded his arms and mugged. "Told you I would."

"Wow, George," she said. "Thank you. Thank you so much."

"Anytime," George said. "Anytime you need an animal carcass removed from your car engine, I'm your man."

Jenny smiled. They stood facing each other in a little pool of streetlight. George took a step forward.

Jenny took a step back. "I should get going."

"I'll walk you home," George said. "Meet the kid. I'll wear a mask."

Jenny was put off by the casual certainty of his tone. *Walk you home. Meet the kid.*

"But don't you have to get to your job?" she asked.

"I'll take care of it later."

Jenny didn't say anything.

George seemed to register her trepidation. "Is it okay if I walk you back? Could I meet your little boy?"

"I don't think that's a good idea," Jenny said gently.

George looked a little deflated.

"Give me your address," Jenny said, "so I can send you your thesis."

George shook his head. A dark look passed over his face.

"Oh, come on," Jenny said. "You'll want to read it one day."

"I don't want it." His tone was clipped. "Keep it. Throw it out."

Jenny nodded. "Well," she said, "I'm glad this happened. Apart from the fact that you saved the day, it was nice to see you."

"You, too," George mumbled.

"Does Dizart know?" Jenny was curious. "Sorry, it's not my business. Strangers are always asking about Freddie's situation . . ."

"No, it's okay," George said. "You and I go way back." He smiled.

"She thought Denis might have suspected it, but she didn't think Dizart knew."

"Are you going to tell him?"

George's shoulders rose in a tentative shrug, but then he shook his head.

"I thought about reaching out to him and confirming it with a test, but I don't see the point." He paused. "Denis was my dad."

Jenny nodded. "I'm sorry I never got the chance to meet him."

"Thanks," he said. "You always used to say that. It was nice."

She exhaled. "Okay. Well." She extended an elbow in George's direction, but he did not reciprocate.

"Could we hug?" he asked. "I swear I don't have Covid."

"Okay," she said.

They hugged, and Jenny had no choice but to breathe in the deeply familiar brine of his sweat. There was a gravity to his scent, and yet its effect on Jenny was effervescent. A few times she began to relax her grip, but George did not.

"I had you," he said when he finally released her.

Jenny didn't know what to say to this.

"Admit it," he said. "I had you with the car story."

"Maybe for a second," Jenny conceded.

George looked pleased. Laughed to himself. With the jaunty swagger of an old hand, he grasped the retractable handle of his bag of tools.

"I *had* you," he said, and off he wheeled, over the bridge and into the November evening's pristine chill, the air above the canal having arrived from somewhere else, someplace far off and unsullied.

ACKNOWLEDGMENTS

Thank you to Amy Williams, Caroline Zancan, Diana Spechler, Frances, Molly, and my parents. Phoebe and Angus, you were sometimes an obstacle, but also the anchor. And most of all thank you to Teddy, my ballast, my partner in the wagon.

About the Author

Kate Greathead is the author of *Laura & Emma*. Her work has appeared in the *New Yorker*, the *New York Times*, and on PRX's *The Moth Radio Hour*. She lives in Brooklyn with her husband, the writer Teddy Wayne, and their two children.